One Night
Out Stealing

Talanoa
Contemporary Pacific Literature
Vilsoni Hereniko, General Editor

Alan Duff *Once Were Warriors*

Albert Wendt *Leaves of the Banyan Tree*

Hone Tuwhare *Deep River Talk: Collected Poems*

Epeli Hau'ofa *Tales of the Tikongs*

Albert Wendt, ed. *Nuanua: Pacific Writing in English since 1980*

Patricia Grace *Potiki*

Epeli Hau'ofa *Kisses in the Nederends*

One Night
Out Stealing

Alan Duff

TALANOA

CONTEMPORARY
PACIFIC
LITERATURE

University of Hawai'i Press, Honolulu

©1992 Alan Duff
First published by Tandem Press 1992
Published by The University of Queensland Press 1992
Published in North America by University of Hawai'i Press 1995

Printed in the United States of America

95 96 97 98 99 00   5 4 3 2 1

Library of Congress Cataloging-in-Publication Data

Duff, Alan, 1950–
One night out stealing / Alan Duff.
p.   cm. — (Talanoa)
ISBN 0–8248–1684–6 (alk. paper)
1.   Maori (New Zealand people) — Fiction.   I.   Title.   II.   Series.
PR9639.3.D792053   1995
823–dc20   95–13244
CIP

University of Hawai'i Press books are printed on
acid-free paper and meet the guidelines for permanence and
durability of the Council on Library Resources

Cover design by Kenneth Miyamoto

*To my sister Josie
and her husband, 'Dee' Walker.*

*And all the other unsung heroines
and heroes of love and humility
like them.*

As always, to my father, Gowan.

Acknowledgments

To my publishers Bob Ross and Helen Benton
for their continued faith, and invaluable advice and support.

Chris Else of Total Fiction Services
for yet again steering me in the right direction.
No better advisor than he.

Ray Richards for his literary agent role.

Richard King for his repeat editing services
and friendship.

Editor's Note

One *Night Out Stealing* is Alan Duff's second novel. Like its predecessor, *Once Were Warriors,* this novel opens another window into the world of the urban dispossessed, in this case, moving at high speed between Auckland and Wellington, the two largest cities in Aotearoa/New Zealand.

Confounding his critics who claim that he is anti-Maori, Duff chooses as his two main characters in this novel a Maori and a Pakeha whose shared values (or lack thereof) are a function of class rather than of race or ethnic group. The implication here is that poverty and thievery are not prerogatives of the Maori as much as universal conditions among the underprivileged. This is how Duff prefers this work to be read.

One Night Out Stealing delves deep into the psyches of Sonny and Jube, revealing a way of thinking and being that is reminiscent of Jake Heke in *Once Were Warriors*. Sonny and Jube have little respect for persons and property. As rich Pakeha become targets for their exploits, my sympathies are torn between the need for a more equitable distribution of wealth, so that people like Sonny and Jube can regain their self-respect, and my rejection of anarchy as a way of life.

One Night Out Stealing, like *Once Were Warriors*, has a ring of authenticity that seduces me to accept the plausibility of the world that Duff portrays. The language Duff employs defies common rules of English grammar in much the same way that its users defy the values of mainstream society. This detailed and colorful portrayal of the internal and external worlds of two creatures of the night, plotting and ravaging the rich, supports its author's claim that he knows this twilight zone from the inside because he has been there. It also proves that Duff's talent as a storyteller, much admired in his first novel, is not mere coincidence.

Readers who enjoyed *Once Were Warriors* will find this novel equally fast-paced, engaging, and cleverly crafted. They will also recognize the fearless but honest portrayal of the lives and minds of urban renegades.

Duff's images will continue to shock and unsettle us for many years to come, particularly now that *Once Were Warriors* has been made into an award-winning feature film. The popularity of the film, Duff's fiction, his work of nonfiction titled *Maori: The Crisis and the Challenge*, and his commentaries in the media have assured Duff a prominent position in the constellation of image-makers who are reconfiguring the social, cultural, and political terrain of Aotearoa/New Zealand.

VILSONI HERENIKO

One Night
Out Stealing

1 Dangerboy Hapi, wearing his face-tattooed snarl, plonked his empty beer jug down on Jube and Sonny's table. Buy me a jug. To Jube.

Jube sort of grinred, made out to scratch his head as he took a quick, sweeping look of how much support Dangerboy might have. Back at Dangerboy he put his hands out, palms upwards, Come on, Danger, it's Wednesday, man. How many round here've got bread to spare on a Wednesday? So what's Wednesday got to do with it? I asked for a jug, not the day a the week. Cos it's day before doleday, Danger. You should know that. Everybody round here's scratching, just like you are, to hang in till tomorrow. Dangerboy's half-mad — the other half dull — eyes bored into Jube's unflinching own. His jaw trembled, like it does with dullards and half-dullards; it's their massive miscomprehension of the world showing through. The jug banged again. A jug, man. But Jube shook his head, Can't. I can't, Dangerboy. In a softer tone that a fool might've read wrong, but not Sonny, who was Jube's friend and flatmate. He knew. Sonny knew it might even be the opposite.

Brown to blue eyeball Dangerboy and Jube locked into each other. Though it was Jube had the softening approach. Sonny shot his own eyes round the mid-afternoon bar they'd been in several hours already, for what support might be for both sides. Not many of Jube's likely allies here, and fair enough too: this was a Maori-dominated bar, and Dangerboy was one of them. So was Sonny, cept he weren't exactly most popular in this downtown Auckland bar. But then it didn't look like a lot of Dangerboy's buddies were thick on the ground or, Sonny then figured, he wouldn't have had to demand a freebie jug in the first place. And wasn't as if Dangerboy'd stepped over from a mob, or even a little group of drinkers. He'd just arrived from over in the far corner where he usually camped, up on a stool he thought was his own, like it had his name on it and just you try and be sitting on it if he wanted it. Sonny saw an old cellmate of Dangerboy's, Ted Roberts, but he wasn't showing much interest in the eyeballing, not one that'd have him running over to join in if it broke into a fight between Jube and Dangerboy. Plenty of ex-cons who'd know both parties, so it mightn't be such an uneven contest, as Sonny might've first thought, should it turn to a group brawl, as things did when they erupted in here. How the place was. People got excited easily. Excited full stop.

One jug, man, Dangerboy in a whining tone. Nope, Jube with a voice on the rise. One fuckin jug, man. The dullard tried to regroup. So Jube was open in his casual cast around the bar for likely supporters. Back to the tank-like Dangerboy. Jube told him, I put a jug in your gut, boy, it's one less in mine. Then he lifted shoulders in a huge shrug, Which'd make me pretty stupid, now wouldn't it, Dangerboy? But Dangerboy only banged the jug again, A jug, man. And Sonny could see Teddy Roberts stiffening with another kind of interest; as well, Teddy had company of a couple of real toughs. Sonny got worried; he didn't like violence, even if he'd been surrounded by it and its results his whole life. (I ain't hit no-one and I don't intend to. Fighting's for mugs).

Sonny knew how much he had in his pocket; on Wednesdays everyone in the Tavi knows how much he or she has, as they do on a Monday and a Tuesday, cos they're the worst days if you ain't scored at sumpin criminal, of hanging out till the dole gets paid into your account. Wasn't a day went by when someone round the regular place hadn't scored at something, but it never happened that a good proportion did and so there was always a closeness of money early week. But Sonny didn't want trouble — and it's always worse when trouble happens when you're broke, for some reason — so he fished out from his total in his jeans pocket of eighteen bucks plus coinage, a five-dollar note. Here. He gave it to the thickset Maori with his penal past inked in blue all over his face in stars and wording and other obvious signs, as if a man like Dangerboy needed more attention drawn his way.

Dangerboy leaned right back on his heels how many Maoris do, with mocking gratitude and yet part of it really genuine. (Maybe they dunno how to show their real appreciation?) Hey, man — he thrust out a tat-covered hand and exposed forearm — puddit here,

Sonny. And Sonny took the hand in a limp shake, that not being his scene all this incessant handshaking went on around here, as if being mostly ex-criminals they were forever doomed to forming bonds of friendship, making promises (that they never keep), expressing emselves the better (they think) for it but mainly when they were drunk or several parts thereof. As for you — *whiteman*, Dangerboy dropped Sonny's hand like a hot cake as he turned to Jube with a snarl. But Jube looked away, waited till Dangerboy was gone and up at the bar getting his jug filled.

Okay, Son, just don't be asking me to make up for your stupidity. Wha'? Hey, Jube, whassa pr — You're the fucking problem. Givin that standover merchant five bucks like that; whyn't you leave it to me? Peace, brother. I was only trying to keep the peace. The peace? Yeah, the peace. Like in this, Sonny giving the two-finger sign the passive way. Listen, wanker, only peace you'll get from Dangerboy is on a Thursday when he's got his dole. From hereon in, man, can't ya see he'll have your number every time? Well, man, who wants a fight over a lousy — *I* wanna fight. Ya hear? *I* wanna fight if some arsehole's gonna stand over me. Shit, I thought you woulda learnt that from all your spells inside, surely? Forget it, Jube, I was only trying to keep the peace. But was I backing down to the man? Was I, Sonny? Jube leaning his face from greater height down to Sonny's face. Till Sonny told him quietly, You better watch it or I'll call my pal Dangerboy over. Holding back his grin till the same broke from Jube, who conceded a chuckle and ruffled Sonny's hair and told him he weren't so bad for a too-kind wanker.

They drank steadily. Not fast, but steady as she goes, in keeping with a near-to-broke Wednesday in downtown Auckland city, where all hell could be breaking loose outside for what it mattered in here.

House of wild dreams and dumb schemes, eh Jube? Sonny at a conversation both could easily hear at the table behind them. Of some scam that no-one'd ever done before, just ripe for the taking, and who was gonna be first cab off the rank before it was too late, the dude was asking. Both men knew the dude, that he was no different to anyone else in this place of jabbering, gesticulating men covered in tattoos to show who and what they were just in case it got missed, in deadly facial and total earnest about some government department scam, how to rip off Social Welfare in one easy pub lesson, long as you're paying for the drinks.

9

Yeah, well, Jube with a shrug at Sonny's observation. Don't mean that some ofem ain't good ideas but. Come on, Jube, here's you tellin me I shoulda learnt from being inside, what about you? What about me? Least I don't give away my money to standover merchants. Maybe you don't. But how many round here you know's been out of jail, out of trouble for longer'n a year? And Jube showing he was prepared to consider Sonny's question as he looked around at the human scenery of crims; everywhere you looked it was crims. With their obvious histories tattooed all over em, and the rare ones that had none or hardly any, like Sonny here who only had a very old boob dot under his right eye from his first borstal lag at age sixteen, no more since.

Jube went, Alright, alright, so there aren't any faces who've managed to stay out of trouble for a year or more — so what? A year's a long time anyway, you know, to be having a good time on the outside till you have to do your next sentence. That's the price ya pay, ain't it? For what, man? For being crooks, hahaha. Ha-ha-ha, I don't see the joke in it, not anymore I don't. No? No, man, I don't. Really, Sonny? Jube trying to make a joke out of it, or else take the piss. (Fuckim.) Yeah, really, Jube. Well, I'll be. So what do you propose to do about it? Hey, I never said I was gonna do — Ya did, ya know. I did not. You may as well've said it. So you gonna come up with a once-in-a-lifetime burg, maybe, that'll set us up for life? And, like, who says you gotta *do* sumpin with your life in the first place? You don't like this life we live? Well, you know, it ain't exactly a holiday on a tropical island, is it? Oh, I dunno. Dangerboy over there could easily be the monkey in the palm tree, so there's a start, hahahaha!

That's funny? Funnier than what you been so far. Know your trouble, Sonny? You think too fucking much. And know what that does to a man? It confuses him, that's all it does.

Each man took his turn to refill the jugs. At four ninety a pop times two. The bar filled steadily, the beer went steadily down. Different dudes came in with sly eyes and whispered to others that they had things for sale. A colour tv, only two hundred. You ain't got two hundred? How about twenty now, the rest over, what, couple a months, you take it tonight? Not even twenty? Okay. Try someone else. Stereos, watches, women's jewellery: Now, this piece'd look real good on your missus, Pete, I can juss see her. Fifty bucks and it's yours. Make it forty then. Alright, break my heart, gimme ten down and the rest tomorrow on a rock-bottom price of thirty. Deal. Puddit here, bud.

But only the desperate sell on a Wednesday. And besides, it's best to take the stuff out of your own social environment, any crim worth his salt knows that. Cept even the wise ones get desperate, cos that's the life. Ain't it, Sonny? Jube at a couple of dudes they knew trying to move some jewellery they were claiming were real diamonds, and they might well've been but it didn't mean a scrap, not in here, specially not a Wednesday. Better to take the stuff to a fence; plenty of them about. They might be rip-offs but least they have the cash to pay on the spot, eh Son? Right, Jube; they must be mad expecting to sell here tonight. Oh well, they'll learn. Jube as if he was the wisest dude in here, when everyone knew he wasn't. (Hell, might not be a single person in here who's wise. Or what'd he be doing here in this low dive?) Sonny thinking. (I'm all the damn time thinking about things.)

Air thick with cigarette smoke and obscenities and waftings of dope from some group huddled up at a table passing a joint or three around; it didn't matter in here the law; only law was the Boss, Mr Reid, Dave Reid, and he was okay, he let things go that would have other publicans on the dog and bone as soon as look at a dope-smoker. Not Reid. He knew where his bread was buttered. Lettem smoke the odd joint and it makes em want to drink more of his piss. Real simple.

The air pungent with smokes from both sources, and the language, the inadequacy of verbal expression having the gaps filled and stoppered by fuckins and cunts and fuck-ings by the few white guys around the place, cos that's how they say the word that their race must've invented. Though who could speak Maori in here? No-one, that's how many. This weren't no cultural gathering place, this was Tavistocks. Where the bus terminal ended — or began — right outside the back-door entrance. And losers and workers — they're just about one and the same — sat forlornly on benches waiting to be transported to some miserable home, to and from some arsehole of a demeaning job, who wants to fuckin(g) work, eh Sonny? Who the fuck wants to fucking work, as broke as we get on Wednesdays?

No-one, that's how many here in the Tavi, you're right, Jube. Who wants to work? I mean, where's the future in it? Hey, who said anything about a future, man? — hahahaha — and it's your buy, boy.

Where the bus terminal ended right outside the door, right there where Sonny was heading up to the bar for refills, where you stepped out at closing time and your voice, your laughter at times, echoed in the roof overhangs where the buses rumbled in and out to drop off and take up the thousands of loser straight workers; the world, it ended there too. No sign, though, up at the back entrance said you can't enter if you aren't one of us. But the atmosphere did. The one that lurked outside the back door and told all but a blind fool that this weren't no place for angels or even fallen ones; it just said so in its own atmosphere surrounding the door. Back and double fronts.

Specially the front, cos that's where the payphone was situated, in the sort of foyer space between entrance and bar, where people got to ring taxis, and taxis refused to come. Didn't they know that? People never did learn that they had to go round the corner to the rank, because no-one came to pick up from Tavistocks, too rough, or else the fare got distracted and no-one else wanted the cab. They headed for the phone when they wanted something, money mostly.

Hey, Mum, can you lend me? Hello, is that you, Aunty Poll? Hey, long time no see; It's me here, Gary, your nephew, member me? Yeah, you too. Look, I was wanting a favour . . . Calling up dumb aunties, estranged lovers, ex-spouses, relations, friends, enemies. It didn't madda, it don't madda, only that it's a lifeline. It's that connection of plastic mouthpiece and telephone cable from here in this dark hole of a world to out there where you believe it ain't so dark, and that the callee has that stuff he'll lend you, let you have, called bread in this place; to keep you going, sustain the lie. Of how your life has become; how far it's fallen.

But your kindness, long-lost aunty of mine, my dearest mum, who I know I only borrowed fifty from last week and shoulda paid it back this week as I said, but, Mum, Aunty, you gotta unnerstan I was on my way round with the bread — honest to God, I swear — when the landlord turned up wanting the arrears of rent I'd been paying off till it didn't suit him, the black Indian bastard; they're all the fuckin same, no trust, no morals. It's just your money they want; they're greedy landlords not satisfied with being rich, they wanna be richer. But, Mum, I've got this money coming next week, and it's guaranteed, so I'll be able to pay you back both lots — Mum? You still there? Aunty Poll? Oh fuck the bitch. Who else can I try?

So how's your bread holding, Sonny Santa Claus? Oh, you know

... No, man, I don't know. So tell me. Jube, do you hear me begging you for any? Nope, not yet you ain't, but you will. I mightn't. But you might. Wait and see. Oh I will, Santa, I will. Though don't expect me to be understanding, will ya? And just take a look at Dangerboy over there; I think that was a twenty he just passed over for his next jug. Oh well, he's your mate I spose, couple of hours back he was. Jube chuckling. And I notice he's looking everywhere but at this table. Now why would — Okay, Jube, you made your point. But I ain't crying about it.

Another jug, a few more Jube exaggerations and lies of past criminal exploits, or car episodes from his catalogue of crazy driving incidents. Till Sonny cut him short. Jube? I've never been interested in cars, you know that. They make me wanna go to sleep, honest. All this stuff about differentials and torques and stuff, it don't do anything for me.

How about sex then — hahahahaha! The tall Jube bent over with laughter. Straightening to find an unamused Sonny staring at him. Oh but you Maori boys are sure prudes. Ya know that? Jube in a voice not too loud that might get taken the wrong way. Better'n being sex maniacs, man. Hey, who's one a them? Jube all mocking innocence. You are. And here's Benny coming our way.

Hey, Jubesy boy! Puddit here, bud! And Jube no better in going along with the act; anyone'd think they were being filmed for the television, this hand-slapping, hugging, whooping, ain't seen you in, what, must be going on a year now? Lookin at each other with that self-conscious, hope everyone's lookin at us manner. It's the beer does it. Oh, and plus the fact these kinda people are eggs, as they call it in the vernacular here. Sonny at the pair with pity and contempt.

So where ya been, Benny? You remember Sonny, don't ya? Hey, Sonny, taking his hand. Howzit? Sonny forced a smile, How ya going, Ben? Long time. Yeow, long time is right, you know how it is — Can I borrow a smoke? Helping himself to the packet before an answer. Yeah, you know, I been around, like. Not as if I been inside or nothin, just laying low, you know? Yeah, we know, Benny; been there done that ourselves. We know how it gets, you know, you feel the fucking world sucks, so ya juss go to ground for a bit, but ya come round, don't ya? Oh sure, Jube, a man comes around. Not as if I walked around with my eyes closed neither. Benny looking at both of them, then at the jugs just filled, licking his lips, dragging on the helped-himself smoke and eyeing the beer. And when he smiled his loaded smile, the tattooed spiderwebs round his eyes made him look old and wrinkled long before his time, as he wasn't more'n the thirty mark, younger than Sonny and Jube. And I did get onto something, I do know that. But it's, like, it's bigger'n I can handle, you know?

Jube leaning forward all ears. Sonny leaned away. (I heard it all before. Next he'll be wanting a beer, just to get him talking.) This job I seen, it's — Sonny didn't listen the rest, turned away, eyes into the crowd. Struck immediately by a question in his mind: My crowd? At the sea of faces, grim, dangerous-eyed, poppy-eyed with the desperates of hanging out for a drug fix, or from too many pills popped, others in exaggerated laughter like they were showing the world how happy they were, when they weren't. Come to think of it, who in this hellhole was happy, like in deep-down happy?

Then Jube broke in, asking Sonny to go get Benny here a glass. And Benny thought he saw his chance. A jug to go with it'd be nice. Said to a point just above Sonny's head. Sonny shot his hand out, It's Wednesday, bud. Buy your own. Benny shook his head. Just a glass'll do then. Jube explaining: Sonny gave a jug's worth to Dangerboy, over there still managing to keep filling his jug. You could say Sonny's a mug for a jug — hahahaha!! Jube at his own humour.

Sonny came back with the glass, filled it from Jube's jug, Here ya go, Benny, get that down ya. Winked cheekily at Jube.

The scam of Benny's was a wank. It was a security van, and his plan was taken from a tv crime series; it had everything except the real-life actors to do the job. Sonny dismissed it first, but Jube wanted to hear more, just in case. So the gun came in, which Sonny thought Benny had left out till he tested the waters and filled his glass again, and not from Sonny's jug pulled close to him either.

But, Benny, a gun's worth a minimum five years and they're handing em out bigger and bigger nowadays — oh, but not that I'm worried about guns. Jube giving his prideful look-around look. I'd use one I had to, don't you worry about that. I was the best shot at the sideshows, knocking over those ducks they have. Even when the smart cunt started speeding it up when it was my shot, cos he didn't want me winning all the prizes. You know, teddy bears and that sorta stuff, as if I wanted fucking teddy bears. But, Benny, we get done with a gun involved, it's a long time in the hole.

Benny open-mouthed in astonishment at that. But how would we get caught? I've been planning this for months. Nah, mate, not for us, Jube'd decided. And the moment was awkward because there was no more to say, nor reason for Benny to keep filling his glass, which is why Jube wised up and positioned his jug out of Benny's reach; and he too turned his back to Benny, so for all they knew — if it wasn't for the drone of his voice — Benny mighta dropped dead. The drone soon dropped out of hearing, and Jube figured out loud to Sonny that getting a free glass at every table was Benny's real go.

They drift over, drift elsewhere. Benny here. Benny gone. Then it was Hitman Peters, going from table to table, did anyone want someone hit, that's my job, as well I waste people. When everyone knew Hitman was fucked in the head — oh, but weren't half ofem? He'd take out someone for keeps for a grand; might even do it for less, specially on a Wednesday. Break someone's legs, wrap a softball bat round the cunt's knees, how I do it, for as low as a hundred. And little huddles all over of dudes planning sumpin, plotting some job, inventing some impossible idea — All roads lead from Tavistocks to jail, don't they know that, Jube? Sonny, there you go thinking again. Always thinking thinking, you'll drive yaself crazy.

Night must've fallen outside. Wasn't visible from where Sonny and Jube stood, their watches told them, so did the clock above the servery that was it twenty past six of a not-quite spring evening, and seven was when these doors closed, since they opened three hours earlier at eight and the law said eleven hours' trading only, even with this lot who'd drink till the cows came home.

A hum was about the place as dudes and a handful of sheilas staggered and rocked from all the day down to drinking, and popping pills out in the toilets or smoking joints right at the tables in tight clusters of mainly young wildbloods fresh outta jail, who really thought they were sumpin else smoking so boldly out in the open like that.

Near everyone humming from the state of being drunk, what it did to em that nothin else does, not anything in and of this life; not even love does it to em, gives em that same sense of soaring immortality and hazy happiness; a kind of confidence hard to believe — that wasn't there to start with — and yet sumpin about the confidence that said it wasn't altogether true, or not so that you'd charge outta here go start chatting as an equal to some straight strangers, or haul it out on the morrow like a charm, a qualification of personal quality, an asset to approach life the better with. You, each and every, just felt real good, but yet not so good you felt it was gonna last. So there was the fear, some of it desperate, that the feeling was gonna go. Wear off. And so they gulped, and they tossed back pills and sucked hard on joints, and always the cigarettes. And the talk poured from near every mouth like pus from a mass social wound.

A figure with a helmet under its arm burst in through the front doors: WHO PISSED ON ME BIKE! And it went quieter in an instant. And the fulla asked again: COME ON, WHO PISSED ON ME BIKE? Then laughter broke out. Though not from the fulla with the helmet and the outraged face. Then someone, looked like Corky Wiringi, walked over to the guy, who no-one seemed to know so must be he was a stranger didn't know what he'd brought his outrage into, and it'd gone so quiet everyone could hear Corky say, What if it was me, man? Just as they could see the guy shove Corky, which meant he was definitely a stranger, and a pretty unlucky one at that. Corky hit him.

The fight seemed a quick one-hit affair typical of Corky. But Matty got excited by it, as Matty was wont to do, and he went over and stuck his nose in. So Corky punched the nose. And Matty's face turned instant scarlet, and his mates didn't like that so they hurtled over, and the fight rapidly spread like a stone dropped in a pond as dudes ran to it, specially the young wildbloods, but plenty of older guys too, who Sonny thought should know better, yet knew they wouldn't cos they didn't want to. So a struggling seethe of blows of fists and efforted breath; head-jolting, yelling, women screaming, arm-flailing, fist-pumping, head-butting. Just another day at the office, eh Sonny? Hahaha. Makes me sick, Jube. I know it does, that's what I'm laughing at, lil man. What, it's funny? Sure is, man; I mean here you are, in this place of all the places, and ya hate fighting. Clicking his tongue. Bit like a doctor who don't like blood. Sonny's eyes on the fight, he wasn't sure why, shrugging at Jube's observation.

The fight spread alright. Must be thirty ofem going to town there, Sonny. And there's Corky, who else? Jube's tone excited, swallowing his beer in hasty gulps so not to miss any of the action. Then through his teeth and in Sonny's ear muttering about he'd be in there it wasn't for the fighters being Maori, near every man jack ofem; they'd eat me alive, Sonny, your brown cousins, I'd be the new target to take their Wednesday frustrations out on. Racism, see, Sonny, it's the other side of racism ya never hear about in this country, it's always your lot claiming it's done — Oh, did ya see Matty throw that fucking right! Oh man, now Corky's heading for Matty.

The fight separated itself off, from those who were in, to those who weren't. And those who weren't, neck-craning, eye-googling. Those who were, an encrazed, struggling mass of bodies. And some of them quite clearly like they'd found something, and the something was stardom, being a star, being centre stage, so loving it. Loving it. Look at em, Jube, they're just kids, kids in men's bodies showing off. Right, Sonny, right, but what a show, hahaha. Best scrap I seen in ages. Just lookit Corky. Man, no wonder he was one of the kingpins at Parry. At Corky throwing big lefts and rights at any head he saw, toppling them like ninepins.

Oh-oh, here comes the boss, Jube at the sight of the giant figure of the publican wading his way through the crowd and bellowing as he came: BREAKITUP! BREAKITUP! I'M BARRING EVERY ONE OF YOU! BREAKITUP! And the spectators groaning, Oh boss! it's only a lil ole fight. Men, as well as the hardshot women only to be found here.

Mr Reid got to the action and promptly felled someone with a huge right. And everyone went quiet for just a second then let out a huge OOOOOOhh! at once. At the boss his power. His hitting power, but too his courage to walk right into the thick of it, specially with dudes like Corky who didn't take no prisoners. So Bull Reid flung a few more bodies aside, hit another dude who shaped up to him — flattened him — then it was only Corky, as the others slipped off into the crowd or picked themselves up and got snatched to safety before the dreaded sentence of being barred could be passed on them by Mr Reid.

Corky? Go fuck yaself, Bull. This is none a your business. Between me and these guys. Corky, the giant raised his hand to Corky in his fighting stance. Mistah Reid, man, I never gave you no hassles, you know that. Corky, Reid was shaking his head, this is my pub. You unnerstan? Yeah but, Mistah Reid, I was only defending myself, come on. Corky looking around him, into the crowd that'd melted into one and all looking his and Mr Reid's way. Corky the manslaughterer — twice he got found on the lesser charge.

Twice he'd done time for it. Sonny, I think Mr Reid might be gonna get his beans here. Is that so? And you'd like that, Jube? Well, you know, Jube grinning but with eyes only for the confrontation, be good to see how he goes with someone like Corky.

Corky, you are barred for three months. Aw, Mistah Reid, I was — Three months, Corky; don't make it worse for yourself. Even from the distance Sonny and Jube could see the hurt in Corky's eyes, and it was an odds-on bet someone'd step out on Corky's side. Which was Dangerboy, who bulled his way through the crowd to stand with Corky, his half-dullard jaw trembling with emotion, and part of it was crawling to Corky, showing his staunchness. Jube chuckled in Sonny's ear, There goes your five bucks. But think of it this way, least Dangerboy won't be around for a while yet to get more fives out of you.

OOOOOOOOHHHHHhhhhh! went the crowd at Mr Reid throwing the first of two punches. And Dangerboy fell down. EEEEEEEEE! as Corky staggered from the next blow. Man, ya wonder why a guy would wanna run a pub like this, Sonny in amazement at the one-man stand against this head-fucked mayhem of humanity. The bread, Sonny, he does it for the bread. OOOOOOOOOHHHHHHhhhh! at Corky falling down on just another Wednesday at Tavistocks bar down by the waterfront with harbour waters outside dancing with lights and churns of vessel movement.

Now the clock read less'n half an hour of drinking time. But no hurry, plenty of places to go to from here. Just that the adrenalin was going in everyone from the fight and Mr Reid proving himself, yet again, so he was God gone up another notch, with everyone talking about him his power, his godliness, and Corky's reign ended. Jube was telling a barely listening Sonny of his own fighting prowess, of how his right was as good as his left, and that's very unusual, Sonny, I can tell you, when in walked Jeep by the back door.

Hey, Jeep! But Jeep just waved at Jube and headed for the bar, now being minded over by Mr Reid himself — Himself — and Sonny and Jube could hear Jeep order twenty jugs for me and my friends please, Bull. But Bull Reid shook his head, Too close to closing time, Jeep. I'd never get rid of you lot. Aw, Mr Reid, my money's as good as the next guy's ain't it? Maybe, Jeep. Maybe not, if you know what I mean. Giving Jeep his hard look. So how many'm I allowed to buy, for fuck's sake? And I thought this was a pub? Jesus Christ, I've got a good mind to take my money someplace else where I'm, you know, re — well, where I'd get some respect. As people moved in on Jeep from everywhere, and the Boss told Jeep he could have five jugs but no more than that. Come back tomorrow, Jeep, with a bit more time and you can order how many jugs you want. Yeh, I'll do that, Mr Reid, I will. Cept it won't be here, I can tell you. Suit yaself, Jeep.

Jeep came over with two of the five jugs to Jube and Sonny. Hey, Jube! Plonked the jugs down, shook Jube's hand, even though they'd been drinking with him last night. Same to Sonny. Puddit here, Sonny, and ask me how I am. So how are ya, Jeep? Oh, you know, Jeep bouncing on his toes moving his shoulders from side to side. You scored good, right? Oh, you know — What, a burg? Mighta been. Well, man, I'd keep it down even in here, the walls have ears, ya know? Jube getting close to Jeep, and anyway he had to cos of the professional hanger-ons milling around, three with his jugs he didn't grab, patting his back, hanging loose till they got more than a sniff of his evident good fortune. Jeep ignoring Jube's advice, blurting out with it, his good fortune. Did a big house in Remmers. Just finished. He patted his pocket. Cash, boys. Heaps of it. I'm made. And Sonny saw Jube's eyes glass over with jealousy.

Jube's hand went out. Puddit here, Jeep. And may I be the first to offer you my congratulations. And Sonny thinking this could be a ceremony, an award-giving ceremony for burglars. So he laughed, Hey, Jeep, ask Jube where your prize is then, hahaha. Though only Jeep, not Jube, laughed.

Bell went. Session in the Tavi was ended. So where we goin, Jeep? Jube with an arm around him. Till Jeep told him, Oh I got a woman lined up. She finishes work soon. Work? You got a woman who works? Yep. Highlife massage parlour. She makes heaps herself. We're gonna paint the town — by ourselves. But here, here's twenty from me for the road. He shrugged out of Jube's embrace, patted Sonny's cheek, slapped Jube's back and nipped his darty-type body out the door before Jube could say, Cunt. Dirty rotten lucky cunt.

They bought some cans for home with the twenty windfall plus a few more added from Jube's pocket, since Sonny was out, to get as many as they could. Back through the bar and everyone asking where was the party action. Party at your pad, Jube and Sonny?

Nope. Nope, not tonight, Jube a bit more mellow than usual, when normally he was on for a party anywhere anytime.

Out in the canyon echo of bus terminal, Jube's cowboy boots clacking on the tarmac they crossed; bus-catchers all around, half ofem drunk, waiting for the seven thirties and seven forty-fives home to working-class shitholes. They're us, eh Jube? Sonny with a little gesture at the waiters. Us? Whaddaya mean us? Us, like in they come from the same, like, background. *Do* they? Jube's question echoing. A large Polynesian woman lifted her head to stare at Jube. Them are us? Yeah, you know — aw, hey, man, are you in a pissy mood? But Jube wasn't answering for a bit; so he was pissed off at sumpin.

Jeep. Why fucking him? Eh? Why fucking Jeep? It's always Jeep who lucks out on a job. Us, why do we get the houses don't have much bread? You tell me what that lil jerk's got I — we — ain't got? Man, I was robbing houses when he was in his fucking nappies. And as for having a massage woman as his sheila for the night — Fuck! Jube near spewing on his jealousy. Magine what sorta tricks she'll know in the sack, Sonny. Oh, I dunno. Ya mean, ya dunno? Dunno what? That she'll know any more than — Course she'll know more. That's her job, ain't it? Her job, Sonny, is servicing clients in the sack, ya got that? Yeah, I have, but that don't mean she — Man, are you trying to wind me up? Nope. Just trying to express an op — Well, fuck your opinion. Jeep's a dirty rotten lucky cunt and I hate him. Stabbing his free finger at Sonny, other arm taken up with carrying the carton of beer cans, Pricks like Jeep, they fall over and it's on a fifty-buck note — Jeezuz. What's his fucking secret? That's what I'd like to know.

Their shoes rubber-padding on the tarmac as they crossed and went through a narrow street to where Jube's car was parked. Buses rumbling in and out behind them. Stars and moon clouded over and it starting to spit. Sonny's whistled tune broken off by Jube telling him to shut it, will ya. Lights out behind em of Tavistocks on just another Wednesday evening. And Jube with an idea that they might go on the cruise tomorrow, maybe the weekend, somewhere. A cruise, man? Where to? Where to, Sonny? How about the fucking moon? Ooo, we are in a pissy. Ooo, we are in a pissy, he says — Who's in a *pissy*? Jube stopped to stare bitterly at Sonny as he fiddled in jeans pocket for the car keys. You're in one. You're in one, Jube repeating Sonny again. So cruise where, man? But Jube gone off the idea as quickly as it'd come. Dunno where. Somewhere we can score good like that fucking dead-lucky Jeep. Hefting the carton over to the back seat, climbing his tall figure in; all long legs and lean muscle and sinew. Expelling on a long sigh as he started the engine, Life, man, it fucking sucks sometimes.

2 Outside some takeaway joint with a name — McTucky's — sounding and looking so familiar lit up in red neon blinking teasingly, cos the name was right on the tips of both their tongues, they'd guessed and guessed earlier to no avail; just this tease of brand name, it seemed, like a bell that wouldn't quite clang.

Main street in Jube's rear-vision mirror, and over Sonny's left shoulder, the more since he was half faced that way, with left leg bent up on the seat, which had cigarette holes burnt in it and picked larger over the years by all the different passengers who didn't give two stuffs about adding to the ruin of upholstery, nothin better to do with their fidgety idle hands not used to work but couldn't stay still neither. Hicktown. Place coulda been a cowboy town from a man his days as a kid at the movies. (When he had hope, eh Sonny? Yeah well, maybe. Maybe it was sumpin I was born with.) Railway line up the street a bit, a man could easily relive the sounds of train rattling over it from his father's job that gave him his daily booze money. Sonny could see in his mind the covered wagons with their orange canvas tarpaulins spotted over with patches. Cruising, eh? This is cruising?

Jube not responding, just staring ahead at the road, where the railway line sliced across, that headed south. At black strip and white centre line and flanked by power poles strung out with droops of wire. Couldn't even remember the name of the town on the sign when they came in from the west. Might've even read Hicksville, uh Jube? Yeah, maybe.

Jube lighting up, staring his gloom into the cloud of smoke. So Sonny not so sure if he should be mentioning it, but he did anyway: So where's these Swedish hitchhickers you were sure we were gonna pick up, man? No answer. We drive, what, four, five hours and not a hitchy to be seen, let alone the beautiful blondes you said. Well, I heard of plenty of guys who've picked up Swedes and they all said the same, that they were easy meats.

Oh yeah but they would, wouldn't they? Who would? The people we know. They're all lying ex-cons who don't know the difference between fact and fantasy, and you know it. The hell I know it — *you* know it, or claim you know it. Trouble with you, Sonny, is you think your brain gives you some kinda, like, licence to sum up people. Cept you're wrong. I know plenty of ex-cons who don't talk the crap you say they do. I — Oh yeah? Name em, Jube. Name them? Yeah, name them. Go fuck yaself. What, you a cop all of a sudden? Name them he says. Yeah, name them he says, cos I know you can't. Name *you* in a fucking minute.

Ooo, my-my-my. Sonny chuckling. Again at Jube telling him what would he've done anyway they had picked up a couple hot little Swedish numbers. You wouldn't know what to do with it, Sonny. No? No. What's an it? Your black lil cock, that's an it. Who said it's little? You don't wanna comparison, do ya? Well, I . . . Thought ya might dry up on that one, Maori boy. Well, size ain't everything. Who told you that? Oh, you know, different women. They're not women, not in our world, they're sheilas. Fucks. Cunts. That's what they are. Women — they're women to me, man. Yeah, they would be, wouldn't they, Sonny, who thinks he's a class up from the rest of us. Hey, I never said that. Ya don't have to — it shows. Sonny shrugging. Eyes to the outside again. Sitting there and thinking, always thinking, a man can't help it. (And fat lotta good it does me).

Life, eh Jube? What about fucking life? Like ya said the other night, it sucks sometimes, uh? You're telling the story. Well, it beats sitting here saying nothin. You know, I had a thought — Well, I'll be — Come on, Jube, I'm trying to be sociable. I was thinking about when you're — a man is sentenced, you know? You're asking *me*? No, only saying. Ya hear your sentence being spoken by the judge, ya know? in that accent they have, like they're English, not New Zealanders. Like them snooty upper-class English ya see on the tv crime programmes. Sonny Mahia, it is very evident you have not yet learnt your lesson, as with you, Jube McCall — Hey, what's your real name again anyrate? Colin, Colin, that's right — Colin McCall; the both of you are professional burglars with long histories of offending, blah-blah-blah — Hey, Son, what's your point, man?

23

Gimme a chance, Jube. I have: so what's your point? I'm coming to it. Then come. But not over the seat if you don't mind — HAHA-HAHA! Oh well, least we got a laugh out of you, Sonny with a shaking of head.

But you know, Jube, you have that feeling of — of kinda like powerless — no, not powerless, it's more like you and the judge are from different worlds. And he's sentencing you — us — from his perspective. Yet the things we do are from ours, our way of seeing the world. What I'm saying is, maybe they should have judges who're from your own backround, who unnerstan where you're coming from? Oh yeah, sure, Sonny. And so they give you a smack on the wrist every time; yeah, that'd be neat. Unreal but neat, ya know?

And anyway, you're taken to the cells where ya wait all day as it fills up with other dudes got jail sentences, so eventually the cell's like the Tavi bar cept smaller and they don't sell beer — hahahaha — but the same shit is going down, ya know? Jobs planned for soon as the lag ends, even before it starts, and this time you're telling each other it's a *cinch*, it can't miss, and ya can't possibly get caught. Yet ya do, don't ya, Jube? We get caught. If not on the job, then after it; cos we couldn't hold ourselves back, had to go out and splash, like Jeep last week, then next day he's just another name in the paper you mightn't a picked it wasn't for remembering his real name was Richard Fleming because you were celled up with him for a bit back in '88. Man arrested in hotel bar with several thousand cash on his person, believed to be — Several thousand? That what it said? Several *thousand*? Yeah, several thousand. Oh *man*, Jube groaning. Why not us? Hey, let me finish my story. Fuck your story. Was getting depressing anyway. Okay okay, just a minute more. You're in the van and the motor-mouths are still goin on about the jobs they got planned, and you — or me, I should say — me with the miseries, with that sentence, three years, ringing in my ear in that crystal-clear voice of the judge's. World outside through the painted slits all normal and going about its everyday straight business — Jube, I sometimes wonder why we keep on like we do, you know?

What, that was your point? Yes. Well, we go get a *job*, ya think? Sonny shrugging, Maybe. Go get one yaself. Work's for suckers, man. Work sucks. And so does this shit town suck. And the burger, now I think of it. And we are out of here, Sonny-too-much-the-thinking-Mahia. We are out of here.

Engine rumbling into life. A promise. Of mighty horsepower to come. Of Jube about to hit the road again. The road out there, up front, but first behind em as Jube suddenly accelerates as he spins the wheel and does a one eighty turn and burns rubber in a long squeal, and his self-satisfied laugh is just a bit louder than that as they take off down main street.

Sonny can hear the judge of his earlier contemplation going through his ritual, his pompous-voiced ritual of expelling him and Colin McCall, here doing his childish car thing, from the society they were never a part of in the first place or they wouldn't be before him getting turned out. Purged. Fucked off out of their law-abiding lives because you two are menaces, to society as well, inexplicably, yourselves; So says the judge. And are you ever going to learn, he asks, and you'd like to tell him, just once tell him: When that big, troubled something inside me unlearns, sir, that's when and only when.

But you don't, you never will, it'd break with the ceremony of you being given over to prison authorities for the specified time in years of the judge's ten-minute deciding. Three years was the last pronouncement, and you had turned to Colin Edward McCall, here driving you down a deserted hicktown street trying to reach the ton before the main street runs out, and told him in that bravado voice, Only a three? Hell, I spected at least a five. Though it hurt. It hurt being hurled from the collective comfort, even when you were never a part of it; it was the thought. Just as the thoughts of now got ended by the scream of Jube braking, then the world turned topsy-turvy as he manoeuvred the car in a spin back the other way. Laughing, HAHAHAHAHA! in joy at his driving skills. What it did to him.

And a funny thing, even as they roared southward again up this still-vehicleless main street of Hicktown. Sonny heard in his mind the chirrup of a cricket. Outside on the ledge, the concrete windowsill ledge of his prison cell. (Remember that, Sonny?) Of just him, lying there awake, Jube in the bunk above snoring, flipping his troubled dreaming mind back and forth in musky, sperm-stained, prison-grey blankets; the cricket outside, Sonny's hearing locked inside. Yet shared. He and the tiny spot of loud-noising life sharing the moment. And whatever the hell it meant in its brief moment of time and placement. Cell placement.

Over the railway line, hitting the road other side in a nose dive Sonny feared would break the front axle. Jube laughing at the sensation. Countryside quickly coming, as the day died in front of them. Sonny catching a sign that read something DISABLED, had him think immediately of Buddy, poor Buddy Edwards, spine injured in a drunken car crash, wheelchaired for life. Imagining Buddy back behind them on the road, stuck dejectedly in his wheelchair in his limbless state, his impossible-to-imagine mind, watching the red eyes of Jube's tail-lights disappearing into the fading day going to dark. Sped off into the evening, where the clouds were a last-light glow of wispy red, and the hills humped up like dead whales.

Buddy not even able to wave goodbye, even if he wanted to, from his misery and profoundly bitter jealousy of the able. (But what able, Buddy? Is this able?) Sonny at the countryside whipping by as just an impression of near-died day. Buddy back on the road, in Sonny, his mind, staring after the disappearing tail-lights on their unusual high plane because of the fats Jube had on back. Watching them, meant to be on freedom's highway, cruisers, like Buddy was, the same highway that turned him from able to utterly unable. Man couldn't even wipe away his tears.

Night folded around them, wrapped em up in a big blanket of car warmth and night-black. Could be their boyhoods, two boys under a layer of blankets peering up at the stars, at a big fat yellow moon and telling spooky things to each other. And laughing.

But this was no childhood memory reawakening; it was eight roaring cylinders passing out the exhaust, designed to sound like twenty. An ugly piece of metal shaping with two adult humans inside; howling tyres, gear-slamming engine changes, creaking, straining metal being wrapped around every curve and bend. And a bad rattle in the back somewhere. The night split apart by the wide beams of Jube's big yellow-eyed monster scything through it. Nothing evoking childhood here.

Every bend and curve and sweep loomed up out of the light-sliced dark as though it offered some mortal challenge to this half-crazed honky, his sense of manhood when he was behind the wheel. Or maybe his sense of manhood full stop, Sonny wasn't sure. Just that near all of Jube was vested here, in this hotted-up machine of his tinkering, fine-tuning between drinking and stoned spells. The straight sections he simply buttoned down the pedal to the floor. The challenges in when the straights ran out — Oh, I love corners. As he took the car to its utmost limits of a propelled weight getting its unsleek length to go round a curve. And the gear-stick middle of them was Jube's six-shooter, he could act it out as though he was the cowboy hero stood legs astride on dusty main street, twirling, spinning, doing fancy fast tricks with his shooter. God help them that they'd reach the stated destination — Jube's out-of-blue Wellington, same place they'd gone cruising to a couple of months back. Where some thieving bastard had broken into Jube's car and removed the sound system. The lot: radio-cassette player and four speakers. Near broke Jube's heart. They were gonna meet up, Jube said, with them same dudes they palled up with in that bar and ended up at their place for the night. Good guys. Thieves, like us, hahaha.

Carton of beer cans at the next town, Dannevirke, since the burgers back in the last town had settled. Lion Red cans, what else? Jube to the dude at the bottom store on another hicktown deserted night. What the rugby league players drink; right, mate? If you say so, buddy. Yeah, I say so, Jube took offence. Paid the guy then told him, I don't like your attitude, pal. You got a problem in the attitude department. So have you, mate, and you looking to causing any trouble I've got half a dozen chaps in the public bar might enjoy crossing swords with you. Fuck you! Jube spat but didn't linger. Took it out on the road instead, if such a thing was possible to add to.

Grumbling at the price of the cans anyway, They're fucking rip-offs these smalltown joints. And they wonder why they get burgled, held up with shotguns? Fuckem, eh Sonny? Packa arseholes the lot of em. *Pfzzzit* of tear tab. Such a *nice* sound, don't ya think, Sonny? Yeah. Sonny already halfway through his second while Jube was having his little moan at the world. Beer helped lessen the fear of the speed — the fear of dying in a mangle of metal collided or flipped at a hundred miles an hour.

Sonny glancing across at the profile of Jube in dashboard glow. An outline of nose eruption and underneath curve of walrus mo. The beer can lifting frequently to the profile; his guzzling long and thirsty. Mm-uh. Wiping at his moustache. Nother can please, buddy. Warming up fast, how he did with the first quickly drunk few. Sonny hoping the pattern wouldn't follow of Jube starting to talk cars. Anything but cars. Oh, and sex. (Maybe they're one and the same thing to him? Power, I dunno.) Passing Jube another can, breaking open another for himself. Night dissolving in the arc of light before them, and closing after. Like a curtain.

(Don't talk cars, Jube. Please. As for being in a cell when he wants to talk cars; not as if a man could say he was going for a walk. Same in here, he could hardly go walking. These car freaks they won't play Scrabble — too hard for em, too many words they don't know. Yet get em onto diffs and stuff and they're geniuses — of a fixed and simple kind. Won't share the giant crossword — same reason: dunno many words. But gettem onto the different timings involved in engines and they're numerical cleverdicks. Yet the same guys can never figure out, in percentage conversion terms, how much time they got left of a sentence with remission deducted. Though Jube fancied himself as a bit of numbers king.)

Hey, Jube, wanna do some numbers? Hey, now you are talking, Sonny boy. Hit me. Okay, add these up: nine, seven, two, thirteen, twenty-thr — Hey! come on now, no twenties, Son, twenties aren't in the rules. I thought you said you were good at numbers? I am but — Well, I don't remember no *rule* bout no twenties. Well there is. So start again. Nope. Sonny, come on. Twenties allowed? *No*, man. Okay: add these; ya ready? Yep-yep, hit me withem. Right: nineteen, eleven, seventeen, fifteen — Hey! come on now, they're all in the teens. Yeah, so? So play the fucking game, man. I am. I didn't do no twenties. No, ya didn't, ya just dropped down one cog and hit me with all teens. Then I ain't playing, Jube. What? You heard. And fuck you too. (Good). Sonny smiling, leaning back and smiling. (Lettim have a little sulk. I don't feel like listening to his talk.) Drinking rapidly himself so to dull that fear.

Soon Sonny able to enjoy the shifts in his beer-affected mind; of perspectives, and of it happening, sometimes, his mind really expanding. So he'd hear music. And see figures dancing intricately involved sequences to that music; seemingly of his own creation, since he never recalled any reference from ordinary life that might've gone toward it. Couldn't. Because it was kind of classical. Like that stuff ya hear when you're spinning the tuning dial in your cell trying to find a decent station, and ya hit onto something that really grabbed you; even though it was obviously highfalutin music, it still struck a chord. A something that you had inside yourself that you didn't know about, not till the fluke radio dial tuning happened you onto this; a marrying-up in your mind, a settling of a peculiar curiosity that wasn't there to start with but just seemed to pop to instant life at the music coming on, and with it satisfying the same something. (Hell, I dunno.)

Once he'd sat on the edge of his prison-cell bunk listening to some opera stuff he was about to spin off till it occurred to him that it seemed to be rolling his entire life — emotional life — through his ears, in his mind, in just the few minutes it took to hear it to completion. He'd wept that day. Just sat on the edge of the lower bunk and wept. And his head remained filled with what made him weep; echoing over and over and over till a screw gently announced that he'd better pull himself together because the main prisoner populace were heading back in from optional exercise-yard walking. He didn't remember if he said thanks to the screw, but probably he did.

But no music now. Nor dancers. Just the stars in their forever mystery, and Jube having a sulk beside him. Hey, Jube, you ever wonder about the stars? Nope. Not even a little bit? Nope. You still packing a sad? Nope. So how come you don't wonder about the stars? Cos they don't wonder about me, hahahaha! Yeah, that wasn't a bad one, Jube. I know it wasn't. Humour's my ace card — when it suits me. That right? You bedda believe it, Son. Wanna hear some jokes? Oh yeah, long as they don't have *rules* you just decide on on the spot. Sonny? Yeow? You're a cheeky cunt. Thanks, Jube. Did you know that the whole universe started with one big bang? Well, I'll be — And that it's expanding and expanding and then it'll reach a critical point so it can't go no farther then it starts coming back in? Well I never, Sonny Einstein who's been doing his reading in the prison library. Jube, are these your jokes you're saying after I've said sumpin? Take em how ya like — Einstein. Hahaha. Night parting outside. The beer hitting the right spots. Speed not so fearful.

They were good guys weren't they, Son? Who, man? Pete and his pals in Wellington. Oh them? Yep, they were okay. I thought we might put it on em. Put what, not the hard word surely? Ha-ha-ha. Sonny, that was very funny for you. Thanks, Jube. But I meant a team-up job. Oh? Yeah, like in we team up withem sumpin big, like the job they'd done day before we met em, the warehouse. What, another warehouse? No, man, just in general. So why'd they wanna team up with us for? Cos we *got on*, Sonny-fucking-negative-Mahia. So? So I got this strong gut feeling that they might have other big jobs on they'd need a bit of expert help on. We're experts? Oh come on, ya wanker, you're making it hard for me to keep my patience, I'm warning ya. Jube, I ain't trying out your patience —

29

Yes ya are. No I'm not; just trying to figure out why these guys we met for one night, even though we did crash at their place for the night, what they want to team up with us out-of-towners for? Numbers, Sonny, that's what. Gophers, extra bodies to carry the stuff off the premises. What premises? What premises . . . ? Sonny, are you taking the piss? No, man, I — Then shuddup, will ya. Hear me out. Okay? Okay, Jube.

Now, I figured having us'd be two advantages: first, we're extra carrying labour; second, we're from out of town so we can arrange the fence to buy at our end, so there's no connection, no tie-up with Wellington from their end, and to tie-up with us on the job itself our end. Simple? Oh yeah, real simple. What's that mean? Oh, you know. No, I don't know, and pass me a can while you're at it. I think it's too, like, loose, ya know? No, I don't fucking know. Are you saying it sucks as a plan?

Well . . . Sonny shrugging, for what it was worth in the part-dark and Jube's eyes on the road anyrate. Hearing Jube's tch-tch-ing, and telling Sonny, Sometimes I wonder about me and you, what we got in common, what use we are to each other with me doing all the criminal thinking and you doing all the dumb-star-stuff think-ing. Ya know that? Well, I have thought about it, Jube, I must admit. And? And like, you know — Don't keep saying you know all the fucking time. Okay, and like I've come to the same conclusions — but . . . Sonny pausing, just to irritate. And it irritating: But fucking what! But there's other times when we do need each other. Oh yeah, since when? Since every week when one of us runs out of bread first and the other one carries till Thursday or the next burglary. And that's it then? Jube turned his head for a second. It's a start, and I ain't heard you complaining before now, other than your, you know, usual grump with the world. Hey, man, you are taking the piss outta me, aren't ya? Nope. Ya are. I said nope, Jube, so come on. Jube not saying further. Onward.

Jube, you ever think about us, where we're going? Oh yeah, all the time, Sonny. (Oh?) Like now, we're headed for Wellington, Sonny, and in a few days we'll be headed to Auckland. We'll be loaded up with hot goodies we might even have a hired truck full a the stuff, which'll head us for the different fences we — I mean I — know. We'll have ourselves, with Pete and his Wellington boys, a massive celebration party with half a k a dope, heads a course, and piss coming out our ears. We'll order Kentucky Fried and

McDonald's at a hundred bucks an order, which we'll feed our party pals with. We'll go to sleep where we fall, we'll wake with a fridgeful a cold piss. And they'll be no shortage of sheilas; I'll pick who I want from the Tavi, hire some I have to, long as I have myself one within easy fucking distance. So, that's were we're headed for the next lil while. That answer your questions?

Sonny waited. HAHAHAHAHA!! for Jube to do just that. Sonny sighed. He gurgled a can from opening to emptying, nearly threw it back up, but held it. He lit a smoke. Didn't answer Jube's going, Hey ya still talking to me? Hahahaha. Not till a kilometre or two went past and the one-hit can'd done its work. Sonny felt better. Better able to cope with Jube, their tangents of difference. He asked again: But seriously, you think about — Oh, every minute of the day, Sonny. Yep, I think about my life, you know, how I wish I was a brain surgeon — no, make that a motor mechanic — Hey, really, Jube? Yeah, really and truly; don't tell me you didn't know that about your old inside cellmate and outside flatmate, now come on, Sonny? You're kidding me, aren't ya? Oh no, Sonny, I wouldn't do that. Why, only yesterday I was gonna ask you, Sonny how do I get myself qualified as a motor mechanic, cos I'm sick of being a thief. Aw, you're having me on, man. Paying me back, eh? Yeh! I'm paying you back. And I don't wanna hear no crap bout going straight, cos I never wanted that not in my entire life. I can't even lie straight in bed, and that's cos I don't want to. I was born bad and that's how I like being. And I'm beginning to worry about you, Sonny-fucking-Mahia.

How come? Cos you all the time think-think-think. Nothin wrong with that, man. There is; it's not right. It don't *sit* right, ya know? It sounds like — makes you sound like some fucking con ready to turn into a nark cos sumpin inside you is busted. Jube, I wouldn't nark on — *I* know ya wouldn't, but there's plenty who're asking me questions about you, Mahia. Like who? Like half the dudes in Tavistocks for starters. Yeah, well, they hardly count. I mean, who the fuck are they? They, Sonny, are your peers, whether you like it or not. Ya got that? No way. They are, Son, and they can sense you ain't one of them no more. One day they're gonna get a little delegation together and sort you out. Nah, come on, why'd they do that? Who've I ever harmed? That don't madda a shit to them; it's how they see you. You know the score anyway; inside you got hassled for being what you are, which is too much of a headman. Our kinda people, man, they don't trust those who live in their own heads, ya know? Half your sentences you spent in the library. And you wonder why your own kind are a bit iffy about you?

Sonny shook his head. Nothing to say to that. Nothin. Not sure if it hurt or he was pleased that his Tavi bar peers saw him as something different. (But, man, I don't wanna be sumpin I ain't. I just want, like, some sorta peace. In my mind, and from there in my life. I wanna turn this fuckin life around; that's what it is, what it's always been — But *how*? How, man?) Oh, crack another can. That always cures it, eh Jube? Hey, now you're talking a language I understand, lil man. Onward.

(. . . like someone's opened a door for me. In my head. This door. Opening, but just a peek, to start with. Then slowly swinging open to reveal this other world — that's inside *my* head? No? Yet it is. And look, there's the dancers; they're men for some reason, and they aren't any particular race, they're just neutral faces that are beautiful but in a strange way. Now they're dancing. And there's music. Oh, don't let me lose this.) Sonny fixing his mind's eye on this event taking place, not daring to move, hardly even to breath. (The music isn't recognisable either. More a beat. Yet there are stringed instruments, maybe they're violins. But the dance isn't like that, violinish, and yet it all fits. It fits. And it's so clear; yet I'm not dreaming, I'm sitting here in this car watching this dreamlike sequence taking place right —) HEEEEEYYYYYYY!!!

The car lurched wildly, crossed the white line, and Jube shrieking his laughter, AHAHAAARRRRRRGGGGH-HAHAHAHA! at the first possum of the night, frozen in the headlamp glare, every little detail of rat-like face and pricked ears as clear as day; picture of dumbfounded unknowingness, thick tail laid out behind it like a veil, a death veil, if they have such things. *Thuck!* Death coming in a glancing blow of rubber at a hundred miles an hour. *Gotcha!* Hahahaha! Man, them possies're sure suckers for death. Hedgies, though, ya gotta watch for the hedgehogs their prickles don't puncture your tyre. Aw, come on, Jube, they don't puncture — They fuckingwell do. (Well, I'll be damned, eh Nose? I don't believe it for a moment.) That right? That's right: hedgies-puncture-tyres. What, you calling me a liar? Would I be so stupid as to do that, Jube? Nah, I don't think you would. But then, with you, Sonny Mahia, a man can never tell. Pass me one.

Little hiss of Jube tearing the tab on the can, as Sonny lit two cigarettes, handed one to Jube. Ta, man. Jube's face slightly aglow as the ember switched on like a light. Bubbling sound of him taking a drink from the can. Outside, reflector strips flashing regularly by. Farmhouse lights on Sonny's side up on a hill. And where, sure as free-range eggs, that window glow was firelight. Fireglow and Mummy-warmth. And her brood sat around the fire, eyes locked into the dance of flames. And Dad reading a story. Tummies full from Mum's best cooking, a roast, no doubt. Okay, story's over, it's dishes time, kids. Aw, Dad. No aw Dads. But can't they wait till the *Cosby Show*'s over? Oh alright then. Their dad'd be one of them kind. A good bastard.

(Not like mine. I hated my old man.) After the dishes he'd help put em to bed, then he and wifey'd go back to the fire. Hehehe. Come and sit down here on the rug, dear. Down she be, legs drawn up to catch the heat around her area. Hon? Hmmm? Come a little bit closer. Smiling at him, his hand reaching out for that smooth line of drawn-up legs. Oh, honey.

Blast of air from Jube's window gone down. Not a sound, though, from the can tossed to the wind. No different, Sonny in an instant reminded, from a borstal minister putting to his youthful, incarcerated audience, Would there be any sound in the case of a piece of ice breaking from a main body if there were no ears to hear it? Really got them thinking. And flummoxed. Stumped the lot of the dunderhead boobheads. Then one dude, Moomoo Jacobs was his name, asked: Whassa fuckin difference? And everyone laughed away their confusion. Sonny still had occasional ice dreams. The break-offs sounded like rifle cracks.

Flash of silver out front and Jube swinging for it. Too late. No thud of impact. Hey, what's a frog doin out here in the middle of the night? Dunno, Son. Maybe it couldn't sleep — HAHAHAHA!

Cans getting warmer. So drinking for effect, not the pleasure of ice chill in mouth, against throat. Just effect. To shut out the whatevers they permanently were with people like them. And don't forget the smokes: that need to suck, to satisfy sumpin of the mouth.

I ever tell you that poem I wrote got printed in the *Star*? Yeh, ya did, lotsa times. And not as if it was printed, man. Was the Memorium column and you paid for it. Okay, okay, I wasn't saying it was a normal poem. But I still made it up. None a that copycatting like other people do in the In Memorium. I composed it all by myself. Wanna hear it? If you insist. But you slow down a bit first. Why's that? So I can concentrate. Okay man, a deal. The engine went instantly quieter. Ya ready? Come on, man, get on with it. Well I'm *sorry*, Mr Mahia, don't want you late for your appointment with the Prime Minister now, do we? Here we go:

My mate Ace, remember the V8s?
Them were the days, weren't they, mate?
Rums and bourbons, washed down with Coke
Hey, givus another bottle, along with some smokes.
You drove the meanest V8 in town.
Had to be you Ace, stead of some clown.
But now you're the All American boy in the sky . . .

Hey, Ace weren't American. Jeezus, Sonny! you interrupted me — and I never *said* he was American. Yes ya did. No, ya spoon, that's just a saying, it's a — You wouldn't understand. You gonna let me get on with it?

But now you're the All American boy in the sky.
But we'll always remember you for giving us those highs
Our day'll come, old buddy of mine,
When we'll be cracking a bottle — No, make that nine.
And we'll toast to speed, and to thrills.
Only wish to God it was me, not you, got killed.
So farewell, dear friend. Your turn came too soon.
But Jube'll see you again, on the dark side of the moon.

Silence. And the car still at its reduced speed. (I can hear his heart thumping. He thinks he's on the tv, in the movies. He's sucking on the emotion like a kid on a last bit of lolly. He thinks —) Makes you feel, don't it? Uh well, yeah. Guess it does. Guess it does. But did it, like, sound okay to you? Yeah, it did. Ya sure? Sure I'm sure. Not having me on, are ya? No way. Thanks, Son. I, uh, preciate that. You know? Yeah, I know. As the speed gradually increased.

The shifts. Beer shifts. Of mood, and perspective. Now attitude as Jube went Huh? at an oncoming set of lights not responding to his foot tap of dip to full to dipped beam. A pause of his anger coming up, then: Give *me* full beam, ya cunt — wrenching the wheel over, taking them to the other side of the white line. Now muthafucka, see what ya made of. Through his clenched teeth, Sonny could hear it even over the constant roar of powerful engine, the shift in Jube's mind. From ten, fifteen kilometres back of getting all sentimental over his late pal Ace killed himself in his V8, to this: *Come onnnnn!* and the floor dip switch a staccato hammer of Jube's foot hitting it. COME ONNNN! Sonny's eyes opening and closing about the same rate as Jube's foot was going on the dip switch. (We're gonna die.) Jube? *Come onnnn, muthafucka.* Jube! *Come —* HAHAHAHAHAHA!! Sonny opening his eyes to see the victory of the other car pulled over off the road with its light going from dip to off. Jube's window belting down, and an arm going out, *GOTCHA! Hahahahahaha!!* His triumph bellowing no different to the earless break-off of ice in remote Antarctica.

Did ya like that, Sonny? Yet nothing genial in his tone — cold. The beer shift had him in that cold mode, and only extremes would briefly warm him. So next it was a truck that wouldn't dip its lights on instant command from Sir Jube. And over he went, to the oncomer's side. As oncomer barrelled towards them maybe half a kilometre away, lit up like a Christmas tree how they like to these truckies, something childlike in their make-up; the dacka-dackadackadacka of Jube on and offing the dip to full. *Me and fucking you, buddy.* The cab outline doing a little wobble of no doubt disbelief. Hey, come on now, Jube ... Once was bad en — *You and me, cunt.* Come on, ya fat prick of a truckie, let's see who breaks first.

The full beam of truck headlight getting through Sonny's closed eyelids. So he opened them — shut em again. *Jube!* Fuck up. Then came a horn blast. Coulda been a fucking great ship bearing down on em in the night. Jube? (Hate your guts, Jube McCall.) Foghorn blast and juggernaught rumble closing. Then it was a violent swing of movement as Sonny caught the da-dada-da-da! of horn. It could have been a long, echoing laugh.

But Sonny not prepared to taunt Jube on conceding. Too risky; he might play chicken to the bitter end next time. Bigger than us, eh Jube? Took Jube some time to respond, and then it was just, Yeah, was a bit. And silence.

They pulled over at a rest area layby. Not far back the sign'd said Wellington was forty kilometres to go. But nowhere to crash, put their heads down. And too dangerous to sleep in a car in the city, ya might get mugged. Eh Sonny? Jube from the front seat and

Sonny laid down in the back, be a bit of a downer we got mugged by our own kind? Sure would, man. Like my sound system, eh Son? Stolen by our own kind. Who'd do a thing like that? They must've seen the paint-job on the car, shoulda told em it belonged to one of their own? Any fucking wonder I got so upset, eh Sonny? Yeah, I don't blame ya, Jube. Was a good system, wasn't it, Sonny? (Shifts. Now he'd shifted to his wanna chat mode. The whining lil boy kinda chat, of just before tuck-in-time: Mummy, guess what happened? But I don't wanna hear his voice. It'll enter my dreams, gimme nightmares. I been to sleep with that voice in my ears, echoing in my head well over a thousand nights of imprisonment. A break. Gimme a break, will ya, Nose?) Night, Jube. Hey, ya not going to sleep already, are ya? Sure am. I'm tired. The thump of Jube turning his sulking form either facing the seat or the underside of his dashboard.

Lying there, sleep not yet signalling it was near; and a man knew his sleep pattern off by heart from them days of prison introspection. Sleep, it was a trickle, Sonny was certain, of this chemical coming from someplace in the brain. And it didn't come then, nor did sleep.

The night chill coming in through the breeze of Jube with his cowboy-booted feet stuck out the passenger's window. Sonny curled up like the fetus every crim is: huddled unto himself, lost of the womb-warmth, Mummy-warmth (that wasn't there to start with), just this curled thing taking comfort from itself, since there weren't no-one nor anything else to take it from.

The stars. Just one opened eye out the window away. A twinkling up there in the forever mystery for all men. Sonny staring at them. Wondering about em. Nothing deep, just a small curiosity and a little larger puzzlement. Hearing Jube's movement then the window going up; must've got too cool even for him, Mister Tough Guy who don't never dance cos tough guys they don't. Watching the unending vista of stars, till they gradually disappeared behind the fog of Jube's always troubled breathing and his not-untroubled quieter own. Till that tiny leak of chemical told him sleep was on its way, if not necessarily peace.

3 In this bar. The same one they were in last visit. Two hours they'd been there, since just after nine this morning; an early opener, like Tavistocks back home in Auckland. Caters for the desperate and the fancy-free. Not forgetting the dregs of society who can't conform. Started off with a handful plus Sonny and Jube, then grew to about the two-dozen mark, and not yet noon. Look atem, they're scum, Jube every so often scowling. Giving off this eerie hum of collected talk. Alkies, near to a man, and no women to be seen. And look at him over there, that wanker, jeezuz fucking chrise but ya don't see that even at the Tavi, eh Son?

At this dude, he wouldn't be more'n forty, meant to be in the prime of his accomplished or contented life and here he was in a sleaze pit, staggering in a tight circle round and round and gibbering like an animal. A fretting one. And lookit them packa arseholes over there. Jube sparing no-one, a group of derelicts huddled at a standing table, in threadbare clothing and with filthy matted hair, but it was their teeth, their mouths that gave them away: gaps, gums, gaping holes in acts of insane laughter — Man, what the fuck are we doin here anyway? Sonny wanting to know.

Pete. We're waiting for Pete to show.

And if he don't?

He will.

But if he don't?

Sonny, he'll show.

By four o'clock, and both of them getting well on the way, the guy hadn't showed. Sonny came back with two more jug refills, asked Jube for some small change for the jukebox. Jube laughed, No way, Maori boy, you'll only play your coon music, hahaha. Then Jube's face changed: Hey? You're not saying you're broke, are ya?

Yep. Broke as. Aw come on, Sonny. No come ons. Broke is broke. Was my turn to do the power bill Friday. Left me with about thirty-five from my dole. I'm here, I been here, what, eight hours, and it's dóne run out, my main white man. Sonny breezy on the beer and no food from since the night before. Jube shaking his head in dismay. But you shouldn't be broke, Jube, are ya? Jube brought out a twenty-dollar note as answer. That's it? This is it, Sonny. How come, man? You didn't have no power bill to pay. I bought half a dozen bullets. Half a fuckin *dozen*? At ten bucks each? Yep. And you smoked em all since, when, Friday? Jube nodded, And you helped. Hey, I had one lousy joint on Sunday; why I agreed with your fool idea to go on the cruise. Let's go cruising, Sonny, that's what you said in your stoned state. Let's go south again, but try the east coast through from Taupo, we might even pick up some Swedish hitchhikers and they are just *born* to love fucking, that's what you said, Jube McCall.

Pete'll show.

Pete won't show, and why didn't you organise sumpin better?

Oh? Like me phoning my secretary, This here's your boss, Girl Friday. Can you phone Pete the Wellington burglar and make an appointment with him? That's a good girl — Oh, and remind me to feel you up next time I'm passing. Come on, Sonny, don't worry so much. Pete and his boys'll show.

Six o'clock and Jube growling at Sonny to slow down cos there wasn't no more bread to buy any more jugs. The permanent drunks around them in their intended states, and throwing punches at invisible ghosts of their forever haunting; flubbed out on their feet, hardly able to stand but somehow managing to; breaking out in weird cries that seemed to source from deeper than even their tormented hells of souls. And their two observers falling into their own gloom.

The laughter, even the encrazed laughter from the brain-addled, more and more sounded like a happiness that the out-of-town pair didn't have. A drizzle started visible through the grimy window that looked over the carpark, where Jube's dirty undercoat-grey monster was parked like some terrible guard creature waiting for its master. And more and more people coming in, but a lot of them workers in workers' clothes and good honest thirsts, and something else enviable about them too. Outside, the drizzle'd quickly turned to steady rain. The pair were down to their last inch of beer in each glass, and staring at it or at the rain shrouding Jube's V8 monster.

Jube grabbed for the smokes, Oh jeezus, not the fucking smokes too; there's five left. Though he lit one regardless, and so too did Sonny. And a moment of eye glance between them had the uneven number remaining in the packet a separate determination on the part of each.

The patronage, who were Jube's scum of earlier, were no longer that; in fact, they took on an air of security that the pair were without. If only for the fact that they appeared to have money enough to see the drinking process to its intended end: oblivion. Not to mention no shortage of smokes. As well, it seemed they had the emotional security of having their own kind to talk to, tell lies to, exaggerate to, laugh with, toast, throw ever-expansive arms around each other. Again, another whole point of the drinking process: to break free.

And it didn't fit. Wasn't right. That they, the out-of-town duo, come to town with their big dreams of criminal teaming, city-to-city A Team of burglars, they who supposedly had the greater freedom and therefore the greater scope, should feel inferior to a barful of alcoholics and enslaved workers. That's it! Jube's fist thumped on the table. We are out of fucking here. Fuck Pete. Fuck this whole town. It sucks. Marching toward the door, scattering drinkers as he did, Get outta my fucking way.

In Jube's car being driven at high speed in the city confines, though not much traffic left of city workers heading for suburban homes. Hey, that's the Beehive, man. Where the PM his-self works. Fuck the PM. Only PM I'm interested in is Pall Mall smokes, Jube fluking the joke. Nor did he laugh. Speaking of smokes, who's having the last one? Sonny not answering, looking out his window.

Sonny?

Yeow?

Where's that last smoke?

Man, it musta smoked itself all up — hahahaha. Though Jube didn't echo the laughter. Just scowled; told Sonny, You'll keep. And try the ashtray. But Sonny shook his head. Man, you and I both smoke em right down to the filter. Take a look anyway. Sonny did so. Nope. Sorting through the pile of filters, ash and matches, and not a butt worth smoking. Jeezuz fucking chrise.

Jube drove them aimlessly. They ended up out the other side of the city, which the shop signs said was Oriental Bay. Jube mumbling that it didn't remind him of nothin Oriental, just another New Zealand bay. Where's the Chink food shops? Rain driven at an angle by the wind. Up a hill off to the right — sea was on Sonny's side, the left — and the houses looked very robbable, so Jube's mood picking up a little. Tanight, bro, we're back here tonight. Eyeing the houses hungrily. And so was Sonny, though his mind as much on the food that might be in the fridge, and hoping the people were smokers, which wasn't very often when you hit a posh home. Not even ashtrays in most ofem.

Yep. Jube turned around up the top of a long, winding climb. This'll do the boys tonight, my lil man. Back down the hill. We'll wait it out someplace we don't get reminded of smokes. And food too, man. And food.

Down the bottom of the hill, turn right. May as well follow the sea, eh Sonny? Round a sharp bend, Jube on the wrong side, a near miss with a car, hitting its horn at Jube and he giving the fingers back. Pulling his arm back in, It's wet outside, Sonny, hahaha.

Sea beside churned up by the wind. Out of the sea loomed a figure on a sailboard. Heyyy! thas us, Son. That's us, at this lone dude in a brightly coloured wetsuit riding his board over a boiling sea. Man alive! Sonny in admiration. And Jube grinning the same. Man triumphing over the elements, Sonny thinking as Jube slowed right down. Till he felt the different movement. Then it didn't seem possible.

Not with how they were feeling. Not when out of their gloom had come that apparition riding the waves, belted along by the wind, and so both had taken hope from the sight. Even with being broke, hungry, out of smokes, you'd still taken hope. So it didn't seem right — it was an incomprehensible wrong and yet it fitted all the same — that you should be chugging to a halt with Sonny looking at Jube staring at the gauge that was reading E for empty of petrol.

And so far from home.

Two drenched lurkers in a city park, waiting for night to fall and a chance to come by.

Sonny, shivering with cold, dreading the embarrassment, the shame of being caught in this position by some happenstance cop, or a sharp-eyed John Citizen; crouched, uncomfortably, behind shrubbery with back exposed to the rolling openness of tree-studded parkland.

Stationed opposite, Jube, across the small chasm of bank divide; and below meandered a path, partly illuminated by spillover light from nearby lamps. Of the kind you see in spooky old English movies, with mist or rain shrouding the scene, the pending scene.

Smells of earth and flower and leaf everywhere. City hardly a few minutes away, though you wouldn't think so with the quiet; only the thrum of rain. The path crossed every once in a while by late-evening hurriers under umbrella, or huddled into raincoat; unknowingly watched by two desperadoes gone of the warmth of their mobile home. And no money to get it going again; it'd been drunk and then pissed, urinated against just another stainless-steel urinal in just another lowdown bar with fellow flotsam. But it'll be a piece a piss, Sonny, Jube's words echoing in his mind as the rain ran off his face in rivers. Soon as it's dark, I'll pick the mark, then I give you a raised-arm signal and you only signal back if it ain't cool. It'll be as easy as that, bud, I promise you.

But Jube's promise that Pete and his boys'd be in the bar was what had them now here in the first place — cos all the bread'd got spent hanging around on a hope, a notion, a criminal wank notion. (Fuck him.) A cinch he said it was gonna be. That was back then, when they were walking their dejected states into town, when their desperate destinies'd seemed twinned. Back then, it was an abstract. Just another Jube half-mad idea: I know! Find a park and mug someone. Mug someone? You kidding? The hell I'm kidding. Never been more serious. But why can't we do a house? No getaway vehicle, remember, Sonny? No getaway vehicle with the park neither. Don't need one. Run across the park's what we do after the biz. And anyone following'll have to the same, right? Don't worry, Sonny, it'll be a breeze.

Yeah, a breeze, a cinch, a piece of piss, an easy-meat bowl-over — fuckin crook-breezy confidence that had nothin' — ever — to do with how things actually turned out. Story of our lives. We fuck up.

Sonny miserable in his muscle-cramping position. You leave the bizzo side to me, cuz — Oh, Jube was so sure of himself at every new turn of sudden impulsive idea he got: Just leave it to me, Sonny my main lil man. Calling a man that cos it made him feel bigger.

First dude I see looks worth taking I'll be onim like one a them big cats.

And now, Big Cat calling from across the way, Hey bro! Saves having a shower, eh? His chuckle no less hideous for the rain part muffling it.

Two lurkers in a city park.

Came the sound of whistling — whistling? Then out of the rain, down there on the eerily lit footpath, a figure striding beneath a big umbrella that exploded in bright colours even in the sheeted wet. Whistling in this? Sonny stared down at the figure, his step-out of dark-trousered leg, his whistling in sharp time to his walk. (Man, to be in his head, eh?) As Whistler marched as quickly out of view as he'd come; and Sonny betting the guy'd be going home to a real nice wife, full of positivism like her hubby: How's your day been, darling? Oh just fine, thank you, and yours? Oh, you know, mustn't complain. Life's too short. That sort of exchange. Kissing each other hello: mmmm-uh! And a mirrored wink for the laters to come. Then the kids, falling over themselves to greet the father. Hey, Dad! Hey, Dad! Guess what? Guess what! (I seen it on the tv. At the movies sometimes. Ya only have to watch Cosby to know that some people they do live really happy lives, even when they're having their downers. Stability. It's the stability they got that people like me don't have, that's what it is. (Is it? How would I know?) Things get sorted out. Problems, big and small, they get resolved. And sure it's only a tv family of actors — but it's still based on sumpin, ain't it? Like, if the acted situation exists, then so can the reality, can't it? Oh God, I don't know . . .)

Staring into the rain-filled space where'd strode the Whistler. Man, I bet he fucks her tonight. Probably why he's got sumpin to whistle about. I would too I had a real nice someone to go home to. Rain, hail or snow, too. Not for Mr Whistler some picked-up slut from barlife sleazeville, or at a party where the sleaze moved their activities to; a sheila who chews gum or smokes a fag while you're trying to reach her, find that sumpin special of womanhood a dude like you needs to find or it's all fucking meaningless, it may as well be a sheep from a paddock, a piece of meat that ya hump in and out of till you're spent. You wanna show her your specialness of tender concern, your depth of unnerstaning, you ain't no Jube McCall wanting only to shove her down on your meat as he calls it.

Nope, none of this type for you, Mr Whistler, you and yours'll be *loving*, and journeying the depths of each other, I know ya will. Not like a Tavi moll who's all wrong timing and harsh kisses and untender touch. And talking like that Lyn of Tawa on the tv: Sunnee, didja like me straightaway when ya firz saw me? Or you'll be inside her and she'll wanna know what kinda car do ya drive, Sunnee? Is it fast? Is it a Vee-ate? So yeah, Mr Whistler, not for you dying inside her because of sumping she said that was not near of the moment.

Ya wouldn't unnerstan, Mr and Mrs, that our girls, our women, are basic functions of crude back motive, of: What's it worth if I let you have your way, Sunnee? Of dry twat and hard-kissing lips. Not for your Mrs Whistler to fail to reach your partner; it, love, is a refined process for you both. It is part of the great reflection of having class and breeding, and a little bit of money probably helps too, though it ain't necessary, not on its own. (I've read it somewhere . . . Oh, I know: was a book, that's right. I was only young, a teenager — Jesus, it was borstal. Borstal. And I was doing solitary. Just sixteen and doing solitary.)

Insolence to an officer, that's what the charge was. Seven days in the Digger on number two diet. Teenagers, mere teenagers, and they were throwing us into cells for periods of solitary confinement, and on specified diets according to the gravity of the crime. Number one was cold potatoes, glass of milk, piece of bread for three meals a day three days on end, full normal rations on the fourth, then back to another regime of number one. It was assumed to be civilised. Number two was dripping to spread on the bread, and porridge for breakfast, soup and bread and dripping spread for lunch, spuds, bread and milk for tea.

They woke you up each morning, the six separated cells of you, at five thirty. A warning bang on your steel door, you had five minutes to get your bed made up in the required bedroll formation. You were unlocked separately to take your bedding to an empty cell, or if occupied, out behind the steel-grille entry door; and you collected it again, under escort, at nine at night. (When I was just sixteen.)

On your second day, two officers came to your cell: one stood at the door, the other ordered you to your feet. Name! Mahia. Bang. He punched you on the chest — Sir. Sir. You gonna be insolent to an officer again. No, sir. *Oooofff*, a piledriver again in the gut. You fell on the concrete floor. He ordered you, GET UP! You did. His pal at the door smirked at you: I don't think this one'll be back here again. They left. You heard the process being repeated in muffled form next door. You thought you wanted to die, at only sixteen, but mainly because they took away your right to reply. Explain yourself.

That afternoon they returned. And you backed into a corner, wondering why they hadn't had enough. But it was an offer. Of two cigarettes if you'd donate blood. They'd also let you have a longer shower tonight as well. You got taken out into the main wing, and it was like seeing it again: it was a big space of landings two high, and steel stairs and echoing screw footsteps and inmates behind cell doors yelling out occasional obscenities.

There were these guys in white coats who smiled at you and were very gentle as you sat on a chair and they put this thing around your arm, which they pumped up. You thought of the two smokes this was going to be rewarded with, and were struck by the kindness of their manner. Too soon it was over, part of you was dark red in a plastic container and a screw was taking you back to your cell, over a lino floor polished over and over by some teenage set of designated cleaners meant to be training for rehabilitation, but really they were learning to be adult forms of what they were then — criminals.

Back in your cell the screw gave you your two smokes and a piece of striker and only one match. Then he left you. So you tremblingly lit the smoke, fearing you'd blow it and have the smokes but no means of igniting. You lit the other off the first and you felt sick halfway through smoking the second. And you felt you'd been cheated.

On the third day they made a mistake: they let you have a choice from a selection of books, most of them insulting nursery-rhyme stuff deliberately chosen by Mr Stone, the unhappy screw on day duty in charge of the Digger. He thought it was really funny just grabbing any old books from, Sonny presumed, the borstal library, except what would it be doing with nursery-rhyme books in a place with young men? But it was a mistake all the same, because Sonny lucked onto a book that from page one put an end to the sentence. An end. They'd fucked up. They'd unknowingly released him with five hundred and sixty pages of freedom. So when the nights came with bedding return Sonny was disappointed. And so the seven-day sentence ended just half an hour after he'd read the last page of the book. And he was still soaring free with its characters and southern American settings and voice twangs and Yank peculiarisms when

Mr Stone opened his cell door and told him it was over and I better not be seeing you again.

All them years ago like yesterday. And what'd a man come to? This? Is this what he amounted to?

The rain came down harder. Buckets of the stuff, endless buckets; pelting so hard it stung a man's scalp, the backs of his hands. Could have been a reminder, in symbolic form, of being assailed by the fists of his fellow prison inmates the first sentence he did, and first met Jube; belted up for being the thinker type, no other reason on earth. For simply having a mind that was curious. (Oh fuckem all, the boobheads of the world.) He tried to tell em he was one of them, he was no threat, and even when he put it to em that if he was so brainy as they said, what the hell was he doing inside, they didn't hear.

They did not hear.

A woman appeared below, she wore a purple plastic raincoat with a hood that was up, and big yellow buttons blurred in the downpour. She disappeared where Jube's side of the bank turned to rock formation. But very soon came another, her arrival being announced by the sharp ring of heel on pathway, clik-clik-clik-clik. When across from Sonny rose the apparition that had to be Jube; yet it couldn't be, it was too real, too crazy, and anyway where was his signal? Nor did his plan at any stage mention a woman being the victim.

But training had Sonny shooting a look over his shoulder for the all-clear, scanning the almost-dark park, then it hit him that the attack was about to take place and that it was a woman. He buried his face in his hands, but that didn't work so he pulled them away. And the figure below was three parts across Sonny's framed vision. And the figure opposite — (*Jeezuz!*) Well, he was flailing. His arms were clawing the air. Then a leg shot out at an awkward angle, then it — the figure that had to be Jube, as unbelievable as it was — flipped entirely. Man, his big spoon feet just went out from under him.

Then down he tumbled, as the unsuspecting woman clik-clik-clikked her way out of sight, though Sonny didn't have his eyes on her but on Jube. Him sliding down the slope all arms and legs, and then an audible thunk followed by a stifled groan as he hit the pathway. Smack dab on his bum. And the would-be victim gone.

Just Jube there, sat on his dumb white arse with hands behind supporting him. And Sonny holding back his laughter for all he could.

Rain falling.

Jube scrambling to his feet, shaking himself. Looking up at Sonny's position, Sonny?

Sonny.

Sonny! The fuck are ya? Sonny? Jube staring up at the bushes. Then behind him. Back Sonny's way again, Sonny! hissing it out. Then he turned and scrambled back up the slope, slipping and sliding in his haste. A few moments to catch his breath. Sonny? Lighter-toned this time. And Sonny stretching the moment. SONNY! For fuck's sake, man, the fuck are ya?

Yeow?

Sonny? That you? Where the fuck ya been?

For a crap, man. Couldn't hold off any longer. Wha's up?

How long you been crapping?

Oh, bout five — hey, I didn't exactly *time* it, man. Everything alright?

Sure is. But let me know next time will ya? I mighta been doing the bizzo. So what'd ya use for paper — leaves? Hahaha!

Yeow, leaves, brother. But Jube?

Yep?

You think I woulda been better sliding down the bank on my arse?

Wha'?

Well I woulda been as clean as a whistle by the time I got to the, uh, the bottom . . .

I don't get ya, man?

Oh, I think you did — HAHAHAHAHAHA!

Know sumpin, Sonny? You're an arsehole.

Woman pushing a pram — (the hell is she doing out in this weather with a lil bubs?) — though the rain'd eased off quite a bit. She was partly beneath an umbrella, which was mostly tended the way of her carriaged child (all tucked up in there) as she hit the lamplight, a portrait of motherhood, leaned forward to protect her child, who didn't really need it. Then gone. The outjutting of rock and night just swallowed them. And one of her elevated observers promising himself that if Jube'd made a move on her he'd've yelled her a warning, and if it still came to it he'd have — (I'd've charged down the bank and knocked him for six. I think.) Sonny hoped.

Next: it might have been a statue, a dark, moving statue wrapped in a stylish overcoat moving quite swiftly, with no heels ringing her coming. An arm across from Sonny shot up, and the figure immediately followed. Sonny groaned inside: it *was* to be a woman. Hating Jube. And himself.

Eyes back at the pathway to catch the shape of Jube loping up behind the coated figure. And fist clubbing her to the ground. Sonny glanced over his shoulder for danger signs; just street lights ribboning off in the distance of wet gloom. Back to the woman and this cry escaping her just a single, O. Like that.

The same echoed in his heart.

Then the two of them, racing headlong through the dark off where the path was lighted; over slippery rolls and down into troughs. Balance an uncanny finding of both them. Running. Running. (We're always —) *ahuurgh*, Sonny sucking in breath — (running from things. Crime deed —) — *ahuurgh* — (cops —) — *ahuurgh* — (from life — *this* lousy life.)

Yet here, between his own sucks and blows and frantic haste, was the other of them, Jube, dragging in breath even as he was laughing.

Two Big Macs with large fries times two, my man, and puddit right here, Sonny, my main man. Hahahahaha. Catch up on all the lost cigarettes, one after the sweet other. Man, is this good or what? Two dozen cold cans, Lion Red a course, my good man, thank you very much. Filler up, please, and ya bedda givus fifty bucks of vouchers while you're at it. Oh, and a carton of Pall Mall filter, make that two cartons, just in case, eh mate? hahahaha. Ya never know when ya might run out.

Off we go, down with the windows, on with the heater, that'll dry us out. Pass me another can, Sonny, I gotta thirst — Like an elephant. You got it, Sonny-boy: like a fucking elephant.

Four hundred and thirty ... forty ... fifty ... sixty — We *still* got four sixty bucks left, Sonny. Oh but can ya *believe* it? Hahahahaha, ain't life sweet sometimes? And how's ya clothes, they startin to dry yet? Maybe you want a bit more speed with the ole heater — HAHAHAHAHA!! Come on now, Sonny, lighten up, bud. The woman'll be okay. She just got a knock on the back of the neck. You're worried, we'll get a paper first thing — that's if we ain't hungover and forget — HAHAHAHAHA!!

And hey, don't the sea look nice at this time a night? Lookit that, a fountain stuck out there middle of the fucking sea. Din't notice that before, did you, Sonny? Hey, come on now, *cheer* up. Get a few cans down ya gut, that'll fix it. It was only a lil whack, Sonny. You'll see. *Read all about it! Read all about it! HAHAHAHAHA-HAHAHA!!* Oh man, but this's too fucking funny for words, man. Pass me another can, bro! Ladalaladedumdedumdedaaaa!

(Life, eh?)

4 Oh man, Sonny shaking his head as he and Jube left the bar, Why do I fall for your fuckin dreams and schemes everytime, man? That's the second time we hung around in that creepy joint with all them wasted alky dudes outta their fuckin heads and us waiting for *Pete* to show up — again. *Again*, Jube. Well, at least we're leaving with bread in our pockets — *Your* pocket, ya mean. You been rationing out that dough like I'm your kid on pocket money. Stopping in the street to stare up at the taller Jube, annoyed that he was grinning. The hell's that look for? Pocket? Money? Geddit, Sonny?

Jeeeeez, Sonny hissing his exasperation. Ya call that funny? Oh, I heard worse, Sonny my main — And I *ain't* your main lil man. Listen, listen for a minute, will ya? at Jube resuming walking, heading for his car. Jube, we can't go on like this. Jube? Jube! But Jube was laughing. In the busy — even for this sleazy area — pedestrian five of Wellington evening Jube was weaving in and out and laughing. And calling over his shoulder at Sonny having to trot to catch up with him, Let's go find another bar. Another bar, eh Jube? You goddit, Sonny. And what, hang around for *Pete* again? Aw, now now, Sonny. No fuckin now nows, man, I'm about sick of this. And why're we hanging around Wellington still anyrate? Told ya, gonna hot that area up the hill where we broke down other day, that's what we're doing. But, man, there's areas all over fuckin Auckland just as good. Jube's head going from side to side. Not the same. Why not the same? Cos it ain't. Sonny behind him sarcasming, Cos it ain't. Cos it ain't. That's a reason, Jube: cos it ain't? Reason nuff for me, Son.

Following the striding Jube, how the beer gave him confidence that he didn't otherwise have; though it did the same for Sonny, he wasn't denying that. (Cept I know it don't make me get that show-

49

off swagger like Jube's got on.) A kid selling newspapers, Sonny digging in his pocket, not even loose change. Hey, Jube, givus some change for a paper. Jube? Jube! at him still walking, having to run around in front of Jube to halt the man. Some change, will ya; I wanna buy a paper. And anyrate why're you still holding out on me, man? I was part of the job. Oh yeah? Yeah. Like as in what? Like as in I kept watch. So gimme gimme. Oh man, but you must think you're sumpin else giving me out the money like that, as Jube made a job of counting out from a handful of coins, How much does a paper cost? Fuck you, man, I'll remember this.

In Jube's car, Sonny scanning the front page. Whatcha lookin for, Sonny-boy — a job? Hahahahaha! Situations Vacant are in the back pages, cuz, hahahahaha. The jerk with his irritating laugh as he revved his engine up, and Sonny didn't even have to look to know that Jube's eyes'd be out on the pavement scanning for fans. (Pathetic jerk.)

Sonny found it on page three; just a little mention, of a woman who'd been assaulted and robbed in a central city park, had been discharged from hospital and her injuries were not serious. Hey, Jube, I found it, Sonny put on a grave tone, gave the same face to Jube as he stopped for a traffic light. He saw the wince around Jube's eyes, then his features tighten, as he stared straight ahead. Sonny made out to be reading direct from the newspaper: Says here the woman is in a serious condition . . . in intensive care. She regained consciousness at one stage and it is believed she was able to give a good description of her attacker — Hey? How come? I hit the bitch from behind. She's lying, man. The bitch is lying. Let me finish it, will ya? Where was I . . . She describes her attacker as — oh listen to this, Jube — as tall, with a moustache, bad breath and very very ugly — HAHAHAHAHAHA!! Got ya this time, Jube McCall. Though the look on Jube's face didn't have him agreeing or seeing the humour. He just drove.

Jube picked a bar at a big-city roundabout, That'll do the boys.

Two jugs, buddy. Lion Red, a course. Only wankers drink any other brand, eh mate? Jube not catching the barman's cold look in reply. Place was quite busy. Least it ain't sleazeville, eh Sonny? Nope. Sonny looking at the pool table. I'll go put our name up on the board. He walked over to the blackboard, nodding cordially to a group obviously playing partners. Maoris. One of them gave Sonny a typical lift of eyebrows greeting of one Maori to another. Made

Sonny feel warm. Even if he didn't particularly feel of any race, Maori or white; as he was in about exact half proportions. If anything, he identified with the Maori side of himself, but hardly gave any of it a thought.

He and Jube drank their beer and watched the games progress till it was their turn. Jube looked at Sonny with that self-assured look of his when he was a good part pissed: I'm feeling like I did in the park other night, bro. Lucky. Puddit here, he stuck his hand and shook Sonny's hand, as if they were about to enter a competition of epic proportions. Sonny let go of Jube's hand quickly.

. . . these two fullas, eh — from Auckland, eh — played us in pool. Came walking in here bout, what time, Bull, ha'pass five? Yeah, ha'pass five, eh, and we weren't even warmed up. Our first jugs. Bull made it a jug a corner, and we thought we were gonna wastem eh. A fuckin hour later and their table's lined up with our jugs. Yeh, in *our* pub, and here's these strangers from Auckland fucking cleaning us up, eh.

So Tama takes over from Bull — eh Bull? cos you're fuckin useless, eh? hahaha — cos he was getting wild at these fullas still winning. Tin-arsing, more like it. They couldn't do a thing wrong. And us getting broker and broker from having to buy em jugs. Tama tole the main fulla, the Pakeha cunt, the smart-arse one, make it singles, you and me, ten bucks a game. But the Pakeha says no, keep it doubles, but ten bucks a corner's alright cos they already had enough jugs to las em all night. Laughing at us, eh? That's what the cunt was doing: laughing at us. So Tama goes yeah, alright, ten bucks a corner.

Well, first game was nothing in it, eh. Was me: I fucked up on the black when they had one more to go. Hey, and the Honky's got the nerve to laugh at me for jawing the black. I felt like jawing him, eh — witha fuckin right. So they won that game. But when this white shet comes over to me, sticks out his whiteman freckle-hand saying gimme gimme, I was this close — this close to up and smackinim one. But Tama gives me a look not to, eh. Not yet. So I gave this Honky shet his ten bucks, and Tama gave his mate his ten — Maori he was too. Don't ask me what he was doing teamed up with a fuckin white wankah like this. Wasn't as if he wassa tough-lookin fulla either, the Maori guy, jussa, you know, a ornry-looking fulla, eh. Eh Bull, the Maori fulla was alright, eh? Yeh, even Bull thought he was alright, this Maori mate of the egg.

Eh, but as if it's not bad enough them beating us on the table, this Pakeha cunt has to start talking league. How Auckland always wastes Wellington. And I tole him, What about Wainui then? How come they won the national championships then, cunt? But he juss said something smart, eh, cos he fuckin knew Wellington's got the best club in the country. Man, was I getting wilder. Felt like going up toim and saying, Come on then, you and me, man. Auckland against Wellington, then see how you go. I'da givim fuckin Auckland alright. Punchland, eh Bull? Give the cunt punchland.

New game. Well, bugger me days if this Honky piece a shet don't up and pot al their balls one turn, eh. Only left em the black. Then the Maori fulla he tin-arses the black, so me and Tama we're doing twenty apiece and juss about broke. Then this Jube fulla comes up with his gimme gimme shet — man, I was just about to up and smackim when Tama's brother grabs me. Coolit, Joe, he says. They won fair and square. I thought he was serious for a minit, eh, till I looked at his face and he gave me a sly wink. So I knew it was gonna be on soon.

The Maori fulla — Sonny — I'll say this for him: he was giving us back our jugs they won earlier. He didn't even want the last ten he and his mate won. I felt sorry forim, eh, what we were gonna have to do to him and his arsehole mate. Not his mate, but him, the little Maori fulla. But oh well, such is life, eh boys? Such is life in the Roundabout Tavern: issa quick and the dead in here, eh boys? HAHAHAHA!

It was worse with this Sonny fulla trying to talk, be friendly, you know? But, man, I wasn't gonna con*verse* witha dude taking my money — and my fuckin pride — so I hardly said nothing back to him, eh. Just: Yep. Nope. Uh. And he wassa smooth-looking dude, eh Bull? Half-caste, eh, he mussa been a half-carse. Looked more like that Eytalian fulla, you knowim, the fulla owns the fishnchips place at the Naenae shops. The one always looking in that mirror he's got by the till at him fuckin self. Well, this's what this Sonny looked like — Well, till we had to make a couple *al*ter*ay*shuns to his face — HAHAHAHAHAHAHA!!! But you shoulda seen what we did to his mate; the Maori fulla got off light.

I go to take my shot and Tama whispers to me when I pass, It's on. So my heart it's going to fuckin town, eh. Cos I'm *dy*in to smack this Honky. Man couldn't concentrate on his shot then; not that it maddered, hahaha, seein as the game wasn't gonna last for much longer. I just whacked at a ball, then it's the Honk's turn. Down he goes and Tama goes, Hey, you moved the white, man. Game shot. Strict fouls in our pub. I never saw the white move, so I knew this was it, cuzzy; we are gonna be getting it *on*, hahahaha. And here's me, here's me making out I wasn't interested but I'm *easing* myself up to where the action was gonna be, my eyes making out I'm half sleepy from the beer — No, make that me making out I was sussing out the lie of the table for my partner's next shot, hahaha!

The Honky goes, No way, bud. You know how they go: Bud. Bud, they call you. Man, I hate fuckin bud, dudes calling me bud. And Tama don't like it either. No way, *bud*, this cunt says, you're juss trying to set us up. And Tama goes, Wha'? What was that, man? And this Jube goes, Can't ya take a loss like men? And Tama steps up closer and goes, What was that you said, white man? And me, I knew Tama wanted that Honky juss as bad for himself, so I moved closer over to the Maori fulla, even though I was feeling a bit, you know, sorry for him, eh. Then I says to him, You're a fuckin cheat, juss like your whiteman mate here. Just to work myself up, eh, cos he really didn't deserve it, he was juss in the wrong place, eh. Oh man, so this Sonny guy looks at me with these big innocent eyes — fuckin near broke my heart, and thassa truth. You know, like a big ole dog wondering what the fuck he's done wrong why you're dealing to him? Oh man.

Man, but I had to do the business right then or I'da never done it, eh. Too soft. Too much the Maori aroha in my heart; and after all, he was one of our own, even if he did come from Auckland. Like hitting your own liddle brother.

I smackedim. Fuckin had to, before his big brown eyes had me up and buying him a fuckin beer! Hahahahaha!! HAHAHAHA-HAHAHA!! I'm a funny bastard, eh? But that's how I felt, eh. But he don't go down with that first shot. No way. And not as if he was a big cunt or nothin, jussa small fulla really. You know, average to small. He just wobbles and then those fuckin eyes're looking at me again! But me, I was too embarrassed he didn't go down, and I could see out the corner of my eye Tama and Marty having it out with the Honky, so I goes, Oh well, in my mind, and let this lil fulla have it — *Boom*. Right between the fuckin eyes. And he goes down.

I look at the other fullas, and hello, this Honky dude is slugging it out with the Motu brothers. They're throwing punches atim from everywhere, but he's throwing them straight back, eh, I'll say that for him. And boy, the looks on those brothers' faces, hahahahaha; were they fuckin surprised at what they'd picked on. Me too. But I still wanted this cunt badly, eh, so over I go. And Tama he's starting to do more dancing and blocking than punching, cos this Pakeha's real tough; and Marty he's got that worried look, not cos he was scared, you know what Marty's like, he don't mind even if he gets a hiding as long as he has a scrap. But he was worried this Jube fulla was gonna clean the both them up.

I seen this gap, eh, in the fulla's guard. So I in — *booom*. Smack on the chin. But when he juss looks at me with these mad blue eyes, I thought, Oh-oh, whadda we got here, a fuckin escaped loony from the sylum? So I hittim again. And his eyes go funny, so I know I've hit the right spot — thank fuckin chrise, eh Bull? As for you, Bull Hapeta, where the fuckin hell were you, now I think of it? What? HAHAHAHAHAHA!! In the blimmin toilet . . . Oh yeah. So his eyes go funny and his guard drops. And, brother, you do not drop your guard when that mad Marty's around, you don't. Cos in he goes, Marty; fuckin fists pumping like Sugar Ray Leonard I tell you. Down the fulla goes, and the brothers are into him with the boot. Kicked the fuckin shet out of him. Then they wanna work over the Maori fulla, eh, who's up on his feet and trying to stop them kicking his mate's head in. But I stopped them, Tama and Marty. Leavim alone, I toldem, he wasn't doing nothin much wrong, was his Pakeha mate not him.

So they drag this Jube fulla outta the bar, throw him out in the carpark. His mate picks him up and we see them drive past, right out that window there, eh Bull? Or were you in the toilet hiding again? And you know what, the Honky fulla's giving us all in here the evils, eh.

He drives round and round the roundabout — tha's why they call it a roundabout I spose, hahahaha — bout four fuckin times, slow as. Slow as, eh Bull? And fuck the traffic too, he wasn't worrying bout slowing up the traffic; just us. Giving us the evil eye. Never seen nothing like it. Not in all the years I — we, hahahaha — we been beating up wankers, for one to go like that; round and round and round, his face all beat up but not so we couldn't see his evils. And Marty wanting to go out and givim some more, but me and Tama said you're on your fuckin own, bro, that fulla's fuckin mad in the head. He mighta had a shotgun sittin in there or sumpin.

The last time he drove past he pointed: one-two-three times, eh. And we could tell he was saying, I'm coming back for you. And I don't mind admitting, boys, it put the shits up in me I can tell you. Mean to say, a ornry fight a man don't think twice about it. But this cunt didn't turn out no ornry fight. Musta done a bidda time inside too, by the tats onim. A fuckin jailbird, eh boys? He and his mate musta been a cupla jailbirds. Anyone here been to jail . . . ? Nope? Nor me. Oh well, mussa been jail made him like that. But wouldn't surprise me he turned up here one day, outta the blue, with a whole lotta mates to get his revenge. And I spose Bull here would just happen to wanna go to the toilet, hahahahaha! HAHAHAHA-HAHA!! Oh well.

And Joe the Roundabout Tavern regular took his eyes half hopingly, half warily around his bar just in case he saw a mug or two he and his pals could beat up on, and just in case yesterday's madman had returned to back up. Then he clapped his hands together: So. So who else's got a story to tell? And everybody grinning, smoking, drinking their beer. You could tell Joe's story'd made em feel warm inside. Warm, excited, and a little afraid too. Of what they weren't used to.

5 Two trespassers sneaked in under cover of the night they best thrive in; poised in readiness for dog outbreak, at first probing of stone thrown from the other side, then another thrown from the shadow of the head-high fence they'd climbed over. Hands gripped to retreat at sound of dog bark and paw crush over the long, sloping lawn they were eye-keened to.

No moon. No stars. Not much light that might pick them out as braced and half turned to the fence. Faint wash of sea down the street residential distance; rhythmic sigh of ocean, and the quick takes of their own excited, fearing breathing. Not forgetting the pain and rhythmic throbbing of beating wounds but a day into healing. Least not that of the taller of the two figures. And too his heart.

Waiting in that eternity it always is; the surrounding picture of darkness and funny residue of light, which maybe is from all the little artificial glows from households, but whatever, it must be a man gets eyes in the dark. He can see things. In outline, but he can pick out tiny details. Oh, but maybe just the senses heightened by being a thief; and maybe it's the more so when you're both fresh and sore with the physical consequences of your social inadequacy, in that your eyes, specially Jube's, seek out — and find — in the dark a kind of atonement? (Well, it's done now. It don't madda anymore, the deed's been done.) Nope. No dogs. Let's go. Jube in control. Jube in command. Jube making up for last night: someone's gonna pay.

Two trespassers transgressing further; flits of swift shadows moved from the fence over black space of lawn to tree eruption. Hand rested against trunk, sharp the feel of bark texture, and Sonny registering the tiny indentations so starkly he could have been stoned. Jube moving off. Sonny in fast follow. Sonny with the rising of heroics. A comic-book star. Paused at another tree. Eyes fixed on the odd shape of house. Could be a movie, even; with them the two main stars, and everyone in the audience on the edges of their seats in admiration of them (me and Jube here). Watching them, their two heroes, as they advanced on their target, big bulk of house up the slope there, roofline hither and thither, a jumble of upthrusts and downward structural angles set against a sky greyed by the faintest of light; of all them houses, the compoundment of home lights, where all the mummies'd put their kids to bed, and daddies'd helped too, and the love'd been long made and they were separate, kind of, in dream now. And two thieves panting unfit bodies up a steep slope, intending to commit crime.

No-one home, Jube through his swollen lips coming out muffled. Like I always say, Son: no-one home at two, no-one home at all. Let's go. Sonny not as sure as Jube, never was; even though the letterbox had circulars built up in it to tell old-hand burglars that the newspapers might be stopped, the neighbours collecting the mail, but unless you had a No Circulars sign on your letterbox, Jube'd chuckingly reminded, ya may as well stick a sign up says you're ready to be burgled.

Off the lawn standing in the driveway catching breath, both of them hands on knees but with eyes wary, observant. Front entrance one of them richy jobs, with big overhang of roof verandah, and a little lightglow on the doorbell so could be seen the solid slab of wooden door in there under tunnel-like entrance of roof and support poles dripping with growth jagged in leafy outline. Brass knocker smack dab upper centre of door, visible in the bell light. (In case there's a power cut?) Sonny wondering about that one as they straightened and headed for the door. Jube trying it, locked. Empty down there in the carport. This was looking a cinch.

Jube led them around the house; slowly-slowly, careful-careful, ya never can tell, ain't nothin written as guaranteed when ya burgling: though it was looking an odds-on certainty. Man, I never seen such a weird house; you, Sonny? It's weird alright. Hope it's weird with the goods inside. Yeah, it'll be, Jube confident in his tone, that mufflement of voice reminding Sonny, as if he needed reminding. (Was a fuckin nightmare. But then so is our life. This very life of right-now: creeping around this big house, looking for best way in.) Sonny not thinking what it might be like to be on the receiving end, not really. Mind not working like that. Not now.

Pausing at windows, none with curtains across, to peer in, scan for movement. Nothin. No life here, man. Jube sounding excited. The hope returned. But I ain't never seen a joint like this shape before. Nor me, man. Check out the size a the fucking lawn, Son. No Neighbourhood Watches here, bro. Jube at the vastness of section size as well trees along the boundary lines, with just small gaps through which hardly a house light shone at this two o'clock of a starless early morning. Man, we could have a fucking party and the neighbours wouldn't hear. I've got a good feeling, Sonny. A real good feeling. Yeah well, let's wait and see, man. Won't be no good feeling the pigs catch us on the job. Wait up a minute, I'm gonna check for a back way out. Aw, come on — No come ons, man, It goes wrong . . . Sonny not waiting for Jube to further scorn his caution, headed up the sloping lawn to where it levelled off.

The surprise of outlook. Of residential spots of light, and the ribboning of streetlamps in that quiet way they get of two in the morning, a stealing morning. It had Sonny catch his breath; was a stepping from one world to the other, which he hadn't thought about till now. Brought it back in the instant too, his and Jube's distance: from them down there before his eyes, fast asleep all the families, might be one or two couples making love. Keening his ear in the idiot hope that he might hear the cries of woman in ecstasy. Then he felt wrong. Not for the thought of love-making, but for being here.

But then it didn't feel wrong, not when he went whoosh in his mind over his life; what else could he have been? So it felt out of balance, not wrong. At odds. With the world, as usual. Of two of society's failures in the process of taking more of their living — the luxuries end — from the same society't kept em alive on government benefits. And Sonny knew it didn't fit. So he turned, not bothering with assessing a possible extra escape route, and he trotted down the slope where Jube was waiting in the shadow of one of the many jut-outs of house structure; a house of nooks and corner crannies, and why, even some of the windows were *curved*. Jube wasn't going to be asking him about his escape route, Sonny knew that, so he just followed Jube in silence as he went back into burglar mode.

Back door was full pane of glass. Couldn't be better, Jube in a whisper. Go check out the neighbours for hearing the glass break, Jube instructed. Sonny did a quick but careful scout, told Jube fine, too many trees, nobody'll hear a thing. Good. Jube ran his gloved fingers up around the door surround for alarm wiring. Sonny flicked on a torch for the sign that declared a place was burglar-alarmed. Nothing. Jube hissed at him to turn the fucking thing off, Ya think it's Christmas?

Jube took off his jersey and wrapped it round his right hand. Sonny stepped forward and ran a diamond roller glass cutter in a practised square adjacent to the door handle, a bit larger than fist size. Stepped back. Jube gave it a little aiming nudge first, then a short hard punch. Broke first time. Sonny waiting for the hiss of triumph from Jube as he usually did. But it didn't come. Only a half-hearted grunt of satisfaction, as if he was preoccupied with his hurt from the beating. But more the hurt to his manpride; that Jube had and Sonny didn't see the point of. Though Sonny knew it well enough. Was the thing that ran through every crim he ever knew: pride. But not pride pride. Just this sullen, dangerous quality, a capacity to be deeply hurt by anything and everything. Then watch out. World, that is. Made em bashers, stabbers, softball-bat club-bers, even murderers, when the pride was stepped on. Real or imagined. Sonny listening to Jube's breathing as he fiddled with the door lock through the hole. Sonny hoping like hell then that no-one was inside, or they'd be the ones copping Jube's simmering wrath.

Inside. That first moment. A limbo. On the way from your domain into another's. Raced the heart, lightened the head, had the face going hot and cold with the flushes. Excited and feared. The stranger(s) on wrong territory. Ya wanted to turn and run, but your other mind was saying stay stay, this could be it. So ya stood there, and ya felt like a lost child stumbled into a somewhere it shouldn't be and not knowing the means, in the mixed-up mind, how to get the hell out. Then the same mind it started moving, rapidly, through the changes.

Sonny remembered the time he and Jube did a place and they were peering through a window when a woman sat up in bed — her shape did — and screamed. Like nothing a man'd heard before, and it'd hurt him. He wanted to yell at her to stop, not to worry they weren't rapists, they hadn't come to murder her, just to, like, steal some stuff from her, preferably cash. But the woman was screaming and Jube was swearing under his breath, then he got louder and next he was yelling at the woman, calling her a bitch, that she should be

59

so lucky he was gonna rape her. Sonny took off, left Jube to his mad devices. Jube came sauntering back to the car parked some hundreds of yards away as casual could be and laughing at the woman her fear and how she oughta be grateful they weren't there to do a bit of *man's* business. Jube informed Sonny as they drove away, did he know women have a very high rate of orgasm when they're raped? That's because it's a woman's secret fantasy to be raped, it's what they all wank emselves over.

Sound of Jube moving, the tip-toeing of his cowboy boots on a hard surface, his outline a tall, swift-moving shape. Sonny wiping at the sweat broke out over his brow and running down his face, the woollen gloves feeling like sandpaper as he wiped. Wiping and letting his mind do its processing stuff that'd give command to his scared stiff legs to move. And it was always like this. Same for others he knew, though not most. Too unmanly for em to admit if they were anyway.

It was a bit like that first chemical trickle of sleep coming on — it felt tremendous. A high on its way. The fear faded away and came great relief and a strange excitement, like some part of you was being avenged, or compensated for the life you'd been given, even the life you the adult'd made for yourself. It was still a making-up. So Sonny moved off after Jube.

Through what had to be the kitchen by the shapes and little gleams of shiny metal here and there catching light from outside, bare though it was, and Jube's frame in outline as he moved across like a huge screen these huge windows, a row of em. And as Sonny followed suit, the city buildings suddenly rose up in his vision and repeated themselves in mirror image on a still harbour. And there ships, strung out with glowing lightbulbs, rows of majestic and bulky steel profiles. (Me, up here looking down on it, like I own this joint. Like I paid to have this view . . .)

The eyes adjusted and, with the added light from glittering city, the room became vast, its shape quite irregular. A big piano with its half-raised lid throwing off the building lights. This was class. What kind of people live in a joint like this? And where's Jube got to?

Found Jube, picked up his distinctive form as he stepped past a tall, narrow window other side of the big ones that had the view. Jube'd give directions in his own good time. Sonny took his eyes back to the big windows, took a moment to figure out that the zips of lights running both ways along a well-illuminated strip were a motorway. No stars. No moon. Yet for some reason getting a thought about stars, how every little dot of twinkle was a huge body and that some dwarfed even the sun. Just dots, yet vaster than everything that'd ever been of mankind and his mad and sad and silly and hideous ways. Then he turned to pick out Jube again when — !!

Sonny sucked in a great breath of total disbelief at the grabbing of his arm in painful grip. Had to stifle his scream. Then came Jube's chuckle, which rose to a rolling laughter, and Sonny whacked away Jube's hand from his arm, You cunt! You *cunt!* And Jube still laughing. That ain't *funny.* Sonny's annoyance growing fear at Jube's laughter seemingly out of control. He started for the door out. Got a few paces then the world flooded with light.

Sonny dropped instinctively to the floor, which brought howling laughter from Jube. Sonny stood up. Jube a monstrous sight with beaten-up face and mouth agape in laughter, Sonny had no eyes for the illuminated surrounds. Ya mad? You gone fuckin mad or sumpin? Brain damage? It's brain damage, man, that's what you got from the hiding: fuckin brain damage. The hell've you got the fuckin lights on for, man? Ya like being inside? Ya like prison cells? Man, I'm outta here. Sonny made for the door once again.

Sonny, Sonny — *Sonnee!* Hold up, man, whatsa big panic? But Sonny didn't stop till he got to the door and reached for the handle. Jube, you are stark fuckin ravers — Ya are! Yet couldn't help but be aware of the strikingness of this house now with the kitchen flooded in light, showing up the huge living-room area where stood that big black piano. And Jube moving over to this big dining table, saying, A note, a note. They left us a note. Sonny not knowing where to take his eyes — on Jube or at this new dimension of living such as he'd never seen. His body still wanting to flee, and warning Jube, What about Neighbourhood Watch, you idiot? Jube stopping at the insult to give Sonny a baleful stare before shaking his head and grabbing up the piece of paper.

Sonny racing his eyes around, but not to take in the sights; he was just scared. Jube, the pigs'll be on their way, man. I know ain't no-one's here but . . . Had to pause to swallow the catching in his throat. Mind with images of police interrogation, of that look the D's get of absolute superiority over you, the caught-again dumb-arse criminal, how they tell you that, in tones of contempt and scorn, and how they still play the roles of good cop and bad cop, and yet it fuckingwell works, after all these years it works. I'm going.

Sonny opened the door and stepped out into the relative night. Got several paces and was about to break into a sprint when Jube began calling him back, Sonny! Sonny! Oh, you just won't believe this, man. Come back! Hearing the command. Stopping. Heart hammering (I don't wanna go back inside. Can't take one more day of it.) Yet Jube's voice echoing in his mind.

He turned, went back and stood in the doorway, immediately struck again by the spectacular dimensions of house interior, its angles, off-white walls and timber bits and pieces everywhere, and Jube over there standing staring down at a piece of paper in his hand shaking his head, whistling a one-note expel of apparent disbelief. Jube, we gotta go — Hold up, Son. Hold up. Jube, we have to — Listen to this, Son. Jube turning to Sonny. His face grotesque in its disbelief, as it was in any expression with his swollen wounds and cuts and general puffiness.

But Sonny with the urgencies, so rushing over to Jube — even as he began reading out loud from the note — tugging at his T-shirt exposed bare arm, Please, Jube. Let's go wait it out. Ten minutes, man, that's all I ask. But Jube going, No, no, listen to this. As Sonny pulled at him.

Outside, the pair of them. Jube complaining it was all panic shit this coming outside to give it time, see what developed from a might-be suspicious neighbour. The fucking note, you wankah, it said there was *money* left for some Oliver dude. It'll keep, Jube. It'll keep. It'll keep, Jube. It'll keep, Jube in sarcastic repeat. It'll keep says the country's most panicky burglar. Well, it *won't* fucking keep. And it don't, Son, then I'm gonna take it out on your black hide I swear.

Waiting down by the fence, in its shadow, Jube with enough sense to hush his mouth for a few minutes as they scanned the neighbourhood — what was visible through the trees right around the property — for lights suddenly gone on. Ears anticipating the approach, the silent approach as they called it, of cops coming to the scene. Then Jube starting up that he knew it was a waste of time, but Sonny saying, Wait on, please, mate, just wait a few more minutes. My mind's juss one big picture of a cell, man, I'm tellin ya. I'm freaked out. Wanked out more like it, Jube unsympathetic.

They gave it maybe twenty minutes. Of watching that house with the lights left on like a decoy. Then back they went, up the slope. Running this time. And Jube giggling and guessing on how much bread there'd be the note said was under the pillow of someone called Ants, of all things; pillow because, so said the strange note, she liked playing Santa Claus where her big brother was concerned.

Inside again and which way to go where the bedrooms'd be? Down them stairs. Jube raced off and slid down the handrails, spiralling his giggling shape down out of Sonny's sight. A light banging on as Jube must have whacked a switch.

Sonny following down a passageway that didn't last long before it curved off to God knows where. No time to take in much except the irregular shape and the pictures along the walls. Jube's head going this way and the other way, he took off up where the passage curved. So Sonny went the other way where it curved again, and there was a door, to his right. He opened it. Wow. What a bedroom. Timber ceilings, the same stark white walls, windows with floral patterned curtains drawn across, two single beds with covers that kind of matched, but not exactly, the curtains, pillowcases the same. Pictures on the walls. A dressing table. Couple of chests of drawers, antique-looking, went well with the timber ceiling. The timber frames of windows. Bits and pieces that said it was a kid's room, maybe a teenager's.

Sonny walked over and lifted the pillow on the first bed, then the next. Nothing. He was halfway out when he heard Jube's whoop. He went after the sound. Found Jube jumping up and down and notes — money — flying all over the place. Sonny grabbed one. A fifty. And lots of them. This couldn't be true.

But Jube was jumping and his eyes, swollen from the beating, were near normal in their gleeful wideness, and then he was grabbing Sonny in a bearhug, lifted him up and swung him round, wouldn't let go even when Sonny said, Easy, man. Spun him a couple of times more then flung him onto a double bed on his back and stood over him laughing and clutching a handful of notes.

We're rich!

The note was addressed to an Oliver. Jube walked around wearing a huge grin as he read from it: Dear Oliver, Sorry we're not home to welcome you but your father was in need of a well-earned break — What from, Jube breaking off, ripping off the poor? Fuck the cunt. Back to the note: You have the Sounds number — Hey, where's the Sounds? Sonny shrugging he didn't know. Maybe it means music sounds, Sonny half joking. Head still reeling with the cash find — but here it is again in case you've forgotten it or misplaced it. Oh, aren't they just so fucking *nice* these richies, uh Sonny? In case he's forgotten or mis*placed* it. Aren't they the fucking pits, man? Jube resumed from the note: Your father says to remind you the money is repayable — Ya get that, man? Repayable. His own fucking flesh and blood and he wants his bread back. Jube sweeping an arm around the room, quite different from the one Sonny had been in and yet sorta the same in theme, or something about it. With a pad like this and he wants his own son to pay him back. Jube clicking his tongue in disgust. Sonny wondering about that himself. Oh well, least he's got the bread to give his son. *Had*, Sonny. *Had*. Jube with a grin. Back to the note: We're back on Sunday week, so of course make yourself at home, darling — Oh, darling, is it? The guy's a man and they call him darling? Man, it's his mother, ain't it? Can't she call her own son darling? Well of course, *darling* Sonny. And are you quite comfy over there on the bed? Could I get you a cushion, *darling*? Ya wankah, you're worse'n this bitch, tapping the note. Jube finishing it with emphasis on the words *Love*, Mum.

He clapped his hands together, time for a beer. To Sonny counting out the money into two separate piles that came to exactly five hundred apiece. Best they'd done in cash in quite a few years. And we ain't even started yet, Jube in that tone of being onto a sure thing, and Sonny still not sure, not till they were out of here. What if this Oliver dude shows while we're here? What, at — Jube glancing at his watch — ten to three in the morning? Anyway, I'll punch his lights out minute he walks in. Now come on, I'm dying a thirst.

Up the stairs into the kitchen, fridge with plenty of beer, but nothing familiar, only these fancy bottles that Jube was having trouble reading the label of, handed a bottle to Sonny. You read it, you're the bookworm knows all the fancy words. Sonny read Alten-mun-ster. Shrugged. Funny top too, how does it work? at the metal piece holding down what looked like a china cap. Sonny pulled at the wire and the cap came off. He tasted it. Mmm, not bad. But Jube shook his head, Nope. It's shit. Nothing like a Lion Red. As Sonny held the green-tinted bottle up to the light and marvelled at the quality seemingly radiating off it.

With the note giving reassurance, and the beers helping in Sonny's case, they quickly relaxed. Jube started walking around the place inspecting this and that. No hurry, Son, no hurry at all. We got all fucking night, bro. Breezy, arrogant in his newly moneyed state.

Pictures must be worth a fortune on their own. Nah, no market for em, Son. But is for these Persians, Jube at the rugs spread out everywhere in the living area on polished timber floor. Man, I ain't seen any of these before, Sonny in immediate appreciation of their intricate patterns and subtle shadings of colour and tone. The surrounds more and more dawning on him, as they also were to Jube, but from his own rough perspective as he stopped before a painting, mostly modern squiggly stuff in bright colours, and sneered at it and tried to pick out the cunts on the vaguely female figures he saw.

Sonny was seeing how everything of this vast living area fitted, achieved a kind of balance that his instincts saw but his mind could not confirm. Not in words. It just felt a kind of perfection. An accomplishment of some great social force, of the people whose taste and eye and selection of architect it was, their force, their membership of some exclusive club — no, class, or maybe they are of an exclusive club that gets together in each other's posh homes and talks about the different styles and all that. So far removed from the son of a boozing railway worker and an equally booze-addicted mother; so far from the chattering, jabbering, face- and arm-tattooed, beer-swilling seethe of the Tavi bar world; so far distant from two thieves entered forcefully into it — and yet they were here, with a start of the cash spoils in grubby-jeans pockets. They were masters inspecting what next spoils to take as they drank their no doubt expensive beer that the label said came from Germany, itself another far-off concept but now being taken, in drinking form, as they were — or Sonny was — drinking in this habitat they had busted into.

Recesses here and there, each with an object in it. And when Sonny hit the main switch for the living room, the place transformed to different shadings of light, not least the recesses where might be a vase, a bowl, a statue figure in wood, in stone, a floral arrangement in a stunningly coloured vase, but with angles of shadow in the recess of each object's standing. Man alive.

*

65

Jube sat himself down at the piano and grinningly plunked out a few unrelated notes. (To Sonny, it felt like a worse violation than actually being here in the first place; with that face-beaten, ugly-smiling criminal dude with his boob dots and a star tattooed under his eyes, spiderweb around his throat, all over his arms from ink-black fingers to curls and twisty tats of red splotch and green over predominant blue. And here he had the cheek, the effrontery, to plonk himself down at that magnificent piece of musical furniture and run his tattooed hands over the ivories. So Sonny said, Hey, you're spoiling it. Watched with secret pleasure Jube's puzzled frown. Spoiling what, man? How could I spoil anything with what we already found and what's still waiting for us? Chuckling. Plunking out a few more notes and breaking out lalala-lalala-lah-lah ending in a giggle.

Hey, come look at our Mummy in the photo. Jube held up a frame. Leering at it, for some reason when why'd a woman have a photo of herself on top of a piano that'd make someone, even a Jube, leer? Sonny went over. Man, she's some woman, expelling a whistle. Colour photo of a woman seated at maybe this very piano with these kids either side of her, a teenage girl and an older teenage boy. Whole fuckin lot ofem are good-looking. Ya reckon?

Jube shaking his head. She's alright, I like the daughter. Bit young, though, but then again when it's got hair on it, it's old enough — Yeah yeah, no need to get smutty. Ooo, my my my, who's talking? Sonny's talking, that's who, and Sonny ain't into little girls. She ain't little, she'd be all of what, fifteen, sixteen? Don't tell me you ain't had a young one in your time? Yeah, when I was young, but not at thirty-four. Oh well, Sonny, each to his own. Ya might prefer darling boy here, uh? Hahahaha. Jube walked away. Left Sonny to stare at the photograph, the woman, her not so much beauty as it was a presence; of self-assurance. And a certain and definite air of contentedness to her. The kids, hard to tell, they were just kids, if a little on the precious-looking side. The girl was beautiful, her dark-haired brother pretty cool-looking too. But it was the woman, the mother, held Sonny the thief's attention.

Jube came back with another bottle of beer. I'm gonna check out the main bedroom. Jewels, my man, that's what I'm reckoning on finding. Oh, and other things too, adding with a chuckle. Sonny followed him downstairs, but not without a parting look at the woman with the high cheekbones and sloping eyes that could be green or maybe blue, hard to say even with a colour photograph. But it was her smile. He went down the stairs with the song 'Mona Lisa' sprung up in his mind, though the woman didn't look like pictures Sonny'd seen of the Mona Lisa painting. Nor was the song in original form of Nat King Cole repeating in his mind's ear. Was Natalie, the daughter, doing the next generation's version of it. He could hear her as if she was following him.

Took three doors of Jube's trying before they found what must be the main bedroom. Inside it was another door, which led into a big bathroom done out in marble stuff and shining hard surfaces of interesting texture and pattern, floor, walls and vanity units. A large step-up bath, a separate shower, plants hanging here and there, and a large clear pane of glass that looked out into a cluster of trees and shrubs packed tight, intimate. Even the towels looked worth a mint. And everything about the place was perfectly neat and ordered: soaps in different places, bottles of stuff. Then the two men's reflections in the wide mirror showing complete and utter strangers come in from the dark; incongruous intruders, Sonny in a black jersey with a few little holes in it and grubby jeans still spotted with his own blood from the beating. Jube different only because he wore a T-shirt, and the blood stains on his jeans were larger, and his tattoos on white exposed arm highlighting their different colours. So did their hair colouring contrast: Jube's brown with ginger streaks in its wild straggle, Sonny's black and wavy. Hey, we sure look chalk and cheese, bro, Jube laughing at the reflection. And check out this bathroom, man, it's bigger'n our fucking flat.

No bedroom in this house could possibly be compared to anything either knew, each having its own distinctive identity and feel. Yet Jube went straight over to the dresser had the mirrors and grabbed up what looked like a jewellery box, flipped the lid and looked in. Sonny waited, holding his breath. But the other just shaking his head, I don't see no Crown Jewels in this lot. He tossed the box through the air at Sonny, you see what you can find out of that lot.

Left Sonny fingering through the items as he went through the dresser, Sonny asking, What're you specting to find in a drawer? Jube not answering, if his giggle didn't count. Sonny shook his head, went back to the jewel box, not knowing value of pieces and never had taken an interest over the years. Market was limited any rate; Sonny'd seen dudes come into Tavistocks and sell for the price of a few jugs of beer jewellery that the paper next day said was worth twenty, thirty grand. So wasn't long of inspection before Sonny put the box back in its place.

Jube was down on his knees on carpeted floor sorting through a drawer of clothing. Bingo. He looked up, smiling his ugly smile at Sonny and out came a glossy magazine in his hand. *Penthouse*. Can ya believe it? House like this and the guy has a *Penthouse* in his undies drawer? And not just one neither, there's a stack of em here. His eyes with that glassed-over look he got on the subject closest his own underwear.

He got up. Staring at the magazine. Seemed to have upset him. Or given him a surprise insight. So what's a *Penthouse*, Jube? Ain't a crime, is it? Ain't a crime is it, he asks. Course it's a fucking crime. Stabbed the mag with his forefinger. Living in a joint like this you can bet your black arse he got here by robbing the poor, they all do these cunts, probably has some high-up job, government or sumpin like that, telling people — ordinary people like me and you — how to live their lives and — hit it again with his finger — this. They have this.

So?

So? he says. Whose fucking side you on anyway? Nobody's man. I didn't know it was about sides. Come on anyrate, we ain't here for no *Penthouse*s. But Jube reached out and grabbed Sonny by the jersey sleeve, Hold it. Don't this mean nothin to you, man, that this guy's got a drawer full of dirty mags? Nope. Well, just you hang around a minute, buster, cos I bet the five hundred I got in my pocket we're gonna find more. More what? Evidence, as the pigs say, Sonny. Gonna find us some evidence of these kind of people's *real* selves. Not that highfalutin bullshit up them fancy stairs in that photo on the *grand* piano, it's the real — the *reeeel*, Son, side down here. He was sweating and had a nasty grin, and his swollen eyes with their bruising looked worse with the glints of evil slitted there. He started on a chest of drawers, and Sonny's heart was beating faster; he didn't know why. Fear of this Jube he hadn't seen as bad as this. Or secret excitement and anticipation at what Jube was going to find.

First thing Jube found of interest was letters. He started pulling them out from their envelopes, scanning through them briefly. Nope. Nope. Not a fucking thing, in disappointment as he tossed each one to the floor when he was finished.

Sonny took his eyes around the room and fell on a portrait of the woman and a man had to be her husband. Handsome couple they made. Sonny wondering what they would think of these two strangers in their bedroom, with one rifling through their privacy in search of what he called evidence, like it was an investigation into these people to prove their guilt already assumed by Jube. But what could a man do but stare and hear in his mind a kind of weak apology for being there?

Come on, man, this ain't gettin us nowhere. And I'm still edgy. This's the longest we ever stayed in a house and I dunno why you decided all of a sudden, after all these years, man, and now you wanna near up and move in. Fine. Fine, go ahead if that's what turns you on, but me, man, I'm goin back upstairs gonna roll up some a them rugs you say're worth a fortune and get my arse out of here. I am, Jube, I promise.

Till Jube held aloft a pair of woman's panties. Then brought the white flimsy garment to his face, Ahhh. Inhaling. Eyes half closed in kind of ecstasy. And Sonny standing there in disgust, yet feeling himself harden as he imagined the woman who wore the garment. He glanced at her in the photograph beside her husband, and when he looked back so was Jube looking at the same portrait still with the knickers to his nose and his eyes screwed up in delight.

Sonny wanted to grab the panties from Jube, hold them to himself, whisper to the garment, which'd then become the woman and she was wearing them and only them, that he was sorry. He weren't like this animal Jube. He was normal. Though his thought sequence of the woman taking him in her arms and the sensation of them making love confused Sonny. Then Jube was tossing panties in the air as he went through the drawer emptying it. Laughing. Sonny stared around him again at this room he and this crazy white dude were violating.

But Jube got sick of it pretty soon and they went on to the other bedrooms; nothing of value, just the same stamp of quality and furnishing and layout taste in Sonny's eyes. With Jube seeing nothing except the fact there wasn't no more cash.

Upstairs and replenished with the beer, which was fast affecting both them, Jube told Sonny to start rolling up the rugs, but only the ones he selected. Cos I know about these things, Persian carpets, I studied em. Which Sonny knew from when they did their last sentence together, and it was the only reason Jube took himself to the prison library so he could look up Persian carpets, check out the photographs of the different weaves, the patterns to look for, what was high value, what wasn't. Jube busied himself getting the stereo system unhooked, as well the television set and the video recorder.

Hey, lookee here, Jube with a cardboard box of video tapes. Grinning in anticipation as he roved an eye over the title labels. So where's the blueys, bud? Took Sonny a moment to realise Jube meant blue movies. Aw come on, man, ya think this dude is perverted like you? He buys *Penthouse*, don't he? So what? And who said it was the dude who's kinky, Son? Might be his missus. (His missus? Man, these people wouldn't call their wives the missus. My old man called my old lady that, like she was a thing. Go ask the missus, he used to say. Sonny had heard his father once say to a drinking mate, Had to slap one up the missus just to keep her quiet. The missus . . .)

Shit, what kinda names're these? Jube frowning into the box of video tapes. Georgian State Dancers? That sound kinky to you, Son? Oh sure, Jube, sounds real kinky. Whyn't you put it on, we can sit down and wank ourselves. Might even be the dude — and his missus — in action. Jube giving Sonny a sharp look. Then he fiddled around with the recorder putting a tape on. And Sonny fetched more beer, and they smoked their usual incessant cigarettes, which Jube just crushed out where he finished one. Sonny'd started off with a saucer he grabbed from the kitchen early on but Jube kept sneering at him for being the goody-goody-two-shoes and how hypocritical it was considering he was in the people's house robbing the place. So Sonny went to the kitchen sink each time he finished a smoke, ran the tap over the butt.

He was coming back from just that when the television leapt into life. Sonny stopped in his tracks in confusion at the line-up of Cossack-looking dancers, as the men came foot-drumming forward through the gaps between the women. Hey-hey! Jube at the sight. Where's the controls, I ain't watching this crap. But Sonny getting him to hold it a bit, May as well watch it for a few minutes more, trying to sound casual, in case Jube switched it off out of spite, or suspicion of Sonny being very taken with it.

Jube let it go on long enough for him to find the remote control, long enough to have Sonny's mind in a spin; for it was like something of himself, his other self, that self that when alone and usually in bed, and latterly that bed'd been a prison cell, in that time just before sleep comes and your mind opens up no different to the unexpected burst-open of a flower. Has you seeing things like you wouldn't imagine could be from your imagination, yet there they were, in black and white at times, but more often in brilliant colours and always — always it was dancing sequences and then musical accompaniment. And it was not derived from anything a man knew, some familiar or even unfamiliar reference that might explain it, how it came to be. Looking at the dancers for the few minutes before Jube knocked them off with the remote, Sonny felt was like seeing his mind, pictures from his mind.

So Sonny dropped his eyes and swallowed a big mouthful of beer at the screen gone blank. Forced himself to say, Maybe there are some secrets in that box, uh Jube? To try and force Jube into accidentally putting on something else of a similar visual vein. And he made a silent vow to himself that he was going to grab that box of video tapes before they left.

They carted the rolled-up rugs and the stereo and television and video recorder down to the carport. Stars were out. Car was parked well away from the scene of the crime; Jube's habit because of its obvious appearance in a well-off area and chance of cops on the cruise. He'd fetch it up for loading the gear into when came the time.

No hurry, no hurry, Son. What's your rush, brother? Have another beer, Jube casual, relaxed about the whole thing. And anyway, we ain't checked out the whole house yet.

They split up, at Jube's say-so. He downstairs again and Sonny up. Check out that door there, Jube'd said before he went down, looks like an office or sumpin. Or it could be one a them walk-in safes, eh Sonny, hahahaha. Left Sonny feeling near enough alone, though glad of it.

Sonny took his time checking out the door at the far end of the huge living area with its comfy sofas and one of the coffee tables a big plate of glass on a pyramid piece of marble about the most unusual piece of furniture a man'd ever seen. At the paintings everywhere, some of them as big as a fuckin dining table, though not this dining table, with its twelve chairs Sonny'd counted and that didn't include the extra two, one at each end. He stopped at each painting, found himself playing a pretend game of a prospective buyer, or an art critic; thumb and forefinger under his unshaved chin — gingerly because of bruising from the punches he received

— roving eyes all over the splash of vivid colours, surprised at how many different textures were there, at the build-up, seemingly deliberate, of paint at various points. Going, Hmmm, now . . . let's see. Giggling to himself. And glancing self-consciously, to start with, over his shoulder in case Jube was lurked up somewhere spying on him.

Was the game he was enjoying more, since the art he didn't understand. Could see the colour appeal, but what the hell they were about he couldn't guess. Nor could he see what Jube'd early been spotting of vague women shapes, not only the shapes declaring themselves to be women but Jube'd seen their fannies. Or why else'd he cried, Lookit the vees! Hey, it's a cunt. Only cunt round here's him, Sonny aloud.

The vases, the carved figurines, the variety of solid objects of art in the recesses, Sonny felt he more understood. Least in terms of their beauty being immediately apparent; didn't need no fancy wording nor education or breeding to understand that a figure of a young woman in black wood was a tribute to physical perfection and womanhood in its youthful prime, and maybe a man even saw the innocence too. Just as he saw in the variety of vases each with a shape that kind of echoed the shape of that woman in black wood, yet of course was nothing like the carved figure and yet for some reason that was the message came across to a man, a thief playing art appreciator.

With no more objects or paintings left to study, Sonny took himself over to the wall of windows to take in the view. Of city-tall buildings down there mirrored in the still harbour. The town asleep, damn near all. The witches' and thieves' hour was this just after four o'clock time. (Man, whole fuckin town's asleep, having their dreams, some'll be nightmaring but most won't. And here am I standing here admiring the view like it's mine. And my mate's downstairs doing God knows what, but he'd better find something cos I haven't forgotten his bet.)

He browsed through the book titles, and for some reason got scared; as if his ignorance would be exposed at just about every author name unknown to him; he who in his world had been beaten up for being a bookworm library-goer in prison. Shaking his head at how relative it all was. A name, Doctorow, pausing his eye for just a moment. Nope. Don't know of him. Name after name, title after title, all of them unfamiliar. So he grew depressed. At his ignorance and these people's unattainable opposite enlightenment. And he sighed and moved away from the bookshelves, shrugging, Okay, may as well be what I am, as he opened the door that Jube'd joked might be a walk-in safe. Chuckling wryly to himself, Might be a walk-in nightmare too. Thinking of a ferocious dog that'd kept silent all this while till the first thief made the mistake . . .

6 It was a study, and you could've swung a few cats in it. Desk a huge timber job with a computer screen and keyboard and some other set-up Sonny had no idea about. This to one side, left of the chair on roller wheels. Bookshelves everywhere, from floor to ceiling. Desk looked straight out a window that showed Sonny's own intrusive reflection. The wall front of the desk had paintings, old-looking and real scenery not like the modern stuff elsewhere. Sonny stepped forward to look at a framed certificate, had his heart leap: the guy, a Gerald David Harland, was a Master of Laws, that's what it said. Underneath it read: Given Under the Seal of the University of Auckland, 1972. Sonny wondering what he was doing that year — Oh, I know. My first borstal sentence. A sixteen-year-old, remember that, Sonny? Had him shaking his head at the comparison; had it, this magnificent house and the taste and quality everywhere, had it all explaining itself. Why he, Sonny the burglar, was here. Why Gerald, the master at his law, was master of this house. And never never would the twain meet. Certificate below the first said the New Zealand Law Society, and then the guy's name again, and that he had a licence to practice for 1992.

Society. The word belted Sonny in the gut: this guy belongs to a society. What society do I belong to? I'm nobody's child, as the song goes. All of us are nobodies' children, every thief, every lowlife tattoo-marked hopeless case of prison time and so-called free time holed up the days and sordid nights in Tavistocks bar and bars like it. May as well be from the moon where me and this guy're concerned. Standing there in a state of shock and total inadequacy. So much so he felt drained, weak, gone of the will to do anything further against this entity enshrined on the wall there, enshrined in

74

the everywhere of this fantastic universe of residence in which he — Master of it — evidently got to work in as well.

He looked at the books . . . *Land Law* . . . *Law of Contract* . . . *Company and Securities Law* . . . *Guide to New Zealand Income Tax Practice* . . . and two long line-ups, one *Statutes of New Zealand*, the other, numbering one to twenty-seven, *Statutory Regulations*. Sonny shaking his head, overpowered by it, the knowledge — the *power* — this man must have. The same guy in the photo downstairs in his bedroom with his queen of a wife, the both of them with the looks; as if having money and status wasn't enough, they had to be given looks on top. And as if even that wasn't enough, they had to be given the serenity, maybe even the arrogance, of their higher class, their greater breeding. Enough to make a Jube wanna punch em out. Enough to make Sonny close to weeping.

And when he dropped his eyes to fight off the urge to weep, he noticed he stood on a silken-like spread of rug that near covered the entire floor area. Had to be Persian. Had to be worth a fortune. Yet he couldn't get himself to start rolling it up. Not a hope. Just stood there staring at his rough running-shoes, his blood-spotted jeans, his black-gloved hands hanging limply at his sides. The same image that took him when he managed to lift his head and saw himself in the window. The class, the quality of backdrop and surround he was forlornly stood in. He forced a smile. Out loud, Hey, I look like the wind juss blew me in, hahaha. The chuckle soft and poignant.

He got an anger up then — (have to, or I'll curl up and die) — tried the desk drawers. Locked. Went out to the kitchen and took a while to find a box of tools in a walk-in pantry, where there was all this foodstuff such as he'd never seen before, in cans and packets and jars, a lot of it bearing foreign-languaged labels. One plastic container had fuckin snails in it. A tin he picked up said it was smoked snapper from Japan; and there was a whole shelf of oils: walnut, olive, peanut, sunflower — heaps of the stuff. Like stepping into yet-another world, another dimension to this house, its unreal occupants. On the way back to the study he paused at the photograph on the piano, stared at it for some time. Shaking his head as he tried to imagine what it must be like inside their heads, the mother and her two precious-looking kids, the girl with them braces things not inhibiting her confident smile one lil bit. He was good and angry in his inadequacy by the time he got back to the study.

First drawer he forced open had him reel away. At the brown folders with green ribbon ties; these might be files on murder cases, on anything. Though when he scanned the writing on the one he grabbed, it said something about Bank Parabas, written in black pen, and below it Futures. Futures for what? What manner of man, of law job was this that he had files on a bank's future — and in the plural. Shook his head, I dunno.

Second drawer jemmied was more of the same. A file read Banque Indosuez, which Sonny figured must be to do with the Suez Canal area, which he thought was in Egypt somewhere. Bor-ring. Down to the third, with a set of three more on the other side. He was down on his knees, could smell wool and a kind of oily smell quite pleasant. The pattern of the rug he was kneeled on was really detailed up close, he ran a hand over it, felt as silken as it looked, but he figured it couldn't possibly be silk, he thought silk was flimsy. Like the woman's panties that crazy Jube'd held up to his nose, and he was doubtless down there now doing more'n just smelling the underwear. Animal. He levered the third drawer open.

Only thing in it was a large brown envelope. Read: Brothel Drawings. Commissioned by Marquess of Salisbury. Photographic Prints. So, taken by the word brothel, Sonny took out the contents. Nearly had a heart attack: it's porn! At the sight of the first of several pictures showing a man shoving himself into a woman from the standing position with she seated on a little table. Sonny stared in disbelief. The woman had one leg wrapped around the dude's back, the other half off the floor. His shorts were down enough to free his rampant sexuality, and the picture of it entering a hairy divide was at once repulsive and a turn-on. Sonny shakingly looked at the next.

Two women and a guy. (Man, what a dream.) The guy underneath one of the women, who was kissing him passionately while the other woman, to the side of them, was positioning the guy's cock into the woman's explicitly depicted cunt lips. Sonny as hard as the guy in the picture.

Going over in his spinning head: This is wrong. This guy's a lawyer and he's got pictures like this. Yet keenly aware of his own excitement. And further staring started the question in his mind: Is it *that* bad? Try the next one.

Little midget guy, looked more like a boy, another lucky dude with two women. One woman holding his penis with one hand and holding up the leg and open thighs of the other woman for obvious invitation to the midget to enter. None of them looked bad. Like in evil. Hell, Jube looked ten times worse'n these people. The women in fact had pretty faces and sweet smiles, and their hair was tied up in similar buns all plaited together how must have been the style in them days, since it was clearly from a past era, maybe last century. Looked English, from all the lace and stuff clued around.

Last picture was just stunning: two naked people, woman and man, with the man standing and holding the woman with one of her legs supported by one of his shoulders, held by his hand, his other hand just visible supporting her weight on her lower back. They were kissing. He was fully inside her, Sonny could see the guy's balls, it was like a mirror. Of himself, of every man how he must look to a third eye when engaged in the act of fucking. He stared harder and close at the faces. Decided it wasn't fucking, it was loving: her eyes were closed softly, and their meeting of lips looked gentle and yet passionate. And for some reason there was a fully clothed woman in the picture down her knees supported by one arm on the floor with the other in the act of wiping the doorframe. Sonny couldn't figure it. Was hardly that interested either.

Back over the pictures again, Sonny noticed a weird-looking woman in the first, in the side foreground; she had a long nose in profile and her pose was real strange, as if she was creeping discreetly past the act taking place behind her. A broom rested against a tall vase near the screwing couple. The vase could have been straight out of one of the cubby-hole recesses of this house. The man's penetration could not have been more clear. Nor erotically done. What with the woman's dress hiked up around her midriff, a breast hanging free and the guy buried into her far shoulder as he went hell for sweet leather. Man.

He noticed the midget guy had a tender reached-out hand touching the controlling woman's face. The guy's eyes looked utterly for the woman he was touching. Her concentration on hand on his cock was more serene than anything. And the other woman wore a welcoming smile.

Jube'd give his right arm to see these, it occurred to Sonny. So he took one last look at each then put them back in the envelope and slid it under the files in the drawer above for good measure in case Jube walked in. Knowing that the lawyer guy would have to know for sure that his secret was known to at least one thief. Smiling at that thought because it gave Sonny a surge of confidence.

First two drawers the other side had more files. Sonny took a deep breath on the final drawer, expecting more sexy material. He wondered if the guy's wife knew. If she was maybe part of whatever sexual behaviour this kind of thing inspired, or reduced them to. Found himself hoping it didn't in fact reduce them: it'd spoil all their exquisite taste, even perhaps the physical beauty they both enjoyed. He paused as he tried to conjure up what a husband and wife might get from looking at these drawings. Didn't seem to Sonny it'd have em bringing out the whips and metal chains. In fact it was easy to see the turn-on, even if it was impossible to imagine these kind of people in the act of fucking. Or even making love. Impossible. Especially the woman.

He was still stiff. And horny as hell. Half hoping he'd find something spicier, half that he'd find much along the same lines. Wondering then what Jube had discovered downstairs. Maybe this couple are sex maniacs; you read about it in the papers sometimes, of some aristocratic lot from England found involved in wife swapping and sex orgies. Come to think of it: what is a Marquess of Salisbury? But he didn't know. And his watch said it was closing on five and time was running out. He worked the two screwdrivers in and levered the drawer open, jumped in alarm at Jube's voice behind him, Oi! followed by his smart-arse chuckle. Whatcha found? At the same time the drawer came open to reveal another large brown envelope. So Sonny's heart pounding that it'd be more of the sex stuff and dreading taking the envelope.

But Jube was standing over him, and his long arm came down all tattooed, and knuckly fist took the envelope. Which had Sonny saying, You ain't seen nothing yet, as he decided on showing Jube what else of the presumed same he'd found before Jube found it himself; asking himself why he wanted to hide this in the first place.

Jube was tearing at the envelope that must be sealed, unlike the one Sonny was bringing out from under the files. Here, check this out. He handed the envelope up to Jube, but with one of the pictures first removed for Jube's instant attention. Sonny stood up. Jube dropped his envelope on the floor, it fell with not a whisper onto the rug. Jube's mouth was open. His eyes as wide as the swelling around them would allow. He walked slowly over to the desk, where he pushed aside a magazine whose name Jube read out scornfully, The *Economist*, eh? The fucking *Economist*, that's what this guy *shows* the world he reads. Glancing over his shoulder at Sonny for a moment. Not *Penthouse*s, oh no, we couldn't have that. Turned back to the desk, and Sonny moved around so to see what Jube was going to do, as well as his face when he took in the pictures.

He's a lawyer too — Sonny watched Jube stiffen. He's a wha'? A lawyer. Look, on the wall right in front of you. Jube straining his neck unnecessarily to look at the certificates, turning then a face on the rise to anger. First we find the *Penthouse*s — his jaw was trembling so much he had to pause — then I find pictures of his wife in — Nah, come on, you're kidding me aren't ya? Sonny in before Jube could finish, it was too unbelievable. This whole fucking house was, everything in it and about it, from the layout to the contents to them fuckin snails in a plastic container in the pantry to the sexy pictures that Jube was already seeing as porn. But pictures of the — of *that* woman? Nah, man. Sonny grinning at Jube, but Jube not grinning back. It's true, Son, as I stand here, I've got em in my pocket — a brief smile of triumph, then back to his angry look — and now — stabbing a finger Sonny's way then swinging it up at the frames and finally at the pictures as he spread them out — a fucking *law*yer? And he had *this*? The finger drove downwards at the pornographic display.

What to say? Sonny thinking. Then — Hey? what about these photos, you for real? I'm for real, Sonny Mahia. Jube's eyes glued on the spread of pictures, his head going from side to slow side, a quick glance up at the certificates, clicking of his tongue, back to the pictures as Sonny asked, How about these photos, bro? Ya gonna show me? But Jube wasn't listening, he was just going, Wow, oh fucking man alive, but I do not belie — He stopped, grabbed the envelope they'd been in, looked at it and read aloud: Marquess of — Marquess? Ain't that sumpin hoity-toity high up? England somewhere? Yeah, I think it is, man, think it is.

But Sonny wanting to know about the other photographs. Then the joke struck him: Hey, Jube, how bout you show me yours; I've already showed you mine? Took a moment for Jube to get it, but then he gave a grin. In my own good time, cuz, my own good time. Aw, come on, that ain't fair. They porno? Might be, Jube with a grin. Come on, Jube. But Jube was back staring at the others. So Sonny finished off ripping open the seal on the envelope he was holding, expecting more of the same as Jube was getting his eyes off on.

A marquess. A lawyer. *Penthouse* mags, pictures of his wife as on the day she was born. Sonny, the fuck is going on here ya think? Just as Sonny pulled out the contents of the envelope he'd opened.

Then they were staring at each other. Then at what Sonny held in his hand. And Jube had a picture in his own hand, the one of the man and woman in standing copulation, kissing as they did. Jube had it to make a point. But the point got blown away by what Sonny found. Then Jube, in as soft a voice as Sonny'd heard from the man asking, Son? The fuck is happening to us?

At all that money in Sonny's hand. Only thing Sonny could think to say was: Now you gonna show me the photos?

They didn't know what next to do. Say. Had to swap over the respective objects in each other's right hand so they could shake; was Jube'd started off the gesture, and Sonny having to hurry over his hand-to-hand shuffle then grab Jube's out-thrust mit. Puddit here, Son. The tall guy's voice still as quiet as a mouse. Sonny too when he croaked back, I think we mighta got lucky, Jube.

But no sooner was the handshake over than Jube turned and smashed his fist into one of the glass-framed certificates. Master! *Now* tellus who's fucking *master*! Yet he was laughing. And so Sonny's alarmed frown went to a grin, then he too was laughing. They were holding hands and bouncing up and down as Jube swung them round and round.

Out in the night they swiftly loaded Jube's boot, and all the rear-seat area, as well at Sonny's feet with the variety of items, from television to several Jube-selected Persian rugs, to the stereo set-up, video recorder, and Sonny'd added the box of video tapes as a last-minute remembering. They pulled, without haste, out of the car-port; and the hills where the east must be were just the faintest hint of a new day beginning, as two thieves of a long and eventful night swigged on stolen German beer and exchanged grinning glances at each other in the dash-lit semi-gloom. And they drove down the winding hill of suburban Wellington by the sea.

No rush, no rush, uh Sonny? Nah, man, no rush. Don't want to be pulled over for speeding till we're home and hosed, eh cuz? Chuckling. Looking across at his partner in an unforgettable crime, and chuckling.

Down on the flat they drove alongside the sea, with the upthrust of city buildings still part alight to greet them and the new day fast coming. Both their windows down and a breeze coming in smelling of sea and telling of early-risen squabbling seabirds. And a couple of joggers running past, towards them; two guys, they could've been cops, or lawyers, as Jube laughingly remarked. Though he didn't, as Sonny might have expected, give them any fingers sign or yell smart-arse comment at them. Just drove with eyes straight ahead, beaming all over.

Hey, Sonny remembered, you never showed me the photos. Oh? Didn't I? Come on, Jube, you got the pictures too. What, ya want it all? Thought you said you weren't into sex and stuff? I ain't. But — But what? But I wanna see what a woman of that kind of, uh, you know, class. Money and class, that's it, what she's like with no clothes, no fancy jewellery — She didn't have no fancy jewellery anyrate. Whatever. Juss gimme a look, will ya. So Jube fiddled around in his back pocket grumbling that it was a fucking nuisance, couldn't Sonny wait till when he wasn't driving? And he handed over three photographs to Sonny. Check them out.

Sonny hit the inside light, taking a breath as he did. It just did not seem possible. He looked. Naked as the day she was born. Good tits. Big patch of brown pubic hair. Could've been out of a sex magazine — No it couldn't, Sonny in the instant realising. She was by a waterfall, leaned against a rock. Her hair was wet from swimming, unless she'd been under the waterfall. So what's the big deal about this? Took Jube by evident surprise. Ya mean, the big deal? She's starkers, that's the big deal. So? Ain't we all every day of our lives damn near? We — Sonny, are you taking the piss? No, man, I'm not. I'm only — Three and a half grand each in cash we come away with. Three and a half grand *each*. Plus all this gear near bursting the car at the seams, and then we find the *law*yer cunt's secret side — his porno side, remember, Sonny-fucking-Mahia — then I manage to find photos — photographic *evidence*, Sonny-fucking-Mahia — of more porno carry-on, and here's you asking me whassa big deal? As Sonny fanned the next two photographs out. The same. At the waterfall. But in a different pose. One with a highly suggestive smile, and one leg placed higher and quite apart from the other so offering a broader view of her snatch. But it was hardly pornographic. The next she was standing with her legs together with her hands up in her longish brown hair and she was laughing. And what a beautiful smile she had too.

You wanked over these downstairs, I bet? Well, I — Ya did. I know ya did, Sonny laughing. But Jube shrugging, and Sonny could tell he wasn't saying all. But too much money, too much twist of events to start challenging Jube. Taking lingering looks at each of the photographic studies, wanting to imprint them in his mind as nothing more than they were: studies of naked womanhood, though what a woman. What a woman, what a house, what finds, though Sonny not sure on the husband; as if he had some God-given right to reverse being in judgment on a respected member of society. The same he and his buddy were now feeling wealthy on. With their vehicle everywhere crammed with easily sellable goods. Plus the evidence Jube was sure he was carrying. Might use it one day, Sonny, with that smart-arse smile crims get when they think they've got life sussed out with yet another harebrained scheme.

Homeward.

7 Straight up the main highway north to Auckland. Jube restrained, but frustrated at having to keep his speed down so they wouldn't have reason to be pulled up by the law.

Back home, their run-down rental house in a run-down city suburb a stark reminder of who and what they were, where they'd just eight hours ago come from. It might've been a dream, it wasn't for the cash and the goods they were unloading out back where Jube'd driven down the drive and parked right up at the back door so nosy-parker neighbours wouldn't have suspicions aroused. Stacking the stuff into the spare room, and Jube beside himself with not joy but glee, chortling that it was like having an extra bank account sitting in store in your spare room with all them Persian rugs, the tv, the stereo, and Jube'd grabbed a couple of paintings just in case they might be worth something. Even a hundred'll do, eh Sonny? Buys, what, twenty jugs a piss, eh mate, hahahahaha.

Showered, shaved — well, Sonny anyrate, Jube's face too sore to be shaving — into clean clothes and off into town. Money to spend.

A menswear shop. Pretty posh one too, up the main drag. Queen Street. Trying on different garments; hard to choose when you get the bread to buy what you want, never happened like this before. Ever. In and out of the changing cubicles, making fun of it to cover both their self-consciousness of doing the unfamiliar, as well as their happiness at being richer than they'd ever been before.

Each with his facial wounds, but Jube by far the worst with his eyes blackened up and bruising yellowing; looking at each other in the next try-on of trousers and shirt. How do I look, Son? Man, that face don't look too clever. Wonder what the shop guys think? Fuck the shop guys, man. We don't go asking em about their private lives.

83

Okay okay, only wondered. So how do *I* look? Sonny presenting himself outside Jube's changing cubicle. Ya look like a Maori boy who got a punch on the snout, but that's alright cos all you Maoris've got flat noses, hahaha. But, other'n that, ya lood good, buddy. Jube looking Sonny up and down. Real good, Son. At Sonny in navy cotton trousers and a grey denim shirt.

Jube decided on what he liked: white cotton trousers with a fancy, bright-coloured shirt with billowy sleeves. Pleased with himself as he stood eyeing his reflection in the mirror, and Sonny thinking Jube was the big buffoon who didn't have no idea how he looked, but nodding at Jube seeing the man'd made up his mind. Do I look the biz or do I look the biz, cuz? Hahahaha. Ya look good, Jube. (He looks terrible.) Tell me I look like a drug dealer, Son, tell me. Ya look just like one, Jube. Thank you, my main lil man. Grinning all over at his reflection, couldn't take his blackened eyes off himself. May as well look the part if I'm gonna join the ranks, uh Sonny?

Sonny taken by surprise. This was news to him. But he shrugged. Whatever turns you on, bud. No turn-ons about it, there's bread to be made in dru — Hey! Ya wanna tell the whole shop? Sonny hissing at him. Alright, alright, wasn't no-one around anyrate. So, at his reflection, I look the goods, right? Right. Pair a shades and ya won't even know I been in a rumble. And — Jube turning to point a finger — them dogs'll keep, Son. They'll keep. Make my pile with you-know-what, now I got the capital, and I'm going back. Ya know that bout me, don't ya, Son? That I got a long — a *looong* — memory. Yeah, bud, I know that. And shades'll do the trick.

They both had to settle for their trousers being pinned up because they were wearing them straight out of the shop, as with the shirts. The guy gave em a look Jube took offence at when he paid for his purchases by peeling off from his thick wad of fifties, playing the man about town. The fuck ya lookin at, pal? Ain't ya seen bread before? Sorry, sir. Sorry, sir, he says, eh Son? Leaning across the counter, tapping the shop assistant on the chest, So tell me how much you earn a week, bud? Sonny telling Jube to leave it; and they paid for their purchases and left, with Jube giving the assistant a parting scowl.

Out on the street — crowded. Mid-afternoon on a Friday, and a nice day it was too. Shoes. We gotta get ourselves some St Louis blues, boy, Jube with a contented chuckle as he led them striding down main street. Into the first shoeshop they came to. Out again; it was a women's shoeshop, hahaha. Jube bought a pair of cowboys with fancy scrollwork, pointy toes and a bit of heel that a tall man didn't need. Cost two twenty-five. Sonny opted for a pair of plain blacks at ninety-nine ninety-five. Jube tossed the five-cent coin change of Sonny's off the counter. Keep it, pal. See what you can buy with it. Out they went. Jube laughing.

Down to the car parked up a side street Jube was sure the parking-meter cops wouldn't go near, to a ticket under the windscreen wipers. He grabbed it and tore it to shreds, stomped on the bits with his new heels for good measure. Sonny catching Jube's look to see if people were watching. Oh, I forgot to buy shades, Jube suddenly remembered. Ya getting a pair too? Nope. You go, I'll watch the car for another parking ticket. Yeah, you do that, and if the guy gives you a hassle, stall him till I get back. Jube with an evil look, and Sonny thinking maybe this new-found moneyed state was doing something to Jube; as if he was out of control, all hyped up.

Sonny watched the unmistakable figure of Jube as he came back along the pavement, with an exercise-yard-style sway to him and wearing his smoky-lensed shades, the loudest shirt in town and more so with the stark white of trousers that already had knees in them from Jube's bowed legs. Boob-walkin, shaded, fat walrus mo and a few days' stubble not hiding the self-satisfied grin he had on.

Stopping a few paces back from Sonny in a theatrical gesture. Laughing. Snapping his fingers and going for the driver's side of the car, patting the smudgy-grey roof affectionately, Hey, car. Sonny getting in other side. Jube tapping the smelly leather-wrapped steering wheel, All I need is a left-hand-drive Yank tank, bro, and people'll think I'm the real thing, big-time dope-dealer. Not the hard stuff, mind, I wouldn't touch that. It stinks, does smack. Turns your punters into corpses and ya have to keep finding new ones. How do you know that? Sonny wanting to know. Cos I go around this world we live in, Sonny Mahia, with my eyes open, that's how.

Leaving in a screech of tyres cos Jube spotted a trio of dudes who'd likely be impressed with a bit of burnt rubber, and telling Sonny, See what them punks think of the horses we got under that bonnet, Son. A sly look in his rear vision to see if he had made the big impression. A smirk of satisfaction that he had. Now, where to for cellies, buddy? Cellies? Oh cellies, yeow. Celebrations, Son, you got it. So where we gonna start? Hahahahaha!

They decided on a bar in central city, down Vulcan Lane. Gimme two double rums and Coke, my man, Jube to the bartender in a loud voice. Showing off to the maybe couple of dozen drinkers, men mostly, in suits, in casual clothes, smartish dress the standard, but not loud like one of the new arrivals was. Sonny glancing around in embarrassment at Jube's loudness and his flashing the roll of fifties.

Hey thanks, man. Jube handing a drink to Sonny and leading them, boob-walk style again, over to a corner standing table, his head going from side to side with his bouncing, shoulder-rolling gait. Cheers, toasting to Sonny's glass, clink. Yeah, cheers, man. Jube downing half his glass in a gulp. Mmm-uh! Wiping the spots from his walrus. Lighting a fag and offering Sonny one too.

Next round your buy, Sonny. But then again we ain't exactly gonna have an argument about it now, are we? Hahahaha. Jube looking all around him for who was impressed with how wordly, how self-assured, how fucking *cool* was this dude walked into their bar. Though Sonny couldn't see no-one impressed.

Back with a refill. Cheers. Cheers. Here's to us, Son. Two best thieves this side *and* the other side of the Bombays, hahahaha. Drinking. And Jube glancing frequently down at himself, his new look. Same as his eyes went all over the bar, specially when he said something loud and intended for attention; but still no-one hardly giving him a glance. So it began to show in Jube first getting louder, and when that didn't work, he got restless and disgruntled. Ain't our kind of joint anyrate, uh Son? Oh, I don't mind. I'd drink anywhere right now.

The buzz of normal conversation not changing — no loud-mouths here, other than the Jube one — just ordinary working people rewarding emselves a few beers after an early knock-off on a Friday afternoon. None of that Tavi staccato howl and yowl, of dudes and sheilas goin off their faces with all the variety of things that afflicted em. No. Just ordinary folk in social intercourse. Nothing tragic in this bar, no fights, no mad incident on the simmer, no self-centred crazies breaking out in their pus-infected emotional states over the world they hated (and the world hates them back). Just ordinary folk.

Smoking and drinking steadily, too steadily for Sonny's liking, he liked to warm up to this pace, not go straight into it. But hell, it was a special day, and he had his share of glancing down at his newly clothed state with plenty of his own pride. Jube not doing much talking no more. Four double rums each, it should've had em both buzzing. Cept it didn't; Jube because no-one was paying him any attention, and Sonny because Jube's mood was spoiling it for him.

Another double rum with Coke. Jube muttering how the other patrons looked like Christmas presents, unwrapped Christmas presents that no-one wanted, in their all-the-same fucking suits and ties. Looking at Sonny, Not like you and me, buddy — (and the word buddy hitting a right spot in Sonny's heart: as if their destinies were always fused, and the world around them, right now in this bar, taking no notice of Jube; but nor did anything about them have Sonny feeling like one of them either.) So Sonny nodding meaningfully, Juss me and you, buddy, you got it, Jube. Touched his glass against Jube's: To us doing it again, bro.

Ya think it's the tats, Jube? Sonny stabbing a guess at their obvious, if unstated, uncomfortableness in this bar of straights. Huh? The tats, your tats, your hands, your throat and that; maybe these kinda people don't like us for that? Oh, don't they just? Jube taking the leap from wonder to certainty. Well they cin go fuck emselves. And downed his drink. Let's get outta here.

On the way out Jube stopping, looking around him challengingly. To a cluster of men standing around looking at a television screen, a cricket match on. Cricket sucks! Jube booming. Then he spat a big hoik on the floor. *And so do wankers who watch the wanky game.* Marched out, with a not-agreeing Sonny behind.

Down the street, Get outta my fucking way, ya straight eggs. Jube in a mood. Ducking into another bar. Gimme two double rum and Cokes. Looking around them, at what kind of bar it might be. Turning to Sonny, Now this looks better. At it mainly being worker types, plus old men seated around tables probably talking about the war they'd fought in a hundred years ago. Taking their drinks and going to a sit-down table near the old codgers. Cheers. Here's to us. Again, hahaha.

Sonny listening in on the old men's conversation, how they do in plenty of public bars that Sonny's spent an adulthood frequenting, always checking out somewhere new in case it — ? In case it held the answers, to life, to why a man goes from bar to bar as though he's gonna find them. The answers, that is. To life confusing, to life always off course, out of balance with the world, the functioning world. (Whilst we, the low-life thieves of this world, we steal from them, and when we can't find the get up and go to steal, we accept their handouts. Cos we're lowlifes, that's what we are.) Sonny lifted his glass in another toast, a bravado one to break up his thoughts: Here's to the best burglars both side of the Bombays, hahahaha. But Jube was already lost to him, Sonny could see; a sullen, almost menacing picture of man supposed to be adult. (Kid, more like it. Just look at him, sitting there hating the world. Can't help himself. Loaded with more bread than he's ever had in his life and still he's hating the world.) So Sonny took his attention to the table of old men beside them.

(Listen to em, talking about the war, the Second World War, they fought in.) Sonny looking at the men, their uniform greyness of hair or else none at all, the lined faces, leathery necks and hands; and yet in listening, seeing how animated they got, seemed they were, a large part of each and every one, set in concrete. Back there, when they were young men at war; recalling the bombs, grenades, cannons and rockets and rifles all blazing away. (They're stuck back in that time frame. Kind of prisoners really. Of an event. So their minds are frozen back there too. Same as us, me and Jube. Cept we were born into our event, and our event is social. It's a social prison we were born into; some get out and others don't.) Listening to the men exchanging war tales. (And me? What's so great about me?) Sonny sighing, finishing his glass, getting up to fill his and Jube's again. (And Jube's right: I do think too much.) Walking up to the bar, trying to switch his mind into no-think mode.

Back with the drinks. Cheers, Jube. Yeah, cheers. I wanna woman, it came surling out of his cut-lipped mouth. Yeah, well, don't we all, cuz? Never said I wanted a girlfriend — I don't. Too much hassle, too much this, Where ya been all night, Jube? Your tea's cold, Jube. Ya never take me nowhere, Jube. Fuck the bitches. Cunts, that's all they are the lot ofem. Sonny narrowing eyes at Jube, asking, What about the woman in the photos? Think she's — Yep, she's no different. Old Chinese saying, Sonny: They all look the same upside down. Sonny only able to shake his head at Jube's warped view of womanhood. And Jube grumbling on about what fucking use was it having lots of bread with no fucking woman to celebrate with you? I'm going for a piss. (Leave you to it, Jube.)

Out in the toilets, glad of the quiet, the break from Jube's gloom, his lip-curling talk whenever he was on the subject of women. Pausing at the mirror to take a sneaky look at himself, head and grey-shirted shoulders. Pleased with himself, how he shaped up, patting his hair, I need a decent haircut, that'll do the trick.

He'd not felt like this, as good as this, in a long time. About as good as that feeling of stepping outside prison gates to freedom. That exhilarating sense of feeling you could do anything, that nothing of the confusing world that'd helped get you inside in the first place could bother you this time. Not this time: this time I'm gonna do it all the right way. (But how long does that resolve last?) As long as the dough does that the Social Welfare gives you on presenting your release papers at the nearest office — the first one you spot from your taxi, hahahaha — a whole three hundred and sixty-two bucks, which feels like a fortune, and, added to the lousy fifty bucks you've managed to save from your meagre jail earnings, ya feel like a millionaire.

It's your head, lightened by the freedoms; so you go to a bar to celebrate, and since it's a morning they release you, it's an early-opening bar. You want to start celebrating, but your body can't take it, the beer, into the system when it's had a year or two going without. So your judgment goes, and all the dudes and old pals are coming over to you shaking your hand, Welcome out, Sonny, patting your back, hugging you welcome to freedom, so naturally you buy em drinks.

Come the night, you don't know where the hell you are, you're half expecting a screw to order you to your cell, but instead you have freedom, and your head is spinning from the beer. You feel sick, then someone shoves a joint in your hand and next you're floating. Not knowing what the hell you're doing, except you're at the bar buying beer for everyone cos it seems like one big party that ain't ever gonna end, then someone's hitting you up for a loan, only till Thursday, doleday, and you're not minding helping an old friend out, after all he was very warm in his welcoming you to the outside.

Then the smoke has you seeing the people around you as a confusing then upsetting seethe that is getting too much. Next you're out on the street and you can't believe it's dark already when it seemed like only a few hours ago you were striding along the same street and into the bar, Tavistocks bar, the good ole Tavi, and now it's dark. Outside and in your mind as well. Taxi . . . where's a fuckin taxi . . . ? You wake up at some pub pal's place, and your money's damn near all gone. You've woken to freedom, meant to be, cept it's not; it's a fuckin nightmare. Of yourself. How you've fucked it once again. One day and you've fucked it. A nightmare cos it's yourself that's the problem. Not anything but yaself. And there ain't no escaping yaself, is there?)

Sonny startling at the sound of someone coming in. Bit like being caught masturbating as looking at yourself in the mirror. Of being caught in the act of wanking off. So Sonny ready with a smile and a greeting to the old fellow who came in, How're ya, Pop? But the old man just looked at Sonny, brushed past him, muttering I fought a bloody war for the likes of you. Come on now, sir, I wasn't even born when your war was on. The old man turning a full-scowling face to Sonny. No. No, you weren't born then by the looks of you. A pity you were now. Hey, come on, mate. And the old man hissing at that, *don't* you dare call me mate. I'm no *mate* of the likes of you. Now off with you before I call the police. Sonny shaking his head, a little hurt, somewhat disturbed by the old man's hatred. (Same as Jube: he's on permanent A for angry.) You call the fuckin cops, grandad. Oh I will! I will, don't you worry about that! the man as he held his cock fountaining urine. Sonny walked out chuckling away his hurt.

Dope-dealers, Jube announced before Sonny even sat down. That's what we gonna be now we got the capital to buy bulk. Oh? Don't gimme that oh business neither, Sonny Mahia. This is the biggest chance of our lives. No way, Jube. Not for me. Ya mean, not for you? Ya smoke the stuff, don't ya? I do. So whassa difference? Bout five years — in the can. Five years? Man, what you and I've done in the last week'll get us a minimum seven at any rate. And who says we'll get caught? Jube with the legend, the question on every crim's lips before he answers it for himself by going right out and committing the crime.

That's what they all say, Jube. — That's what they all say, Jube. Fuck what they say. Jube thumbing his own chest, his loud-shirted chest with the spider-web tattoo conspicuous the more with the colour contrast, It's what *I* say, okay? Okay, Jube. But speak for yourself. Oh, I get it, you've all of sudden hit the front moneywise and you're thinking it's gonna last forever? Nope, I ain't. But I ain't doing no drug-dealing. It's only grass, Mister Goody-goody — Don't call me that, if you don't mind. I get sick of you calling me that. Well ya are. I'm not, and nor'm I gonna be selling dope. Suit ya black self then, man, cos I am. Up he got. Come on, this joint sucks too.

Marching along the street. Three, four, five fucking grand a week — a *week* — they make, and here's you telling me you don't wanna know? Nope, I don't, Jube. Son, I know one dealer makes *ten* g a week. That right? What's his name? He — Hey come on, smart-arse, you trying to take the piss again? Nope, just wanted to know his name, and how come I haven't heard of him? We live together, don't we? Yeah, and more's the pity. Suit yaself. I fucking will. Yeh, so will I. A gap opened between them, Jube creating it by striding out.

In the car. Where to, Jube? Fuck-nowhere, bud. You're on your own and so am I. Come on, man. No fucking come ons. You wanna stay a burglar nobody, that's fine by me. Me, I wanna *be* someone. Turning his face to Sonny. Telling him in a quavery voice, I wanna walk into places and have people say, Hey, that's Jube McCall the big-time dealer. Ya hear? I wannem looking at me — at *me* — everyone, and eating their rotten lil hearts out at what I got that they ain't. Women, I want women crawling all over me for my bread, for my being the bigtime dealer that no-one but no-one fucks with. Ya hear? I want to buy the fire power, brother, so any arsehole fucks me around they're history. Ya hear? I hear, Jube, loud and clear. But that ain't what I want, Sonny in a quiet voice. I know, Sonny, I know you don't want what I do; ya never have. And now — looking hard at Sonny — I realise you and I, bud, are on different wavelengths.

Jube starting the car and pulling out into the traffic. Where you taking us, not Tavistocks I hope? Oh no, not the Tavi, Sir Sonny. How about the Regent? Or perhaps the Hyatt? Or would sir prefer somewhere in Parnell perhaps? Up your black arse, Sonny Mahia. Man, is it a *crime* to not wanna go to that fuckin same bar? But Jube was away again, sulking, brooding, whatever process it was that lurched him from one mood to another.

Drop me off here. Jube braked sharply. Glad to oblige — sir. With his door half open, Sonny was struck by something out of the blue. Jube? Jube, them photos you got . . . of, you know, her. The woman of the — Nope. They're mine. And you ain't havin em to wank your little brown cock over. Who said anything about — Well why else'd you wannem? I — Sonny didn't know. The question'd just come out of nowhere. And still it pressed within him. Okay,

Jube, but then I'm claiming the other pictures, the drawings ones, if it's finders keepers. Up to you. Jube's glare visible even through the tinted sunglasses. Nope, not a threat, but fair's fair. What, so you'll swap the porno drawings for the porno photos? Yeah. Though I wouldn't call the photos porno. No? No. What, three photos of the wife starkers, and sitting in their own little envelope in the hubby's undies drawer, and he with his stack of *Penthouses* and the filthy drawings, and you saying it ain't porn? So what you think the bloke is doing with all this stuff — research? Nope, but the photos aren't porn. So what do you wannem for? To look at, man, Sonny getting embarrassed about it. To look at, or wank at? Look, Jube. Look, and then wank? No, just look. You're a liar, Son. Am I?

Jube sighed, lifted his rump to get out the photographs. Here. Have the fucking things. But the drawings are mine. Passed them across still in their envelope, and Sonny's heart skipping a beat thinking of that woman's nakedness exposed behind just a thin wall of paper. His hands trembled slightly when he took them. Now get outta my sight, Sonny-fucking-Mahia. Ya make me sick. And don't come looking for me at the Tavi cos I won't be there. Oh? Where — Mind ya business, Jube with a crooked smile. Oh, hey, Jube? What? You couldn't lend me ten bucks for a taxi home, could ya? Sonny with his best innocent face till Jube's look of outrage had him breaking out laughing. I'll pay ya back on Thursday, cuz.

Jube revved his engine up, but with a small smile on his dial as Sonny got out. On ya bike, Sonny Mahia, Jube chuckling softly through the passenger down window. Then he was gone. In a roar and burning of rubber.

8 Mightn't be barely enough room to swing a cat in, but that hadn't stopped Sonny setting up his bedroom with half the stolen stuff from the burglary: stereo, with compact disc player, television and video recorder; he'd even grabbed one of the Persian rugs and spread it out on his bedroom floor. Wow, now lookit that. The image pleased him almightily. I feel like I got class (hahaha). He had to juggle the bed around to get things in and looking reasonably orderly, though to his eye they didn't fit: room'd been too much of a crash-pad, a place you slept, and now and again brought a woman, some lowlife scrubber picked up from Tavistocks, or who'd attached herself to you because some of them scrubbers're like that, they just latch onto someone they think is an easy mark, get free drinks off him all night and make promises with their eyes.

Comes home because she ain't got nowhere to stay, her old man's kicked her out, or she's been booted out by a landlord for not paying the rent at her mysterious somewhere, which she'll only ever state in vague terms. You get home and she's the most unromantic thing you ever knew, and never mind them wild promises in her eyes the long, horny night; she can't kiss, she can't respond to foreplay, she can't do nothing to you in return, she won't even talk cept to say, I'm tired, Sonny, I wanna go to sleep. The morning, eh? Yeah, yeah, the fuckin morning. So morning comes and you're nuzzling up against her, Hi, hi, you sleep okay? But she spins away, tells you to fuck off. Gratitude, eh?

So the room didn't look right with its expensive insertions. The wallpaper was peeling, curtains old and faded and thinned by years of sunlight, a dull green, more yellow. Set of three drawers, a big wardrobe with an oval mirror and a small table by the bed, and that was it. My world.

Sonny looking at it not only in its new light but how it was before, and how long he'd lived like this, in flats all over town, in between prison sentences . . . Anyway, not a time to be thinking like that. He dug out his wad of money, kissed it, spread it out on the bed cover in two rows, chuckling. I oughta play a game of patience with it, hahaha. Cept every face was the same: a fifty. He wondered why the guy would keep a money tin with six grand in it in his desk drawer, whether it was for emergencies, but why'd a rich lawyer have an emergency involving money? Or for his son, the Oliver guy in the note that'd given Sonny and Jube the first grand. And then to find this . . . Shaking his head in sweet disbelief, and still with that old familiar feeling that it'd get taken away, that some mistake, some fuck-up on his part, or else it'd be Jube fucking up, either way would have the law getting hold ofem first. Then, almost inevitably, the courts sending them both to prison again. With a stern lecture from the bench, of course. Justifies the judge's highly paid existence.

Maybe the money's a cash job the lawyer wasn't paying tax on? Who knows? Sonny rubbed his jaw thoughtfully, So where does it go now it's in our hands? Didn't take an instant for the answer to come back: on booze and dope and running round in cars, that's where all crooks' stolen money goes. And, not for the first time but with more clarity than ever before, the sheer waste of it struck Sonny.

He gathered the money in, back to a pile again. Promised himself he wouldn't waste it, but then again how not to? For it was a world there in front of him at his fingertips: I can buy clothes, eat whatever I want, drink in better bars than Tavistocks; I can *be* anything I want. But I ain't gonna be no drug-dealer, no way. They suck, drug-dealers. Ain't got no morals, no principles; they'd steal from their own mothers. And as for the types they supply, they're worse. Just dopeheads and crims wanting to be out of it the whole damn time. (Like me. How I used to be. But why? Cos it dulled that constant pain in my heart in every crim's heart. Cos we're, all of us, part or wholly broken. From our childhood. But hell, I dunno. Maybe it's just that we're weaker than everyone else, or everybody from rotten childhoods'd end up criminals. We're just nature's rejects.) He clapped his hands together, there I go again, thinking doom and gloom even when I got all this bread, these new things in my room. I'm no different to Jube: no matter how good the going is I'm still angry. So enough of that, brother Sonny. Get with it.

He cracked a can from the six pack he'd bought. Opened a packet of cashew nuts — not peanuts. Cashews, bro. Hahahaha. He'd grabbed not one packet but two and, while he was at it, some other nuts that'd long intrigued him whenever he went into certain liquor outlets that sell the other bits and pieces for parties. He ate a mouthful of the cashews then opened a bag of pistachios, had a little difficulty getting the part-opened shell off. But, man, it was worth it, he'd never tasted anything like it. He ate several more. Sat down on the bed and consumed the lot, the last nut as good as the first. Unbelievable. Another dimension to the world, there in front of his nose every day he and Jube went into the Green Bottle liquor store on the way home. Oh, and that's right, I forgot, the photos. He pulled out the envelope, but shook his head, no. Let it keep. Save her for later.

Instead, he sorted through the video tapes. Some were bought jobs, like different operas with a photograph of what must be the set, or others had a single photograph of mostly a guy with a beard and a foreign name, Pavarotti. Others were obviously home-made, off some TV programme, with the details scrawled in either the guy's hand or his wife's. Delicate but precise writing, Sonny had an idea it might be the woman. But Sonny wanted the Russian dancing one. He found the tape, read it: Georgian State Dancers. TV1 '85. No photographs, just the neat writing on white inner paper. He was feeling excited.

After he'd got the tape readied to play, Sonny went back to the box, in case there was something of more interest than even the Russian dancers. Might be a blue movie as Jube'd first predicted. But ya never knew. But nothing of title on the spines of each tape suggested some pornographic secret about to be revealed of one Gerald Harland, lawyer, of Wellington. Then he found another home-made job, labelled: Penelope and Antonia playing piano duet. 20 mins. (Ants aged 11) 1989. Sonny figuring from the photograph atop the piano in that house of the woman and her two kids, that the Ants was Antonia and she'd now be aged, what, fourteen or fifteen?

He switched the light off after pushing the play button and sat on the side of the bed in the dark. His heart rate was up, and his hand rested on the envelope containing the photographic images of the woman who now had a name: Penelope, in the form of any man's fantasy — naked.

Began with the piano sitting there on its own. Sonny leaned

forward open-eyed at seeing the familiar, like his mind was on replay of being in that house. He saw the floor-to-ceiling windows beyond, glanced down at the rug his feet were on, but too dark to know if it was the same pictured in this screening. Then two figures came on screen from opposite sides of the picture. The woman. The daughter. Fumbling for his cigarettes, not wanting to miss a moment. He found them and lit one. Stayed glued on the screen.

. . . Hello, hello! Mrs Harland was smiling serenely to Sonny. Hello to you too, Mrs Harland. Sonny bright-eyed with disbelief. My daughter and I shall play a piece by Liszt . . . Her perfect teeth in this most extraordinary of smiles. Sonny could see her eyes were green, and she had unusually dark eyebrows for someone with brown hair. Her speaking voice was sort of English, like on — I know: *Upstairs and Downstairs*. And she is definitely upstairs. He could but shake his head in awe, and draw hard and frequently on his cigarette.

And I'm Antonia, the girl came in. This is, in case you weren't aware, my dear mother. Smiling at her (dear) mother, then back at the camera. (It must be the father videoing it.) The image faded for a moment then came back from a different perspective: of the pair viewed from the other side. Daughter in the foreground, and a lovely picture she made; even at eleven a man could see her womanhood not far below the surface. Again, shaking his head in mute admiration; as well, a sense of pitiful comparison coming on.

The mother began playing first. And her voice, just slightly deeper than normal, somehow became mirrored in the notes she was running off her fingers. That the piece was good or bad, Sonny had no idea; just his raw instincts and untrained ear telling him he was hearing something pretty good. The daughter came in, down at the deeper note end. Sonny had plunked out a few notes himself on that very instrument. In that very house. (Why, I have even seen that woman there in the nude. Photographically.) Yet it seemed inappropriate that he turn on the light and take pause of what Jube called the evidence, stolen from her, her bedroom, her own bedroom. He just watched.

And a spell got cast. Which did not break till long after the piece was ended and the smiling images had gone and the screen was just a fuzzy white glow. Piano notes played on in Sonny Mahia's mind and he felt confused. Damn near crying.

Light on. Now what? The Russian dancers? Sonny in a bit of a daze, as well as ashamed of himself for getting so emotional over a video recording of a couple of snob bitches, mother and snotty daughter, playing their fuckin piano. So fuckin what? No need to cry about it, Sonny the Wimp. Magine what they'd say at the Tavi they caught you not only watching this but crying over it as well? I need another can.

But sitting down on the end of his bed, Sonny recalled more than a few times of fellow prison inmates, cellmates, exposing their true selves. Specially when they were asleep; teeth-grinding and whipping around in their sperm-ridden blankets, groaning and crying out from troubled mind; the child in each and every crim wanting not vengeance but love. Sonny'd long figured that of himself and ilk. Bawling. In their sleep and bawling, whimpering, Leave me alone! Leave me alone! . . . Uh, love . . . love me, eh darl? Love Ted . . . Ya like that name? Could ya love Ted?

Sonny remembered specifically a big tough dude, a gang member, he was celled up with for two months who damn near every night broke out like this in his sleep. Love. That's what tough Teddy was secretly about. He just wanted love. So Sonny didn't feel so bad about his outbreak. And the music and the images of the players still lingered in his mind. He got up, put the tape on again. But this time with the light on. Though he still did not find it in him to look at the photographs.

No tears after the second performance; instead, a feeling of perplexing sadness. (I know: it's the gap. The difference. Between us.) Sonny got an insight. (And — and, and it's to do with me and my hopes — No, not hopes. Sumpin else. Sumpin else . . .) But it would go no further than that.

He finished the can, opened another. Lit a smoke. Ate some cashews. Not as nice as the — he had to look at the label on the empty packet — pistachios. He stroked the pile of notes, spreading them out in a fan again. Smiled at them. Picked one up and kissed it. Said aloud, Is this what it's like to have money? You're happy all the time? But he knew he wasn't, not all of even this short time — less than a day — happy. But it sure as hell beats being broke. (Hope that lady in the park is alright.) A sudden reminder from thinking of being broke. And miserable. And so desperate. Then nothing better'n a mongrel, even if it was Jube did the business on the woman.

97

(I was still with him. Didn't see me saying no to what the money from the woman's handbag bought us. Mongrels. We crims're always a few bucks away from being mongrels.)

Then he took the photos out of the envelope.

And gasped.

And felt his guts heaving with an anguish as well as excitement and then a deep, deep wanting. (I want you, lady . . . Not to fuck — *not* to fuck, and yet that too. I'm a Teddy Nathan, lady: I just wanna be loved . . .) Staring intently at one of the photographs. The overall picture of woman shape. Then the specifics. Her face, its serenity, like the piano-playing image of her was serenity. Hair in wet tangles. Those dark eyebrows rather heavy of growth too. So sexy. And he could hear her voice — exactly. It was astonishing. She could be in the room. No she couldn't. Woman like her wouldn't set foot in a hole like this. Nor would she expose herself like this for a mongrel. Sonny fought to get back to admiring her.

The triangle of pubic hair and just the start of the divide visible, a sight. But not only the sight, for now she had a voice, and a personality, or what little was in his mind from the video recording. And she had movement now in this same smile frozen on the glossy paper. Legs well shaped, athletic. Breasts ample. And her eyes, so open and honest. Who but Jube'd see porn in this? (So why am I as stiff as a board then?)

He lay down on his back. Grinning at the thought of the stash of over three grand beneath him. He held the one photograph up in front of his eyes. And masturbated. And when it was over he wept again.

Sonny stood before the mirror looking at his image, grinning. Not bad, not bad, even if I say so myself. This was his next sequence of being alone, not able to find sleep nor tame the restlessness, and don't forget the nervousness that hadn't gone away for — must be near a day. So looking at how he scrubbed up in his new clothes. Need a hair tidy-up he decided. A real expensive job for once. One of them fifty-dollar numbers, but not a blow-wave; I hate blow-waves, they look false, they don't move in even a gale, it ain't natural. Just want some quality.

The nervousness persisted. It felt like he could be ready to go out on his first-ever date. Yeah, that's how it felt. (And not with her,

Penelope, neither. Much too high up in the clouds for this boy. Who then?)

A name just came to him: Jane. Popped up like that in his mind like an introduction. She even had a voice, and it was low-toned like the goddess's was, cept it didn't have that clarity of pronunciation. Couldn't. Not a likely girl of my meeting. Jane. Just a plain Jane. (But not so plain she'd be unwanted by other men. Who wants that? I don't.)

The new shirt gave him a sudden itch, which he relieved, catching his mirrored image in the awkward position of hand reaching right over his shoulder to the itchy spot. He turned it into a little dance of silly steps, then flopped around body with the arm dived over his shoulder and the other between his legs. Hahaha.

He knew a Jane once. She got killed in a car crash. Wasn't her driving neither. Never is the woman. They only get to die, or end up horribly injured, in wheelchairs even, in the name of the driver's manhood. Like Jube's manhood is on the road, encased in the act of speeding. Jane's boyfriend was driving. She got killed and he lived. Guy still drinks most days at Tavistocks. Plays the tragedy to the full, even though it happened a few years ago. They do that, do Tavi regulars; they squeeze every last drop from everything and anything. Life, even. But their life: in the fuckin pits.

It's always the woman gets hurt or killed, same as they get beaten up — in the name of manhood. Poor Jane. Even if she was a bit of a typical Tavi scrubber, she didn't deserve to die. No-one does. Not even Jube. Enough of that, Sonny shaking his head in a deliberate gesture to ward off darker thoughts.

The Cossack dancers, that's what's next. He got the tape, read the handwritten title again: Georgian State Dancers. Frowning. He thought Georgia was in America: tough-guy country, where the whites're like Jube McCall, cept they hate anyone with dark blood like I am. They hate the world, from what a man understands, like Jube does. (Ahh, but come to think of it, so does every Tavi regular hate the world. It's the condition, brother. Part of being the condition, hahaha.) He reverently placed in one of his drawers the piano-playing duo. Mine. They're mine, and definitely not for Jube's eyes.

The dancing was stunning. Had Sonny standing up and stay standing in open-mouthed astonishment that such virtuosity of movement could exist. Disbelieving. This was a Pandora's Box, the whole experience, from first sight of that huge modern house thrusting up out of the dark of angles and slopes and protrusions, to now this. He hadn't even touched the beer can he'd started before the tape came on. He rewound it then started it over. This time he did a couple of imitation steps to the male members of the troupe: guys in Cossack dress, high leather boots and billowy shirt sleeves and fur hats.

Sonny fancied himself a dancer — of crude skills compared to this lot, but endowed with an inborn rhythm, an understanding of beat and how to express it in body movement. Lot of Maoris could. Must be in the blood. Hah. Like crime is too? He thought of the high proportion of Maori people in jails. But shrugged it away: I ain't no genius, don't ask me why this is so. Like I said, might be in the blood, a certain passion, a subsequent lack of control, cos the passion got the better of the mind and common sense went out the window. Hell, I dunno.

Was past eleven o'clock when the tape was through for the second time. Jube'd be coming home soon if he hadn't picked up a woman and gone somewhere with her. But Sonny wanted to see one more tape, and enough beers in him to say to hell with Jube coming in on him. So fuckin what? He my boss or sumpin? He sorted through the tapes. Tried one that said Verdi's *Nabucco*. That'll do.

Bor-ring. How anyone'd want to watch this kind of crap was beyond him. But he kept watching if only that he became a little bit interested seeing people dressed up like they were. And then something happened: group singing . . . Man, that's kinda cool . . . Sonny listening and watching hard now, as the voices began rising, then they fell again, then — LAAHHhh — as they reached up, grabbed a high note together. Man. This wasn't bad after all.

It got so that Sonny saw the triumph in the song, even though it was in foreign language; it was the way the singers built and built, how his own skin broke out in goose pimples and his chest swelled up, even his chin was lifting higher and higher, as if someone'd told him: Stand proud, man! Lah-DA-DAAAA!!! dadada, lada-da-da-da, it went like that, men and women in a kind of ordered frenzy. Melodic, sure. But alive — *alive*, cuz.

Sonny wanted to be part of it. Of them. The group. In song. In joy. Of meaning. Of learning. Of being a member of a something that'd got itself organised and then trained into doing this. Opera? He guessed that's what it was. Man, for all he knew they might be men and women prisoners putting on a musical over in, where? I dunno, Russia? Italy? Germany? What kinda language is it they're singing? Then sounds from outside had him sighing, and he quickly stopped the tape playing, readied himself for the Jube and probable company onslaught.

(Man, this is unreal: from that world on screen I been watching all night, to Jube arriving in his throaty-engined car with its specially designed exhaust he is convinced really impresses people with its growl. He'd be in the company of, what, a Tavi scrubber, or a girl from the massage parlour around the corner to the Tavi, and there'd be a few hanger-ons cos Jube was flush with bread, and hanger-ons they're no different to flies zooming in on free pickings. They'll be sucking up to Jube, playing on his stupid vanity, arms around each other thinking they're all mates even when they know they're not, they'll be stoned as well from dope, all arvo and night toking, and the shit'll be pouring from their mouths as it has been all this time getting out of it. Yet still they don't, and won't, know.

HAHAHAHAHA!!! Jube's cackling laughter. HAHAHAHA-HAHAHAHA!! Another couple of cacklers with him. And was that the softer giggle of a woman Sonny heard? Oh well. Can't beat em, join em. And he opened the door and closed it quietly after him. Hey, Jubesy babe. Flat. Sonny's welcome, flat.

9 Endless, man. The days. And the nights. Just endless.

Was bread did it. Having plenty of readies. That's what was doing it — lettuce, man. Loot. Three and a half grand of it. Oh, and that gear stashed in the spare room (and that fucking Sonny thinks he's gonna keep that stuff he clouted on, the stereo and tv and even a Persian rug, he's got another think coming. It's ours. Not his. *Ours*. In fact, was me who told him to grab the Persians, that ignorant brown prick wouldn't know a Persian rug from a Persian cat — HAHAHAHAHA!!)

Day started when it started, ya know? HAHAHAHAHAHA!! Well it starts when a man wakes up, course it does, it could hardly start when he was asleep — HAHAHAHAHAHA!! Yeh. Might be morn. Might be the arvo. Didn't madda. Ya juss woke up when ya wake up. And first thing't hits you when ya do is that you ain't broke. You ain't broke, you're rich. Like in *rich*. And as you're reaching out for your first smoke of the day the grin's starting to spread already: Hey, I'm rich. HAHAHAHAHA!! Mmm-uh, so the smoke tastes even better than it anyway does.

Ya lie there smoking, grinning away, and going over the night — well, the day too, seein it started at, what, usually by twelve — in your mind of that booze ya drank (and bought for people), the joints you smoked, and the laughs ya had all arvo and night till seven when the Tavi closed and you all moved up the street, through the bus terminal, to another pub of your regular going, and drank more piss, went outside to dack up with a few of the boys, back inside for more laughs, maybe some crim talk and a bit of good ole bullshit. For free. Well, may as well be free since it was only stolen money giving a man (and some of his buddies) this good time. So that's how the day began, the way it started — in a way — of you laughing and getting up soon to go do it again. A-fucking-sweet-gain.

It'd been like this for, what, a couple of weeks? Years? Hell, who knows, and who the fuck cares — HAHAHAHAHA!!! Might be you woke up with a sheila beside ya: huh? where'd she come from? But afraid to check her out too closely in case she was a dog, cos she was sure to be at least half a dog — what else would a guy like Jube McCall pick up bring home? Elle MacPherson — HAHA-HAHAHA!! Chance be a fine thing, eh Jube?

Ya know ya musta chatted her when you were out of it, that she musta got more and more beautiful the more double rum and Cokes ya got down ya; rolling over to her, with eyes part closed, but a morning hard-on that'd satisfy a fucking elephant (cept I don't fancy an elephant — HAHAHAHAHA!!). Grab her hand and shove it down on the old fulla, just to let her know you were ready for her, and let her touch what she was gonna get. Feel that for a boner, babe. And waiting for her to respond. Hey? You awake? Ahh, now that's more like it, at her giving it a squeeze and a few pumps with a hand that'd be thirty, forty (hope she ain't fucking fifty; God, I'd die) and a Tavi heart going on a hundred. Grabbing a handful of her box (man, least it's nice and hairy) and rubbing your mits all over the hair, then a finger probing for the crack (hope it don't just fall in, that there's a bit of resistance). Feeling yaself drawn to her naturally, of wanting to kiss her, but not wanting either because she'd have morning breath and your own breath'd be hardly Old Spice; and anyway something about kissing a mole, a Tavi mole, the intimacy of the act (I dunno) that turned a man right off. (Reminds me of my old lady, me mum. As if I was kissing her.) Yet still drawn to the face, till she said she wanted a smoke first. Fuck the smoke. Ya wanna smoke, babe, get down on this cigar, hahahahaha. And shoving her head down under the blankets. She protesting, This early in the morning? What, ain't it your shift? hahahaha! Geddown, woman.

(Now, what day did that happen? I can't remember.)

Jeezuz wept, but I need a bloody torch down here! HAHA-HAHAHA!! Don't you worry bout no torch, babe, you won't have trouble finding it. It's long and hard and sticking up in the air — HAHAHAHAHAHA!!! But she threw the blankets off. And don't shove it right in neither. I'll choke. No, I wouldn't do that to you, babe, Jube as the mouth'd enveloped his cock, and he looked down at the sight and it pleased him mightily, her tangle of hair part veiling her mouth with his tool sticking out of it. Ahh, babe . . . Closed his eyes. Opened them again when he heard her tell him, And don't you come neither. I hate come. Oh no, babe, I won't come. (Just a little shoot, maybe. Hehehehe.)

The act of being done arousing other feelings in him too. Of a certain hatred welling up. For her, the scrubber. For all women who allow themselves to turn into scrubbers. Hated em. Women, scrubbers, my mother, the fucking lot, even as he found pleasure in being mouthed by the same. Even as he felt his climax — the first, mind — building. He hated.

URRGGGHH! Mmmmmmmmmm — UHH! Jube spurting and the scrubber choking. He with his hand tightly down on the top of her head, keeping her there. She struggling, having muscle spasms. He wanting to punch the bitch. Then he was spent, so he sighed and groaned at once and let go his grip. And up she came: YA CUNT! I COULDA CHOKED TA DEATH! HAHAHAHAHAHAHAHA!! Jube didn't care. And he easily parried her feeble blows aimed at his head as he told her, Go brush ya teeth, bitch. You're dribbling. HAHAHAHAHAHA!! (God, but you were born with one sense of humour, Jubesy babe. Hahahahaha.)

Now, was that a couple of days ago? Man, I can't remember. But she sucked good, and when I got hard again she weren't too bad in that department neither. Might be worth a try again some other time. Nah, too much of a dog to look at.

But damned if he could remember what day that was; he didn't even know her name.

Wasn't only the fact that he was richer than he'd ever been in his thirty-five years on earth, was the stuff stashed in the spare room (and Sonny's room, the cheeky bastard) and to top it off there was the unemployment benefit stacking up in his PostBank account that the dumb government mugs paid in automatically every week without fail. The rent, or his half, got automatically taken out in turn from the same account, and with a rental supplement it hardly made a difference to the dole, so it was near on one twenty a week. Not much when ya live the life, but ya get by; and there's a whole city out there of dumb-arse straights working for a living that you can pinch a bit from. (Or a lot, hahahahaha!) It was too good to be true.

Waking up, and getting round to thinking next about turning

himself into a dealer. Smiling at that. Feeling very nervous in his stomach too, at the prospect, the status he'd gain. Not to mention the big bikkies. Very big. As for Sonny's crap about it being worth a big sentence, hell, wasn't anything worth that now they had so much form? And not as if it was smack or coke, no way, not my scene, I never touch the stuff, even as a user — a potential one that is.

Picturing himself driving an American left-hand drive, symbol of the big dealers, of getting the looks from everyone, of envy, jealousy, admiration and not a little awe. Awe, cuz, cos ain't many in our world can pull up the necessary bread in bulk to buy a reasonable quantity. No, they just live hand to mouth, as the counsellors in prison tell us we got to stop. Oh yeah? How? Well, Jube had the how now. (I have it.) And thinking of that made him near ball with happiness, though he wouldn't have, not him. (Do tough guys dance? Hahaha.)

Outta bed; think about being a dealer again soon. What's to eat? Into the kitchen. Man, it stinks in here, don't that fucking Sonny clean up after him? Oh, forgot: was me and a couple of the boys last night. Or was it the night before? (Hahahahaha!) Don't madda. I don't give a fuck. Looking in the fridge. Nothin. Only Sonny's leftovers of some Chink takeaway food. He can keep that vege three bits a fatty meat, it ain't for Jube. And come to think of it, a man ain't seen Sonny down at the Tavi in, what . . . ? A little surprised that he had no idea; a little worried — but just for an instant — that this wasn't a good way to be. Not when you didn't even know what day it is. But what the hell.

Sonny came up in his mind again; thinking about the lil jerk, his stand-out difference among his own kind, or meant to be his own. But when Jube thought about it, Sonny'd never been one of them — (Though have I? Course I have. Have I?) — lil black shit, too much thinking, that's his trouble. He'd be alright if he didn't think about every damn thing. Plus he wants to go straight, but hey, don't we all? Does he think I don't wanna live in a nice house drive a flash car, have no worries bout bills? But how?

Thinking then of his money stashed inside his mattress, where even an experienced burglar'd be pushing to find the slit along the join line into which he'd slid a good portion of the money (but not all of it or a man couldn't flash his roll, hahaha), and glad — glad — of having it because it represented so much, perhaps virtually everything, of the crim mind, the crim number-one goal in life: to have money. (But why? Oh well, have to ask Sonny that. He's the thinker, I'm the doer — HAHAHAHA!)

Looking around the kitchen and realising the mess was his, not Sonny's, oh no, not Sonny fucking Mister Clean Mahia, his voice echoing in the thin walled room. Jeezuz I'm starving. Getting out the foil container of Sonny's, may as well take a look; looks like chicken . . . more'n three bits too. Maybe I should try it. Nah, deciding not to. Grab a pie on the way to the Tavi. What time is it anyway. Ten past eleven. Well, I'd better hurry, hahahaha. Might miss my noon deadline of the last few weeks. Or is it days?

No time for a shower. Don't madda, everyone else in there stinks the same; some'll've been up drinking all night and carrying on this day; some out stealing in the night and'll be wanting a drink to settle the old nerves, and to celebrate, specially if they struck it lucky. As well sell gear, even at eight in the morning when the Tavi opens; ya never know your luck, might be a wharfie come in from night shift. They got plenty, have wharfies, fifty grand a year, min, a man heard they get, lucky bastards, though who'd work a fucking nightshift loading ships? Not Jube, thas for sure.

Out to his car parked on the street. Varoom, varoom, haha-haha. And away we go. Warming it up for a few moments then planting the boot. (Oo, I love this.) Roaring down the street, knowing some'd be hating it but plenty others'd be admiring a man, how he drove his car, even the sound of it'd have more'n a few green with envy. Eat ya fucking hearts out, fuckers.

At the intersection having to stop for a long flow of traffic. Tapping fingers on the leather-wrap steering wheel, smoking, look-ing at the world passing by, at a group of Pacific Island people, mostly women, hating them, for being fat, every one ofem, for wearing them big long dresses that go to the ground (Any wonder, too, it's to hide the fat. Who'd root one a them? Not even I would.) with them stupid flowers, they even have shirts with the fucking things plastered over em. Fat, always smiling, and laughing, and fussing over their fat little kids, what do they eat the day long getsem so gross? Them and Maoris, just the fucking same: fat, lazy, and aggressive when they've got a few beers in em. Cunts, all ofem. (Even Sonny?)

Even Sonny. He used to be my mate. But he changed. Sumpin happened to him. Stir-stick, that's what it probably is. Gunning into a gap in the traffic, waving out his window, thanks, mate. Why can't they all be like that? Joined in the slow flow, easy about that — to start with. Then getting wild that it must be some cunt, a woman he'd bet, somewhere up ahead driving two mile a fucking hour not thinking bout no-one else, oh no, just her selfish self. So pulling centreward to check out what was happening, but couldn't tell. Left, and seeing there was space enough to get a car up there — if two wheels went up along the footpath, hahaha. Let's go!

Tooting his triumph as he raced along half on the road half on the pavement. Ya mugs! Ya straight fucking mugs! Feeling not only triumphant but bold. As if that was what separated him, Jube McCall, from other people: his willingness to do this kind of thing. Finding a space at exactly the right moment and into it, laughing, shaking his head at himself his mad boldness; knowing it was the quality about himself that was gonna make him a dealer. Boldness. Guts. (I got spunk.) Hey, a dairy. He slammed on the anchors. A pie.

A group of them gathered round a table, elbow height, who sits down in this joint, man, it's bedda to stand, y'cin see wha's happening round ya, the fights, the whispering, the huddles of crime plan, of scam scheme, of rort rip-off, and ya wanna hear the variations these people get on taking the Social Welfare to the cleaners — it's art — and anyway, standing is sumpin crim types — and their associates — kinda seem to prefer. To keep on guard, maybe.

Air heavy with smoke, cigarette smoke. (Too early for a joint, for most of us: spoils it getting the high too early. Bedda to wait till, what, round mid-arvo. Yeh.) Fags being dragged at, rolled-up make your owns, hanging on bottom lips and stuck to the skin, jammed into the corner of the mouth tough-guy style (like on the movies, kiddo); smouldering away in overflowing ashtrays centre-table, burning against match-sticks, filters, on the built-up pile of ash debris, mounds of black and grey pile-up with protrusions jutting out, could be mini-versions of a discarded building site; burning away between nicotine-stained fingers, near all of them bearing tat marks, symbols of their worldly status: LOVE and HATE and MUM (but hardly ever DAD) permanently etched, some fingers trembling with the shakes of too much the candle (and the smokes, cuz) burning at both ends; jugs spread over the table, and glasses —

plenty beer, bro! — cos Jube was buying. Eight, nine, ten dudes and a cupla sheilas, and around that same number of jugs, though the group kept getting added to so Jube was always gonna be behind in matching it for jug buys, though who gave a fuck, long as there was *some* jugs there for filling up the ole glass. (What, it has to have a fuckin name on it, cuz! Hahahaha.)

Tats, man. Everywhere. Tats. Marks of each his and her past and still burning present; windowed behind layer of skin over hands, up arms, around necks and up under throats, beneath eyes, on forehead, on chin, and ear lobes, you name a place. The passport that got you in where nothin else would. (Yet how do our numbers still get penetrated by undercovers?) The passport to crim country, even though it was the same country, borders had to be passed within. The electric-needled entry to crim territory; the cotton wound around a needle and soaked in ink woodpeckering designs like passwords, cuz. To getem in with their ink-pictured own.

Eyes mostly on Jube, or they didn't stay off him long. (He might up and disappear! Hahahaha! And so would our freebies.) He'd cracked it, but he still hadn't said; say that for him for a big mouth: he hadn't said a word. Plenty hints, though, but they were the usual Tavi shit of breaking into a flash house and finding sumpin or other. If it wasn't a mechanical cock, it was evidence of some straight not so straight, how they were round here. Lies, but. All of it lies. (Long as the drink still keeps flowing who's arguing?)

Jube telling little jokes, and everyone laughing like hell, even though they were weak ones ya get from bubblegum wrappers, roaring with him, whacking his back, Jube, you're sumpin else, hahaha. Seeing as how he was in the chair. Ha-ha-ha as ya helped yaself to one of the jugs, oh, and may as well grab a smoke while you're at it, seein as Jube was so kind to buy a load of packets from the machine, Thank you, Jubesy babe. You very kine. Hey, tha's alright, Joycie honey, hahahaha. (Ha-fuckin-ha, whiteman, trying to buy your way in with the Maoris. But you won't. You ain't one of us, can never be. And it ain't juss your skin, it's the coldness of sumpin about you. And your sex too. All the damn time you get it back to sex. Well, us Maoris might be bad, specially in here, but most don't go for that sex stuff. Not like you, Jube McCall.)

The jugs, first of the (free) day going down quick (real quick). Oh, now would ya lookit that: the jugs're done gone — HAHA-HAHAHAHA!! Everyone laughing along with one of the guys, a white guy too, at how he dropped his hint so cheekily, but the rest ofem with their dog-cunning eyes on the floor, at their street-scuffed footwear, or on a new pair of runners from a shop bowled over the Shore a few nights back and ended up here for only twenty bucks a pair (well, they'd hardly sell em singly — HAHAHAHA!), or around em — hi, Duke; Hey, Lonesome, how ya been, kid! — but only very fleetingly at Jube, cos it was careful careful don't rush the man, don't crowd him it might scarim off, he might take his generosity elsewhere, or he might stay put but only buy for himself, in which case it weren't no point in putting up with his wanky company, the guy is an egg, make no bones.

So they stood there in this kind of awkward silence, which only Jube's telling of another little joke filled, cept no-one did much laughing at this one, or not till Rula Jones piped up: Hey, any chance of some refills there, handsome?

A brief moment of silence, of Jube stopped halfway through his (stupid) joke, then his hand dived into his jeans pocket and out came a fifty. So everyone broke out laughing and some were saying, Hey, good-looking, how bout over here? Hahahaha. And it felt, it seemed, as if a good time was being had. A real good time. They must be. Or why were they laughing?

Hey, no worries, no fluckin worries — HAHAHAHA!! — Jube at himself, his generosity, his funny play on the word. More, when a few of them echoed the words: No fluckin worries, bud! HAHA-HAHAHAHAHA!!! And they could see on Jube's face how he was loving this, lapping up being centre stage; and that he could not see, astonishingly, their barely concealed contempt for him. (But ain't eggs and dipsticks like that?)

Jube bought another round. Close on fifty bucks it cost him. Ahh, but what the hell, eh boys? (The girls don't count. Not till later when he's hanging out for that other side of him to be fixed up. Then they'll fuckin count alright.) What's fifty between mates? Not seeing their contempt, nor Joycie's hatred, her hatred of most things white, most things about white people which she loathed before she was capable of giving it attempt of understanding.

Margie came in and joined the group: Hell*ooooo*! everyone. With her limp wrist carry-on, her hideously made-up face and hair-do up in a beehive, her silicone breasts showing ample in a low-cleavaged dress hugged tightly to her falsely represented body that wouldn't even fool a blind man. But she was alright, she really was;

she had a heart of gold, and anyway she'd been around as long as the city of Auckland had, near. She even had a television documentary done on her (you bedda believe it, honey chile) and she was a cheeky sausage so no-one showed any surprise when she immediately spotted who was in the buying chair so went straight to the mountain rather than the mountain having to go to her, as she told the mountain: Mmm, what a man, as she rubbed teasingly up against him. Everyone laughing, genuinely laughing, with no edge nor side-on nor undercurrent because the transvestite was very very funny. Though she'd better watch her act didn't push even the galoot Jube McCall too far, or she'd cop it. She might be funny, but weren't no-one gonna step in bat for her, not a tranny.

I hear you got one a foot long, Jube McCall, she was saying in that lispy voice they have, as she helped herself to a jug with a glass produced from her handbag, a champagne glass, a tall, flute-shaped one, which she broke from her teasing to describe as just that, but you ignorant bastards and bitches wouldn't know cos you got no class, now where was I? Giggling. Everyone grinning. Jube reserving his reaction, though it was plain he liked his cock being referred to in such terms because he said, Who told you that, Margie? They're exaggerating. Looking falsely outraged. It's only eleven inches — HAHAHAHAHAHA!! But no-one laughed, only gave token grins because his timing was wrong. Any anyway his vanity was too obvious and too big. (Like your whiteman hooter, arsehole).

Eleven inches! OOOOOoooo!! now that's — that's — itth gi*nor*mus, dear! Margie pouting at Jube, but wary in her cunning eyes. Okay, I was lying, I was lying, it's ten. Ten? Ten. Really? Yeh, really. Wanna see? Do I what? I mean it. So do I, honey, hahaha. And everyone laughing at the exchange, or they did when they saw Jube laughing. Man, you coulda heard em around the corner, up Queen Street.

HAHAHAHAHAHAHAHAHAHAHAHAHAHAHAHA — A — HAHA-HAHAHAHAHA!!! Laughing at Jube telling a gum wrapper (un)funny. Cos Margie'd brought out some dope from her handbag and they'd smoked up large; the stuff was more'n a buzz, it was sensay-shan-nell. And life seemed so incredibly funny, everything about it; and every time someone said something — even Jube — it sounded so funny, and when one started, the others joined in because even laughter, other people's, sounded so marvellous. And you could've looked into the open mouths and read them like medical records, of people not well, unhealthy, furry-tongued, swollen of gum, ulcerated of gum, and giving off telltale stenches; same in the eyes, a knowing person'd read em like charts, like maps, like storyline reading all the way from some hell to another.

But what madda? What madda? Eh Rula? Eh, Rula. This's our place, the Tavi, it's where we belong, it ain't hell. Who said it was hell? It's fuckin heaven, eh Rula? Eh Mitch? Eh Dave? Eh Joycie? (If you say so.) We're one big (un)happy family here, aren't we, boys? Hey, yeow! Yeow! Puddit here puddit here (puddit anywhere you like, honey, cept not up my fanny).

Even Jube here, he's our mate. Right, boys? Right. He's been kine to us — *kine*. He's kine for a Pakeha, how many Honkies you know who's kine? Not many, eh? Hey, Jube, throwing arms around the tall whiteman, we're your frens, eh bro? You-are-kine. Ya know that? You bought us drinks all fuckin day long, you-kine. *Kine*. Ya hear? And ya don't hear, I'll punch your fuckin lights out — HAHAHAHAHA! Only joking only joking, I wouldn't hit a kine fulla like you even if you do got white skin — HAHAHAHAHA!! Hey, only joking'gain, only joking'gain.

Uh, Jube, you wouldn't have a spare twenny on you, would ya, cuz? Juss till tomorrow, you know? You know how it is, eh bro? You're one of us. You're white, but we look on you like a brother. And my cuzin, Hepa here, could I ask for a lil old twenny for him too, it's juss that we gotta go, you know, over to Mangere, and we got no petrol in the car, so it's juss to get us there cos my brother owes me heaps, eh. Only till we get the bread off him, Jube.

Not a set of eyes missing Jube shelling out a couple of twenties to the Timu cousins, even when Jube thought he was being sneaky. Not one brain behind a set of eyes that wasn't planning an elaborate sob story for Jube's ears.

And each man, and the couple of women, as well the transvestite, an aching readiness of timing waiting to select Jube's demeanour, his changing demeanour, his mood. Like throwing a big punch, it had to be right or you were gone. Then one of them making his move: Uh, Jube, like I been wanning to ask you a fav — No fucking way, Nick. I juss did two ofem favours. What, I'm Santa Claus? Where were you when you had bread a couple a months back and me and Sonny were hanging out? Well you know, man, how was

I — You knew alright, Nick. So don't play me, bud. I ain't no wanker the wind juss blew in.

Wrong. Nick's big hit the wrong timing. Nick sighing, taking his defeat with outside calm acceptance, but inside hating. Even though he'd been recipient of Jube's favours the whole arvo and into the evening, he still hated.

But the others smiling their fawning dog-cunning smiles at Jube, each believing his story, his timing, his big hit was the one. And the night wearing on.

What day izzit . . .? Oh, muss be a Tuesday, the solo mum (sluts)'re out in force with their benefit money; meant to be for the kid or kids, but they come in here with their toyboys attached, spend the day and evening boozing, buying beer for the toyboy. And the toyboys they all have that proud look like they're bein kept and they're proud of it, very proud. Crims, most of em, the toyboys; so any wonder it's pride and not shame they feel, cos how many crims've — what do they call it again? — values, thaz it. How many crims've got values? None, tha's how many. Sweet fuckall none. So they help their solo-mum sheila spend her government benefit then when it's time to go home giver a fucking, they say, no way, I'm off to a party at Joe's place, and I need some bread to buy some beer. So it's a gimme gimme, or else. Or else the dumb broad gets her head punched in and then the toyboy still takes her money cos tha's how the crim is: he's low. (Like *looooww*.)

But aren't we all, hmmm? Joe to Jube, and Jube looking at Joe and goin, Huh? The hell ya talking about, wanker? Low, Jube. We are low, agreed? Well, I dunno about that, speak for yaself. Hahaha, ruffling Joe's hair. (They like that in here, their hair bein ruffled, makes em feel wanted. Loved, even.) You out of it, Joe? Sure, I'm out of it, but, Jube, we are low, man. Lookit us, Joe sweeping an arm around the place. Take a look, bud.

At them grinning, exploding in laughter, being expansive in acts of affection (false affection) demonstration, using theatrical gestures, flowery gesticulations and facial expression poses, ain't hard to pick up on it, not'nless you're blind, and ya don't see many round here tapping white canes on the cigarette-butted, beer-sloshed, spit-spotted, blood-dripped, vomit-smelling threadbare carpet floor, now do ya? And this was only a part of the bar Jube was having pointed out to him. The stoned part.

So they went inside their heads, and saw and discovered things none of em had a means to convey, nor did a one have it in him or her to understand, that what he and she was seeing was some kind of raw truth. They couldn't. Fuckin head'd explode. Just as attempts at trying to relate what was goin on in the head, the stoned-out head, just came out messy, stupid, didn't make no sense; so the heads moved in perfect time to the jukebox music — to the *sounds*, cuz — they could hear every note of voice and instrument, hear every subtlety; even see the big picture of what means and what is musical composition. (And it seemed so *simple*.) But they couldn't word it, couldn't word it, can't word it, can't can't don't wanna, won't ever . . . What day izzit again? Oh, Toosday, tha's right, why all the solo mums're out in force.

They could see each other as well, how each and every of their stoned, drinking companions was, how the dope bled to the outside the different qualities of each person, good and bad, insightful and disturbing. Sillier and sillier.

Some wandered off to the front-entrance foyer, where the pay-phone was. Who zat? Zat you, Boydie? Boydie, get Maku on the phone. Pleese. I *said* pleese. (Fuckin wanker.) Hello? Mak? That you, brother? Iz me. Toby. Yeh, Tobe, bro — *Tobe*. Hey-hey there, brother a mine. How you holding, bro? Come on . . . Juss till Thursday, bro. Only need fifty. Or they'll cut the power off. They will, Mak. They did it larse time and they'll do it again. Pleese, bro. Pleese? Uh? Uh? Man, I'm desperate, brother, really am, eh. Wha? Oh go fuck yaself, gi*mme* a fuckin lekcha. I'll fuckin remember this —

Be seven soon. Closing time. Head off to the next pub closing time, hahahaha. And outside, out the front doors (not the back one that opens out into the cool shade of bus terminal roof overhang, where ya choke on the diesel fumes, and ya startle for just a briefly sobering moment at the sight of life's lonelies and forgottens and weirdos and freaks and nature's fuck-ups of physical disability, ugliness, hideousness, repulsiveness, life's saddies, life's miserables, the terribles, and all the poor waged workers, the suffering abused housewives (on earth to be fucked and beaten and made house slaves of), the maddies, and then there's the children (growing up seeing this and only this as their horizon, some fuckin horizon, cuz, some fuckin horizon) growing up sad and the sad turning bad), well not out that way but out front, out front, outside, man, past the telephone lifeline lieline, this time of year the outside world'll still be bathed in light; and even if it's cloudy there'll be that extra quality of light when it's thrown off sea, off harbour; and down a bit the businesses being busy, the joggers, office-worker late-night workers, running along catching their proud reflections in shopside glass, angled shop windows. Other side fishing boats coming and going (and another load of hash slips into the country, come the long way from shady, exotic beginnings and spy-like journey, just to end up, the better part, in the mouths of lowlifes funded by government to smoke the stuff — Oi, pass it on, pass it on, man, I ain't had a toke yet —)

Oriental boys fast headed down street, not see Tavistocks sign, too busy looking for Massage sign, need girl, white girl, blonde the bess, they bess for Oriental boy who only know black hair, yellow skin, we like white skin, blonde hair, specially down there, we pay more for that. Travelled all that water with only woman wet on Oriental mind, which not so inscrutable when you look close. Lady massage girl, Blonde Queen, I alright, I clean, I clean, Japanese and Chinese boy he clean, so no rubber, lady beautiful girl, no wubber pleese for clean Chinese Japanese Korean boy.

And the massage girls bringing in early-evening earns for a quick drink say hello to some of the Tavi regs, to the lowlife mirrors of herself, and tellem lurid stories of kinky filthy horny perverted customers, clients; and everyone laughing, or scowling, or looking astonished at the extent — the *extent* — of behaviour gone beyond even their depraved condition, of man, mankind his fantastic sexual scope of bent and twisted and warped imagination turned to real-life pictures with simple handover of the cash: Do it this way, lady, sweet blon white lady. Show me it, show it to me (ahhhh), let Oriental boy gaze upon your blonde (pure) sexual loveliness. The gals telling em this, the Tavi regulars, but only surprise and mirroring and envy and part disgust getting through to em, not wisdom, can't be wisdom, cuz, hahahahaha, wisdom's an open door in ya mind, eh, and if it's closed, it's, like, closed, eh. And no amount of hammering'll open it neither. No amount.

Outside, outside in the lovely (for all they knew nor cared), the sun starting to dip, making the harbour waters golden. And the boat and ship churning giving the water this kind of sheen that danced with silvery reflections and threw mercury shade and rounded water texture movements to any observant eye that weren't drunk out of its skull and/or stoned to the eyeballs.

114

More and more going out to the payphone, to beg and plead and implore and lie for the stuff that'd keep this lie going, the same stuff they go out steal for — bread, baby — cos it's what holds the emotional fort, keeps the emotional wolf from the door of your tormented condition. (But not so tormented you can't telephone a con to the callee other end, laying it on thick, with that plastic mouthpiece in your tattooed hand signifying the degrees of your pathetic duration, telling the tale of your unhappy endurance. Mum? Mum, I need some money.)

Such a nice evening outside too.

10 Oh, and during the night, not that night though, too out of it that night, but another night, this sheila comes in, eh. On her own. And a looker too. So everyone thinking she was a new girl started at one of the parlours, probably Class Touch, Big Pete's joint, but then again she didn't look like no hooker, not even to them in their drunk and stoned states. Too sorta confused, of eye and demeanour; the way she looked around her unafraid of eye, only a little surprised at being somewhere unfamiliar, and maybe getting confused at all around low-life patronage eying her; them, the regs, figuring how she, the lost-looking entry, would be seein em; so grinning amongst themselves and giving her looks varying from mock hostility to false innocence. Then everyone could see she was kind of sick, in her eyes, in her innocent unfraidness of not alarming, let alone bolting, at the sight of what she'd stumbled into.

Not retarded, no, she wasn't that bad. Ain't as if her head was rolling all over the place and her tongue was hanging out, not like that. But she looked lost in her facial composure; the skin was pulled tight and she had make-up that'd seen a few tears in the last little while, though she was covering up as if she was okay.

They swarmed over like flies. They didn't give two fucks bout her looking probably a bit wonky in the ole head, the brain department (so who's sane around here, hahahahaha!), they only wanted to fuck her, the men did; and the women wanted to smash her up, lure her out to the toilets and scratch her pretty face to shreds, comin in lookin like that. The men only wanted what was up her short skirt, to go straight up to her, no kiss my arse, nuthin, and hike up her dress and enter her twat, her strangely different womanhood (might be sumpin different for a change). Drooling over her cos whoever scored'd be having the prettiest woman he'd

116

ever had in his life (his unhappy duration), and that's the whole point, ain't it, to fuck the best-looking sheilas you can? So wha's ya name, darl? Jube was one of the first over to her. The first to slime over.

And the other fullas gathered round her like she was being auctioned, calling out their bids of introduction and lewd comment; one even calling out cock size: as if that was the sole reason to bring her sad-faced existence in here to, of all places, Tavistocks, to give herself to the bidder with the longest cock. But why, even Jube wouldn't talk like that and expect a result. Can I buy you a drink, doll? What's your name? My name's Jube, hahahaha, and you'll have to pardon the ole eyes, darl, but I'm, you know, out of it, eh. But not *that* out of it, if ya know what I mean, hahahaha. What was that you're having? Bourbon and L and P? Lady, it's yours. Come with me up to the bar, and you wankers take ya fucking eyes offa her cos she's spoken for, ain't ya, lady? Smiling at Jube. See? Tole you wankers. (hahahaha). And you cin take your dirty paws off the nice lady's bum too, Pedro. Think I didn't see ya? Hahaha, ya gotta watchem in this place, lady — What'd you say your name was?

Maria. Now that's a nice name. Maria. Jube eyeing the woman over her face, into her eyes as far her obvious condition was allowing him to probe, glassy that they were even though they were a beautiful doey brown. Knew a girl called Maria, back a few years now. But she wasn't as pretty as you, lady, tha's for sure. You're not from one of the parlours, are you? No, didn't think you were. You got too much class, huh? Hahaha. Drink up, Maria, plenty more where that comes from. Jube flashed his wad of fifties, his diminishing wad; even though he didn't see it as that. Still felt the same as when it first started, this dream run that bread and only bread can buy. Come closer, hahaha, I ain't gonna bite ya. He'd looked round him at the competition he'd beaten to this woman. They're the ones to watch, Maria, them creeps out there. Here, down that and I'll buy you another one. (A double. No, make that a treble, hehehe).

She downed the three-shot of bourbon and Lemon and Paeroa, as Jube merely sipped on his drink, wanting to stay in shape enough to really giver one if it was gonna work out that way. Eyeing her. All over. In a state of disbelief, or half belief, that he, Jube McCall, could be in such attractive woman company when he'd spent his adult lifetime in the company of sluts and low-lifes and scrubbers. Something was definitely wrong with her, she was spaced out and she

117

spoke in unrelated spurts of silliness in a lil girl voice (which turned Jube on.) Drink up, drink up, Maria, hahaha. Betcha ya don't remember my name? Thought you wouldn't, hahaha. (But you won't forget me, the man, lady.)

Third drink into her and Jube was hustling the woman out. Come on, kiddo, let's go somewhere classy. Alright? Yeah, sure it's alright, hahaha, I can tell. Ya like big cars? Take em or leave em? Wait'll you see mine. Oops, did I say sumpin wrong — HAHA-HAHA, I never meant it that way, Maria. The woman'd nodded at Jube's suggestion they go someplace else, just nodded and looked at him trustingly with those big brown eyes even more glazed by the double and triple shots of bourbon Jube'd fired into her. And the dudes catcalled and whistled and glared and teased at Jube walking out with the spunk, the mad-looking sheila he'd pulled before anyone thought to take advantage of her state, her pitiful condition.

Here ya go, darl, climb in, hahaha. The laugh catching in Jube's throat cos he was hornier'n a bull. And ya don't have to wipe ya shoes before you get in, hahahaha. Hearing his horniness in his own laugh, and his own nervousness at anticipating this event. (Man, wild horses wouldn't stop me now.) In his side looking at this dream stumbled in from the evening. He took her to another bar, a bit flasher. More our own kind, eh Maria, hahaha. Drink up. She drank. And night fell. Try another place? Sure.

Eyeing her as she got into the car, catching a flash of uncovered thigh when her dress rode up as she got in, he holding the door playing the gentleman. (And was that white flash I saw her knickers?) Jube had to swallow repeatedly, and he dry-retched when he walked round to his side of the car, carrying a six-pack of beer. Go somewhere to enjoy the night, yeah? Okay. Fine, the dulled creature'd said. Off we go. (Hahahahaha!) His hand trembling with the key in the ignition. Penis as hard as a rock.

The woman spoke in her dreamy tone as Jube drove. She was away with the fairies, but Jube going, yeow, hey! and nodding as though in perfect sympathy with the woman; her disjointed tale something about supposed to have taken her lith-something pill, that she was a maniac depression or sumpin, in that freaky voice of hers that was really a lil girl's not that of a woman with as fine a body as Jube'd ever seen other than in *Penthouse* magazines, and even then.

Talking to him in that lil girl voice that was turning him on, stirring up his sex juices sumpin terrible that he could rape her on the spot, cept it wouldn't be rape, not since she was in the car of her own accord, and anyway it's not rape it's only a fuck. One fuck is all it is and yet they give out big jail sentences for it, for a lousy fuck that the sheila can take anyway, no different to sticking a tooth-brush in her mouth: a quick twirl around and it's over. Was how Jube saw it. But rape was worth more and more these days, and look at that dude they knocked back his parole even though he'd done seven years cos of the public outcry. (Fuck the public. They're a buncha cunts anyway.)

What problem is this, Maria? he'd felt obliged to ask even though he wasn't thinking bout no problem cept what he had of himself down there — (HAHAHAHAHAHA!!!) — and hearing her mumble about the lithium pill again and the maniac depressive disease she had. Yeh, yeh, sure, Maria, I unnerstan. Know how ya must feel. As they drove through the city out east following the sea. Hey, now lookit that for a sight! Jube in false appreciation the sight of sea dappled with light reflections and streetlamps bouncing yellow off the waters and little humps of waves.

They'd passed a walking couple along seafront and Jube'd felt a kind of empathy with them: as if he and this mad woman were more or less in common with the couple, cept they were driving their partnership not walking it; but this could be his sheila, his main gal, her obvious, uhh, condition aside for the moment it took to run the thought through its shortspan course till the main one came back to the fore. But till it did he glanced over at her frequently, thinking she was one fucking stunner and that people'd be looking at Jube with envy and jealousy and hatred that he had a woman so attractive, the other guys wanting what he had of getting to (shortly) stick one into her, dip into her honey pot (hahahaha) but more, her beauty: that a man wanted so much to have at the same time he wanted to hurt, for some reason. Since, if he couldn't have her for keeps — not if she was sane, he wouldn't've had a chance — what was the point of fate turning up with her if not to hurt her?

All this going on in Jube's mind but not so much words as a series of feelings and impulses connecting up with thoughts. Think-ing it was ya never saw the goodlookers ever at Tavistocks cos the guys'd only wanna hurt em rather than treat em like goddesses, Goddesses never stayed long with low-lifes, they suss a lowie out pretty smartly, so the rare beauties that did stumble in like this one, well, they get what they deserve don't they? (And anyrate, it's only one fuck. Just one fuck. So what's the fuss about?)

He drove. She mumbled. He hardly heard her. Just rambling she was. He drove and she rambled and he got hornier by the second. He headed out to a spot he knew'd have no other cars parked up there, cos it wasn't romantic, had nothing that'd attract cars to park up.

His heart rate doubled. He'd kept glancing at her as he drove, making out he was all genuine ears for her forgotten lith pill condition, even as he sized her up for getting her to go down on him. He'd like that. More than like it. But then he decided she was a bit far gone that she might bite his cock off, so he gave that idea away, even though he hated not to get her down on him.

Out of the blue she groaned. What the — Hey, you okay, Maria? Yes, she was okay. Just that she should've taken her pill. Not *the* pill, hahaha, Jube was hoping like hell since it'd be a signal, a sure signal of consent, which he could tell the cops with a straight eye and an indignant tone if she cut up rough. She wiped at her brow in anguish and Jube used it to reach out a touch first her shoulder in apparent sympathy and then it fell on her knee, rested there. As his heart pounded and his throat clammed up.

There there, Jubesy's here, babe, ya don't have ta worry. Ya sure? she'd asked. Sure I'm sure, he'd turned a full face to her of lying innocence, smiling, as he crept the hand a little higher up her leg; feeling the bare skin, the warmth of her womanly blood inside, the tremendous sickness, nausea it induced in him. And he heard his words stick in his throat as he slowed and turned into a little tree-studded bay. And switched off the engine. So just the boom of his heart pounding in his chest.

He worked his hand up, still facing the sea, and making comment in a catchy voice of how cool it looked with a moon dancing light on it and there must be no wind cos the sea was like glass, as were her thighs as smooth as glass, and she wasn't saying nothin, not even pulling away. He was telling himself to keep cool, keep cool, seein as how there was no resistance, so what was the hurry? But another side of him was equally in despair that she might suddenly pull away from him, slap his face, yell at him (and so hurt me), and that feeling won. He pushed straight to the objective.

The hemline of panties was almost too much to bear. The finery of pubic hair hint was even worse. He leaned across, to kiss her, but mainly to work his hand up under the garment. Which he did. And things went kind of blank. Something did.

Not blind, but lost of a sense of his whereabouts; only his hand, his urgently probing, thrusting fingers fiddling away in there, had him of any state of word thought. He thought: I'm there. Man a fucking alive I'm there!

Dampness and hairiness, and then the definite feel of inner thigh muscles relaxing. (I'm in? I'm *in*?) Unbelievable. And he told himself: This bird ain't mad, she's hot to trot. And felt that he'd picked her up on his own merits. Which swelled his heart with pride and turned his mind to a murderous possessiveness.

Oh Maria . . . (God in fucking hell, but don't let it end, don't let no-one stop this) . . . Maria . . . probing her dampness, stunned that it was turning to a wetness. (She's mine.) My pill, Jube . . . I should have taken my pill. Oh Maria . . . I'm spaced out, Jube. My head is all freaky. Oh Maria, you're the most beautiful woman I ever knew . . . As he worked his fingers inside her, over her genitals, claiming her womanhood. Oh Maria. Jube, my pill, I should've taken my pill. Where am I? How long've I known you? Forever, doll. You've known Jube forever.

Maybe it was the way she was easy, a bowl-over, Jube didn't know, that he'd got wild with her. That he'd suddenly seen her in this light of not being what he thought she was, that she'd let him down, brought crashing to the ground a precious and grave concept of his. Which is why he found himself hitting her. With no reference point, no values to take from the bottomless pit of himself, his morals-bereft condition. But thinking, even as he plunged sexually into her at the same time he punched her with a left and a right, that he was in the right, for it wasn't *his* fault she'd let him down with her being not what she made out to be, that she was no different to a Tavi scrubber; she was even worse than that because she had offered no resistance.

And he'd muffled her screams — no, they weren't screams, they were just moans, of pain, but mostly echoes of her horror, confusion at his assaulting her — with a forearm whilst he pushed in and out of the wretched woman. Hating her. Hurt with her, that it was her, not him (not fucking *me*) who'd let him down.

As outside a full moon fat with nearness to the wretched Earth climbed higher from the sea it'd risen from. And the same loomed up above the roofs of closed early-opening bars like Tavistocks. And the man'd cried out his climax and then it was gone, in an instant. All his rage and hurt feelings of being tricked, she — it. It could have been a slight disagreement now spent of its energy and its meaning. So he lifted her bloodied head and kissed her sorry. I never meant ta hurt you, Maria. Though he knew he did. As the moon rose higher above a sea unruffled by wind or vessel or sea beast broken briefly of its glassy surface. And a woman cried. And her assailant drove away from her wandering state.

11 (I love this one best.) Sonny in eager anticipation of the video tape starting up on screen. Eager and excited, and with a kind of preconditioned hurt coming on, but not a — not a self-pitying hurt, more a kind of door being opened to himself. An aspect. (An aspect of myself, that's what it is.) As snow fell on the street and on spire-roofed church building, and people hurried into church huddled up in big coats and fur hats, then the big wooden doors closed and the scene was just of the small village with snow coming down and not a soul in sight. (But it's coming. It's coming, Son.)

Sound of throats being cleared, then the doors opening and this priesty-looking dude gesturing come, come inside to the warmth (and something else). (The camera) moving inside, sound of heavy thudding of doors closing behind. A deathly quiet, figure of Jesus with down-slumped head and outstretched arms pinned to his cross (and only his, since he gave a cross meaning when no other victim nailed or strung to it did), more coughing, people moving up the aisle, past decoated and hatless worshippers, staring ahead. Silence.

Then massed voices, men and women, in short opening. Then a powerful bass voice breaking out as his large form came closer till he was a face on screen, with mouth set in brief silence as his backing choir did a sequence. (Haunting . . . it's so haunting . . . and yet it's a church service?) Back came the guy, his voice filling the room his image was screening in. He climbed his powerful voice to the high notes and so the room reverberated, and Sonny's mouth opened and made faint imitatory sounds, but so faint even he couldn't hear them, nor did he desire to. He didn't know he was doing it; that his mouth was open and moving mutely in a kind of hurt awe. Hurt that his life had not known this, that his upbringing (my fuckin raising, you dog parents) didn't tell him nothin about this kind of side to the world, that it was there, available, on video tape, tv, record, cd, tape, that it was *there* all this damn time and no-one'd told him.

No-one'd said, Hey, Sonny, catch this, man, it's this music, Russian music, I think, called Slavonic Liturgy, and it's sung by a choir of exquisite blend of tone and note contrast of high women and deep male and lots in between, and it's led, you better believe, by this big fulla, eh, and he has this most unbelievable voice that shudders the walls he's screening in, and breaks the watcher out in goose-pimples, all over goosies, man, with the power and passion of his foreign-languaged delivery. But that's alright, the foreign words; it don't madda, Sonny, what maddahs is you, bro, and your experiencing it for the first time; even though this ain't the first time, it's about the fiftieth.

You know it off by heart Sonny, we know that, but it's as if you've been your whole life deprived. Or why else would it have you tingling and goose-bumping and stomach-aching all over? And why else'd it have you all over with the familiars, the familiars of knowing this, of having heard it somewhere but the only somewhere could be the back of your mind, maybe your dreaming mind, can't say, nothin to refer to, no reference point, just this terrible and beautiful at the same time achingness of feeling you and the music, you and the entire concept of music and sole male lead ringing out his notes of personal triumph. Come over with the familiars of this being an emotional reunion with, funny thing, yaself; like you and yaself'd never quite got it on till now; like you and yaself were two different people who knew each other but not well enough to know that they were one and the same thing, but now brought together by this music. By him. Boris, the label on the tape read, and so did the credits at the end, but which a man'd hardly ever seen because he was reduced, every time, to tears bubbling out of him, like a spring, not the dark-shed waters of pain ya can't rid yaself of, but a spring.

And Sonny's mouth stayed open, but now and then sung along with a now-familiar melody, with made-up words but as close he could get to the original: Boshayyy — BOSHAYYYYaayyy — the word its own downward progression of notes that'd he'd finally perfected in imitating in style but not substance. (Haha, not substance, cuz. Could never match Boris there.) Though it was good and satisfying to be able to use his voice in such a new way, hear it echoed, as though the television screen version was himself, in accomplished form of that latent potential practised and practised and trained up to this perfection and power (oh, man, I'm come over in goosies again) as the singer surged to new heights of note reach then fell away to an aching semi-sob of phrase ending.

Sonny knew about phrasing in music, half the jail inmates in the country know, it's in their blood, Maori blood most of em, of having music and emotion and ya life in a wasted heap in some prison cell, slumped (like Jesus, except we don't die for no noble cause, let alone all of mankind. We just die, have died, are dying in our hearts . . .) on a bunk listening to the radio, some pop station, hearing the songs so clearly, and knowing your cellmate so well you ain't scared to talk about phrasing with him and you discover he's just the same of ear, of unnerstanning. He digs where you're coming from and you dig him, so why can't it always be like this between you and cellmate instead of the wedge that comes between you and your intimate private exchanges of maybe, quite possibly, even unnerstanning life itself? Or certainly a part of the musical aspect of it. (Aspect, see. It's to do with aspects, is life. But it needs someone, or something of your raising to point out the aspects, the diversity of them, what they can do to you that years and years of incarceration don't and can't, and yet so many of them in here could be awakened to emselves by just this very experience — But hold up a minute this is getting to another good part.)

Of women taking the choir lead, and Boris now and then in seeming reply, as though they were asking him something and he was replying. Then he, Boris, taking completely over, but only for a goose-pimpling moment of note reverberation, when the peeling walls seeming to shudder, tremble at the force and beauty of sung and hung note.

(Oh God oh God, what is it, what is it of me, of man, of life, of all life but this life too, that a man, this man, has to go out and steal himself — Yes, himself; steal himself. Break into someone's home in accidental search of himself. What'd I do? Wha'd I do that gave me the mamma that couldn't cope with life so drowned it in drink, and the father who was the same except his losing state he spat at, threw drunken punches at, he cursed it and is probably still cursing it, life, his life, that he didn't deserve what it did to him and he did to it. What'd I do, what'd I do, God, that life gave me this beginning and the growing up inevitable outcome that the same life, the same country, the exact same citizenry rights gave Mrs Harland.

The music became sweeter, the women taking over and singing in a chant-like churchy way that had Sonny lifting his head and half closing his eyes in a pious manner, only half knowing he was doing so, with puckered lips and supplicating hands up at chest level. (Now listen to this) at men suddenly taking the choir lead, and one voice just discernible above his pals of, Sonny figured, a middle note range; for maybe a couple of minutes before they died away and then came Boris. (Man. Boris. BO-RIS.) With just the male choir humming in the background as he, the male lead, made careful song statements, like someone arguing a case in a musical court. Up and down the scale of tone advocacy, in and out the gaps of verbal opening. The women coming in quietly in the background and —

Now Boris dropping; a plea for mercy. (For me, Sonny, his client. Ask for mercy on my rotten soul, Boris.) Now the choir joining in his plea (on my behalf). Sonny sad and smiling through a film of tears at that. (For me? For lil ole me?) Tapping a forefinger on his shirted chest. And the choir singing Hallelujah, hallelujah. Back to Boris putting in final mitigation to God (to the jury of my mind, my life's jury sat in judgment on me), to the world, on Sonny Mahia's behalf a simple plea: Let me grow to what I shall. No more. But no less neither. Juss let me grow, through this, by this, in standing here like some child discovering the world for the first time, as if surrounded by the mirrors of my dreams, what I have perceived in my dreaming mind, that state of being not quite asleep, entering the territory where instruments trumpet your arrival (at yourself, at the point within man, maybe all men; no, not all men or Jube'd be in that too) to this, uh, place. Yeh, place. Location in your mind, your soul therefore, where meaning articulates itself and God don't exist so much as this kind of god in yaself, but not one who needs bowing down before, just this sense of great place journeyed and reached in your mind.

In your mind. (And does everything else then follow? By and by, does it follow?)

Spreading his arms in keeping with the spreading of voice from the main singer. A brief pause. Then Boris back with a kind of trembling announcement, a series of them, like a monk at a monastery, like some religious dude calling from the turnip-top spires of a Middle Eastern country. Like much of man and his pious belief was encapsulated in that final stream of announcements — pronouncements. Sonny standing ramrod straight. Boris calling from the hilltops the church spires the mountains the very heavens. Sonny's arms outstretched and raised to the ceiling, it could be the heavens it was the heavens. And his face, his cheeks and neck and too his arms, broken out in goose-pimples. The choir taking hold of the ending, the impetus, the launching Boris had given it and lofting emselves into glory to God and god and no gods and a mere human god standing with upraised arms and bumpy skin and heart and bone and neuron workings. As bells tolled. And voices shook the church walls. And bells tolled. And tolled and tolled, jingajingajing, jingajingajing, as one man cried. (Let me be.)

12 Jube woke, reached for his smokes, hahahaha, as he always did of the last few weeks, head registering that he had a hangover — so what's new, hahahaha — lit the smoke, lay there appreciating it as he went over his mind the previous day. (Oh, that's right, that mad bird. I fucked her.) Broke him out in grinning. He concentrated his mind on the event so to get best appreciation of the body he'd possessed; felt annoyed with himself that he hadn't thought to switch the interior light on in the car just to get a look at her, at her box, her piece of snatch, object of every man's dreams (yeah, even him, master pillar of society fucking lawyer with his *Penthouse*s and them weird porno drawings that I got sick of looking at cos they ain't as porn as I thought, sumpin loving, almost, about em, and who the fuck's on this earth for that — HAHAHA!) so dammit. He smiled: But she was sumpin else in the sack, even if I did find myself (surprisingly) smacking her around. Dunno what came over me. Musta been the way she just put up no fight, and a beautiful thing like her? Her fault, not mine, for being so easy.

So he lay there and smirked for a bit over that and then he thought about his money, as usual, and how good it was to be rich — oh, and plus that gear out in the spare room, and he hadn't forgotten Sonny clouting on half the equipment, though that was cool, Sonny'd have to give em up in time. Then, *ping*, like that it went in his head as if someone had shot a pool ball across the flat of his mind when he wasn't expecting it. He reached for his trousers at the side of the bed, at the same time a shaft of light, a sunbeam found itself on his bed through the slit of just-parted curtains above him. And he smiled at that, thinking it was an omen. A good one of course. Out he came with the cash from his right pocket; always the right pocket, never anywhere else, creature of certain habits that he was.

Wha's this? Looking with surprise at the amount he had. Can't be. At the three fifties, a twenty, a five and some shrapnel. Felt his face redden with close to despair that he might've dropped it, or been robbed while he was drunk and out of it on dope. He tried the back pocket. Nope. The other back one. The left front one. The same right pocket again. Nothin. He threw the blankets off (there weren't any sheets, too much bother) got out of bed. On his feet, his fully clothed feet cept for the cowboy boots, the ones't were new not so long ago but had long lost their shine and their novelty. Just boots now. That he put smelly-socked feet into when he woke and as often as not didn't bother to take a shower cos it was wasting good drinking time (hahahaha).

He stood there scratching his stubbled chin, over scar tissue that'd formed from the beating in Wellington, reminding him for a distracting moment that he had a long memory and that they'd keep, the black arseholes did it to him, and Sonny, I spose, if you could call his a beating, was more just a couple of punches then they let him off cos he was a darkie like they were. But they'd keep.

Now, where would I have hidden the rest of it? Looking around him, annoyed that he had a hangover because it was spoiling things, had him in a mean mood when normally he'd been waking the opposite. And to think last night, too, he'd fucked a sheila more beautiful than any he'd fucked before; far more beautiful. He hoped she was okay, he didn't mean to hurt her, not badly, just a few slaps to show her she was a slut when she didn't have to be, and maybe a man was thinking he was slapping her out of her — what'd she call it again? Maniac — or was it manic? — depression, that's it — maybe a man thought he was slapping her out of that? He shrugged. It didn't matter. He'd got his rocks off, that was the main thing. The only thing, in fact. Now where's my fucking bread? I used to have thousands. What if I've blown it?

The thought near took his legs out from under him. He bent down to tear up the loose lino floor covering, and immediately his face flushed and his head registered a sharp pain. He stood up. Felt dizzy. Lit another cigarette off the one going in the tin-can ashtray. Mmm-uh, that was better. Back to the lino again, he hauled up a sheet to the sight of nothing but wooden boards smeared in glue with fibres stuck to them. Nothing. And it felt like someone'd hit him.

He kicked the bed over to get at the next sheet of lino. Nothin. Fuck. Now where? He ground his cigarette out on the floor before letting the sheet drop back in place; gut with that sick feeling — and it wasn't the hangover — like the same when you know the judge is gonna give it you, that he's had enough of your constant reoffending, your lies in the stand, your not guilty pleas. Sick. Cos an inevitability was gonna happen.

He felt like stabbing someone in those moments. The image of his Croc Dundee knife in his car boot came to mind. Standing there, wanting to plunge some cunt, as he tried to think where he'd put the bulk of the money, and that awful feeling in his gut spread. Oh jeezuz, but of *course*, he grabbed at the blankets, threw them on the floor and hefted the mattress up, chuckling to himself for forgetting his hideaway, blaming it on the hangover, and too much celebrating being a success (for once in my life) and far too much dope; it was turning his brain. (Maybe why I hit the girl last night?)

Mattress one of them kapok jobs that absorbed the dampness of the bedroom, the whole fucking house, which'd have to have an Indian landlord; it just couldn't be an ordinary, decent white, oh no, has to be a black bastard from Bombay, Jube supposed, with the cheek to charge rent for this pisshole, as he plunged his hand down a carefully made slit at the join so even a thief couldn't find it, felt around in the kapok, arm shoved in to the limit, arcing his feel as he moved slowly back out. That sinking feeling again. Of having blown it. Of all that fucking bread, all them golden opportunities to finally turn his life around. He could've bought half a k of good shit and doubled his investment in a few days, more'n doubled it; coulda done it again — *and* had a good time while he was at it, selling to different dudes he knew in bars everywhere, on the circuit, even out in South Auckland there's plenty of dope money out there even with the high unemployment, cos dopeheads, man, they find the bread — and before a man knew it he woulda been worth *thousands*. Instead . . . (Oh God) he put a hand to his hammering forehead and groaned. As the process of alternatives rushed in to fill the gap, ease the pain.

Sonny. That's who Jube thought of first. I'll borrow from him then go straight out and buy some wholesale bulk dope, fuck messing up like this again. Anyway, Sonny owes me: was me who picked that house, he only wanted to beat off home with his whipped tail between his legs, and even when we were in there he didn't want to know anything about it. Yeah. Jube fast rationalising.

I can borrow, what, a grand? He'll have a grand left, might even have two, I ain't seenim in the Tavi, not once since we struck it rich. Ain't hardly seen the lil brown jerk fullstop, just pass him in the passage, Hey, Sonny, how ya doing? You studying or sumpin? Whyn't you come down to the Tavi and drink with the boys for a change? That sorta thing, but Sonny not interested and Jube'd not bothered since Sonny was like that; more and more, even before the big burg score, Sonny'd been acting stranger and stranger. Stir-crazy, that's what Jube was convinced it was with Sonny. I seen it happen to plenty of dudes: the years inside just up and get to em out of the blue.

Shit, he must have fifteen hundred left anyrate. I'll borrow the lot and go buy, what? Should be able to get it for two ton, two and a half, so what's that divided into fifteen hundred? seven and a half. I'd easy get three fifty retail — nah, more'n that for good head. Four. Four hundred easy. So what's that times seven and a half? licking his finger and doing the calculation on the gathered dust on his chest of drawers. Came to three grand exactly. Had him grinning, at the irony of it, of this three grand and a half near replicated with this new scheme, it was just like conjuring up money again, and wondering why he hadn't been doing this, dealing in dope, before. Then he remembered it was a capital problem before: no capital to start off with, story of every crim's life. I hold back on paying Sonny's bread back I can buy three gs' worth and turn it into six — *six*? Hey, six grand, man, from just a borrowed fifteen hundred start. Smiling broadly because the idea, the plan was so simple it couldn't possibly miss.

Hey! he remembered another source of money. His own money. The accumulated unemployment benefits paid into his PostBank account, minus the black arsehole landlord's automatic rent payment, Jube's half of it, though most of that was made up by the rental supplement the dumb government mugs paid. And he began laughing. Because it added up to around a grand. Oh well, in that case, he lit up a cigarette and puffed expansively on it. The feeling in his gut gone in the instant. Even the headache was only half as bad.

The mind was suddenly clear as it next occurred to Jube — (of *course*!) — that there was the spare-room stuff, plus what Sonny claimed for himself, the stereo and tv and video player, they'd be worth, what, fifteen hundred . . . ? Narrowing thinking eyes at that as it occurred that he'd not even pay back the fifteen hundred — Nope. Too much. Stuff wasn't worth that. But be worth a good seven, eight hundred, what we could get in a pub for the gear, easy. Make it a grand and divide that by two and means Sonny is only owed a grand, plus a little bit of profit for lending me the bread. But then again, if it was only for a couple of weeks how much profit was Sonny entitled to if he wasn't doing nothing himself? Jube decided three hundred was a more than fair return.

Then there were the Persian rugs, six of them, that'd be worth at least five hundred apiece, they're Isfahan, so there's another three g, and Sonny won't know how much I got for em. I'd give him three hundred and tell him he was lucky to get that, the ignorant black prick who don't know nothing about valuable things when he walks right over them in every posh house he's ever burgled.

So. From a point of bleak worthlessness the figures now added up to beyond Jube bothering to calculate in terms of doubling again when converted to dope and then cash again. For all he knew he'd be a millionaire within a year if the figures kept compounding like that, and nothing was surer that they would. Long as I make the first move. He lit up again, thought about it; tossing up whether to have one more day and night on the bash and tomorrow it'd be on, or do it now. Fuckit. Now, he decided. Not tomorrow — now.

Down the passage he marched to Sonny's room, hearing this highfalutin music as he approached, and remembering through the haze of drunk and stoned memories of coming home of a night that he'd heard the same issuing from Sonny's bedroom then. He frowned, wondering if was them video tapes, but shrugged what did it matter? He thought he'd best knock seein as how he was gonna touch the man for fifteen hundred, standing there for a moment as he readjusted his calculations to now include his unemployment benefit savings of a thousand to the scenario, as this weird singing came from other side of the door. A guy. Deep voice. Big voice. Singing churchy crap. What, Sonny's gone religious? Jube shook his head, grinning, no way. He lifted his hand to knock, noticed the time: 10:43 digital read-out. Well, how bout that? I'm up early, hahaha. Knock-knock.

Sudden movement in there, Jube had a good mind to burst in see what Sonny was up to. The music cut off. Maybe he's got a woman? The thought stirring Jube's loins, and so did the picture of the depressed woman, Maria, come back to his mind. (Ahh, she felt so good.) Standing there, caught in his sexuality, his sex-driven mind; seeing pictures, having thoughts, loins stirred to an urgency of need. Heart with a faint kind of longing. Mind feeling murderous even as it felt horny. Twats. All the world's twats, God, givem to me. Let me have em. Let me look at em the day long as I suck piss and I get sucked and I suck numbers and I suck twats. Give em to me, God. As he swallowed a lump in his throat, and hoped to hell Sonny didn't have a woman in there it'd tear a man part with jealousy, nless it was a scrubber. Maybe I caught him wanking, hahahaha. I oughta step in right now, I might catch him with it in his hand, hahaha. Nah, I wouldn't do that to you, Sonny boy. Thinking of the times he'd been caught in the act himself over the years of prison cells, having to share frequently. (Your privacy, your partly frightening privacy, having to share it with another con when it was that you could hardly share it with yaself. Not in terms of facing it you couldn't. You always had rode with it. But never — never — stepped off a bit to look at it. Couldn't. I might be —) He knocked hard on the door. Hey, what's going on in there, bud. HAHAHAHA! The laugh more intended to relax Sonny, put him at ease that he was here as a mate, an old pal.

Hey, my main lil man! Gimme some skin! Gimme some skin! Jube as he grabbed Sonny's hand from his side and shook it like a long-lost pal. And noting, in the instant, how different Sonny looked, how changed; but thinking it was he himself was hung-over, and unshaved for a few days, unshowered too. So how ya been, man? Running his eyes up and down Sonny's relatively short height. Telling him, ya look good, bro. I mean *good*. And meaning it. What, you went and bought a secret youth potion with your bread? Hahahaha. Eh? Eh bro? That what ya did? Appraising Sonny again — and Sonny for his part not exactly spilling over with welcome; with, Good to see you, Jube — seeing that he had another new set of clothes, not fancy but not shit either.

It's your hair, you had a new hairstyle, right? Sonny nodding, and looking just a little too cocksure for Jube's liking. Not that there was any denying the man was a handsome little critter, for a Maori, they usually have flatter noses and thick lips, but not this one; and that hairstyle brought his looks out even better, though Jube knew Sonny never saw himself as having looks, he never had, and Jube'd never been able to figure why. Even the hard-arses in the Tavi said Sonny was a handsome little critter, and if the sheilas there still didn't fall over emselves wanting him, it was only because (Jube knew them so well) they found Sonny disturbing (too fucking bright for em) and that his sensitive side threw that kind of woman off the Sonnys of this world. What would they know, the scrubbers, about looks and sensitivity? Jube of a sudden washed over with empathy for Sonny and not knowing why. You're looking real good, Son. He ruffled Sonny's hair, noting how clean it felt, how it shone. Then he took his eyes around the room.

At the set-up of stereo and tv and video recorder and the bed moved to the far wall and the wardrobe out at a funny angle, even had a Persian on the floor. Then the penny dropped: That box a tapes, they have a bluey amongst em? Jube gleam-eyed and expectant. Till Sonny shook his head with a grin and said, I doubt it. Aw, come on, Son, this's me. Jube. Your old buddy from way back, hahaha. Not a one? Uh? uh? Jube for a moment recognising something of himself in the way he wanted Sonny to confirm the lawyer's kinky sexual tastes as further revealed. That he wanted Sonny to confirm it, just as he was inside poised to get instantly angry at that confirmation. Except Sonny laughed and invited Jube to take a look for himself, pointing to under his bed. So Jube accepted this and took his mind back to the business he'd come for.

So where ya been, Son? Oh, you know, around. I ain't seen you, man, cept to pass in the passageway, hahaha. You been keeping alright? Yeah, I have. Not gone religious, have ya, hahaha. Hardly. Glad to hear that, bro, I was getting a bit worried when I heard, you know, at the door, the shit playing. What was it? Oh, nothin much, just something on tape I kinda like. Not church though, was it? No, man, not church — well, it was kind of church but I aint churchy. Hahahaha, that's good to hear, bro, cos I was getting really worried that you not coming to the Tavi ever since we hit it off, that it'd gone to your head, the bread, maybe even the stir-crazies. Ya know?

I ain't stir-crazy, Jube. Stir-sick, yeh. But not — Man, I know that now, I can see it. You look alright, in fact like I said you look real good. I, uh, I been missing you, bud, Jube dropping his voice to just the right volume. But Sonny only shrugging; You know, the times we shared and that . . . ? But Sonny just staring; hard to say what he was thinking. I was beginning to think I'd maybe lost ya, like as in moved out, hahaha. That you'd up and run off with your money. Or maybe you've spent it, hahaha. Jube's heart soaring when Sonny shook his head adamantly. No? You haven't blown it yet? Hahaha. His laugh reading back as nervous even to himself. Me, I spent a bit, tha's for sure; you know how it is, the Tavi every day and them bludgers into ya for a free beer, a touch-up here, one there, before ya know it you've gone through a couple of hundred. Doesn't last long does it? Not even all that bread we had, hahaha. But that's what it's for, eh Son? To blow. Jube talking faster than he normally did, and hardly able to stop himself.

I got a plan, Son. Having to wait even when he was chafing at the bit to run off at the mouth. Dope. Dope, Sonny; that's where it's at. But Sonny shaking his head, Told ya man, not my scene. But you go ahead, you got your own bread to buy the stuff, but not for this guy, Jube. Hey, come on, man, you ain't even heard me out and here you are wiping me. I ain't wip — Ya are. So let me have my say.

We did the burg together didn't we? Jube swept an arm around, And this stuff you got set up here, it's ours ain't it? Half and half, uh? Sonny nodding at that, and Jube thinking he was getting on top. We got the rugs and the couple of paintings I just remembered in the spare room — oh, minus the one you got on the floor there, hahahaha — the rugs'll fetch a ton apiece at least. Halves, Sonny. We're halves in that too. Same as if we get pulled over the burg, we'll be doing the same sentences, probly in the same cell — HAHAHA! Like we can't away from each other, eh Son? Slapping Sonny on the shoulder, laughing. Then there's our bread we both got saved up in bank accounts — 'nless you spent yours, no? Eyeing Sonny carefully. Nope. Ain't touched it. Same, Sonny. I'm the same: I haven't been near my dole account. Innit great, Son? Yeah, it is I guess. You guess? Only guess?

Sonny shrugging that way of his. Then telling Jube, You told me those rugs'd score two hundred apiece. Did I? You did. Well I was just being, you know, on the safe side. So we don't get disappointed, hahaha. But then again, maybe you got your own fence outlets who'll give us two ton each for em . . . ? Eyeing Sonny with confidence and waiting for Sonny's eyes to drop to concede the point which he duly did. Right.

So how much ya got left? Jube after drawing in breath and

himself to full, hopefully intimidating, height while he did. Oh, you know, enough. Enough how much? Enough, bro. Come on, Son, this is fucking business. I said I don't want — Business, Sonny Mahia. To double our bread. Well, maybe not double, not for the first few buys but eventually we would. Magine the set of wheels you could buy with a few extra grand in your pocket, Son. I ain't got a desire to have wheels, man, you know that. Well ya must have sumpin ya want? Not really. What, not *any* fucking thing? A woman? Sonny with a grin. Jube grinning back, Now that's the Sonny I know, hahaha. Even though it wasn't.

Time Jube was through he had fifteen hundred of Sonny's two thousand remaining of the three and half, and he had Sonny digging out his bankbook to withdraw the accumulated dole payments; chuckling, making cracks, reminding Sonny of the good life that money buys. And while we're at it we may as well sell the rugs. You don't want this one in your room, do ya? You do? Okay, have it. It's yours, bro. Pat-pat-pat in false affection on Sonny's head. Both of them loading Jube's car boot with the Persian rugs, the two paintings.

Oh, Jube remembering again, the gear you got set up in your room, that'll have to go, or . . . ? Playing with Sonny now. So how much is my half, Sonny'd asked, looking like a child afraid of having his most precious possessions taken from him. So Jube went, Oh, make it, what, we'd get easy a grand, twelve hundred for it, so make it six — no, five hundred. You owe me five hundred for my half. I can't be fairer'n that can I? (Hahahaha.) As they walked, Jube an arm around Sonny's shoulders in an expansive show of affection that was more a show of superiority.

First the rugs; turnem into cash. Oh, and the paintings. Hahaha, as he drove to a bar where one of the city's big-time fences drank. Feeling like he was on air, driving on it in this case and walking on it when he strode into the White Heart Tavern up a side street off the waterfront. On air because he had total of two and a half grand from Sonny, his own withdrawn thousand of savings, and the seven Persian rugs he was guaranteed to get five ton apiece for and the paintings, one a McCahon, the other a real old New Zealand scenery job, they'd fetch a grand between em at least.

And just let the fence try the they're-not-worth-anything trick with Jube: he'd bowl the guy with knowledge. Indepth knowledge, from studying several books when he was doing the sentence before last on rugs from the Middle East and Turkey and Pakistan and even India, and don't forget China too, specially their silk rugs. Setting his mouth in a cocksure line at the thought of blowing the fence away with pure knowledge. Specialised knowledge. (Hahahaha.)

Jube made a beeline for Percy, the fence, surrounded at a standing table by his watersider mates. Jube with his sleeves rolled up high so Percy could see from the tats he was no undercover trying to set him up. Jube'd anyway met him once before, with a pal who was selling to Percy; Jube didn't rate him that much from that one meeting.

Percy was fat. But powerfully built. Hard-looking too. His eyes. He could've been any one of the wharfies he was drinking with — and was — it wasn't for his other side activities, which the crim world said made him a handsome living. But Jube wasn't worried by the man, not his rep, nor his hard-faced demeanour. (I'd stab the cunt he pushed me the wrong way.) Jube thinking he meant that threat.

He proffered his hand: Jube McCall. We met once before, I was with Rocky. Percy stared at the hand. Rocky? Yeah, Rocky. We met in here. (You smart prick, shake my fucking hand.) So? (So? he says?) So I'm introducing myself, bud. And the guy's mates pausing in their drinking to look at Jube, some with hard eyes. (Fuck em. Think I haven't seen hard men in my life?)

Alright, so you've met me, whatever you said your name is. Anything else? Jube dropped his hand. (You cunt. I'll remember this.) Was wondering if we could have a word? Looking at the faces fronting him. In private. The fence broke into a grin, an ugly one at that, And why would that be? Jube just had to shrug, he wasn't expecting this. And Percy (the Pig) running his eyes up and down Jube's length, then drawling, I'll say one thing: If you're an under-cover cop, then God help this town's police force — HAHAHAHA-HAHAHA!!! Percy laughing and his pals with him. Had Jube's face reddening.

Jube shrugged again (I'll fix him), Suit yaself. You wanna turn your nose up to a good earner, that's fine by me. He turned and started walking away. (Take that you arsehole.) Smoking inside at Fatboy, who called him back, Hey! Hold up a mo. Jube stopped, took his time in turning around. Place his bunched fists on his jeaned hips, So you wanna talk turkey? Feeling like straight from a movie: heroic. Tough, uncompromising. (Don't you mess with me, fat muthafucker.) Yeah, why not, Fatboy conceded (wilted, more like it.) He nodded to his pals and they took up glasses and jugs and moved to a table nearby.

So whatcha got, uh . . . ? I didn't catch your name. Yes ya did, but the name's Jube. (Beat you every time, ya wanker.) Okay, Jube. So whatcha got for sale? Colour tv? Video recorder? Asking in a mocking tone, as if he'd seen it all before and he was gonna batter Jube down before they even started. Till Jube said through half-lidded eyes, Oh, just a few Persian rugs. Seven. Looked the guy square in the eye, though that was harder to do than normal cos of the fat around em. But Jube knew he had this guy, he knew it.

Persian rugs, eh? Rubbing his fat jaw, then shook his head. Nope. Not interested, bud. (What?!) Jube arched an eyebrow. No market for em, Jube. No market . . . ? Nope. So even if I was interested in the first place, there'd be no point: I can't move em on. And *if*, as well, you had receipts to prove purchase, even then I couldn't look atem. Seeing as how — he paused and his eyes hardened — you and I don't know each other, even though you say we do. You get me?

Yep, I get you, man. Fine. Fine by me. Jube felt hurt. Not just taken aback, but hurt. Belittled. Done at his own game of being the tough guy. So he turned again. Fine, Percy. That's just fine by me. Started walking. Again.

Waiting to be called back, except it didn't come; not a word from Fatboy behind him. So Jube stopped, turned. Fatboy Percy the Pig was staring at him — or straight through him. Jube couldn't read the guy, not one word on his unspeaking face.

So what would you offer? Nothing, Jube. Come on . . . Jube started back to Percy, brought to a halt a couple of steps short of the table, not wanting any closer because it would demean him more. Make an offer. Offer's nothing, pal. Don't you under — Come on, they're worth four or five grand apiece, maybe more. Oh? How do you know — I know, buddy. I made a point of studying em. (Take that, arsehole.) Really? Yeh, really. And what university would that've been, my friend? No university, pal. So where'd *you* study Persian rugs — Persia maybe? Hahahaha.

I got two paintings too. One's a McCahon. You heard of him, or didn't they teach you that at *your* university (try that shit on me.) A McCahon, eh? Hmmm, now you're talking. (Oh?) Jube was surprised. What do you want for it? I — Well, I was thinking — I thought if you bought the both — I take it both are McCahons? Nope, just the one. Other's a olden-day thing, mountains and that, in one of them fancy frames. Frame alone'd be worth a couple of hundred. Yeh, sure, Jube, I'm into buying picture frames. There's a huge market out there — Okay, okay, what's your offer? What's your asking? I — Make it a grand for the two paintings and — Nope. Not interested. Eight hundred for the paintings and four ton apiece for the rugs. No. Sorry, Jube, but that's my final answer.

What, on everything? Everything, Jube. But man, we are talking tens of thousands here and you're — No market, pal. Who do you know in your world who buys Persian rugs, specially at four hundred apiece and then I've gotta turn a profit, so make that, what, a grand a rug and your market's dried up. If it ever existed. What about rich people then, they must buy Persians? Do they? Sure they do. Then go sell to them, Jube. I — Hey, come on, man, what the fuck is this? Percy shaking his head and clicking his tongue and then sighing, Jube, Jube, Jube.

He drew in a deep breath then out it came. Trouble with you local-yocal tealeafs, son, is you lack what we in the trade call, uh, discernment. You either grab the obvious, like tvs and stereos and video players, even microwaves, but ya don't think to follow the marketplace trends in these things, to find out that the price of these things, legit, has been going down and down and down; even average worker people've got these things nowadays. Yet you guys are still asking prices that were around in the early eighties. And ya wanna know why? The fat swelling of self-assured features thrust itself at Jube. Cos your kind is in and out of the slammer, more in than out, so ya lose touch, son. With reality. With what's going on in the world. Not a fucking one of yous bothers to *find* out about the changing world. Percy spat out the emphasis, and Jube was trembling with humiliation and his heart ached to do bodily harm.

You don't pick up even a newspaper; that'll tell you all you need to know of the world on the day — how it operates, what's, as you people say in the vernacular, going down. He shook his head. Only time you lot pick up a newspaper is to read your name, or one of your dunderhead crim mate's names, on the court pages and think you've made the bigtime. So okay, you say you got seven Persian rugs and at least one painting by a well-known New Zealand artist? But what does that tell you, Jube? Tells me you're a fucking con act, buddy, that's what it tells me. But Percy didn't blow up at that, just shook his head in that parently manner, Jube, Jube, Jube.

Your world is all Jubes. The lot of you're Jubes of no homework and no understanding of the — I didn't come here for no fucking lecture, man. Well I'm giving you one, bud, and you don't like it you know where the door out is. So make me an offer and I'll be glad to find the door.

Fifty.

Fifty for what?

The rugs.

Fuck off.

No, you fuck off. Fifty for the rugs — each that is — and two hundred for the paintings as a favour for your disappointment over the rugs. And Jube standing there, deep in his humiliation as his mind went through the rapid process of rationalising. Then he sighed, lit a cigarette, drew deeply on it, blew frustrated smoke in jetstreams, and said, Yeah. Alright. And Percy smiled, offered his hand, which Jube took instant delight in staring at without taking the fat-digited object in his hand. Then Percy followed Jube out to the car and they drove to a carpark, where the rugs and the paintings were transferred to another vehicle, and Jube delighted again in not taking Percy's handshake a second time. They went their separate ways.

Took a little while of driving before Jube could settle himself down. By then the processes had him fixing on the money he had in total, just over four thousand dollars, and just a deal away from doubling. Then he'd do it again. So the lightness of being returned, and he felt kind of invincible, and very very clever, for having turned the morning's grim situation into so much in so short a time, despite the rip-off Percy the fence. He'd keep. He'd get his one day. (Soon as I'm rich from dealing I'm gonna hire some heavies, have em around me, send em out on memory catch-ups — hahahaha — to ask em who the fucking hell they think they are now. Hahaha. Varoom, varooom.) Picturing in his mind the looks of surprise and then abject apology (but no way, bud. No fucking way) at sight of Jube arriving with his heavies, seeing himself in drug dealer dress, flashy the way they do. With style. Panache. And that certain arrogance of men with money — lots of it.

He drove south, along the motorway, to arrange a meet with a drug contact. And he thought of the rugs, the tens of grands' worth of handmade rugs from far-off Iran, or Turkey, how it was ironic that their price at source was added to along the way then the process went back to original again: a lousy fifty each. And for what? So the proceeds can be pissed up against another hotel stainless-steel urinal like all deeds of criminals do? The waste did occur to him, which was why he laughed, hahahaha, because it was such a joke. Such a joke.

13 The snow fell. The credits rolled up on screen as the bells tolled. Sonny filled with a wanting for woman. Not just any woman, but her, the one in the photographs with her hair in wet strings and the sparkle in her green eyes of water and sumpin else naughty, but pure still, about her.

The bells stopped tolling, the screen went white, and Sonny stared at the photographs, at the screen then back to the photos again, shaking his head. No way. Can't even fantasise a woman like her. So he flopped back on the bed, let his mind play snatches of music from the tape, wondering too what was becoming of him.

Jane. That name again came to mind. (That's it: Jane'll be her name.) Of this imaginary woman of his yearning since the other, Penny, Mrs Harland in the photographs, was unavailable. Because she was unreal. But Jane . . . ? He conjured up a picture of what she'd look like, decided she couldn't have any resemblance to Penelope Harland, that she'd have to come from the world he knew. Tavistocks. That'll do. I'll have met her at the Tavi. He closed his eyes to let the images take shape; and a face, of a woman, soon formed, and she weren't nothin special, not of facial feature nor anywhere near of that suggestive sexuality in the eyes and languid poise of the stolen photographs. Nothing like that. Just a Jane. A plain Jane for plain Sonny.

So talk to me, Jane. No virgin neither. No such thing at the Tavi. I'm no virgin, Sonny, he could hear a voice in his mind telling him. Saw himself cupping her face in his hands, telling her it's alright, who said virgins're any great cop? It don't madda, Jane. It don't madda, honey. But Sonny, she was saying back, I've slept with a lot of guys around here — Shooshing her with a gentle hand over her mouth, Don't madda to me, Jane. It don't. (Cos I'll find her purity spot. I'll locate the place in her secret being that ain't been touched,

142

tainted, poisoned by the Tavi bar inhabitants. A place that'll be just like mine, like the place I found through these tapes here, even in the photographs beside me of her, Mrs Harland; a place of my own purity, that ain't been touched — no-one can touch it, I know that now — no madda what I been through. No madda what. And maybe it's been there all this time — Of course it has, Jane. In my secret being and your secret being too.) So talk to me, Jane.

She'll have a tat or two, of course she will; to signify where she's come from and where she assumed she was headed. (Till me, that is.) Sonny smiling up at the ceiling, hardly knowing if it was evening yet or still the arvo. Didn't matter. Nothing maddas, cept me and Jane. You still there, Jane?

The tats'll be a boob dot under her right eye, from a borstal lag when she was young (and mixed up, and hurt — *hurt*, dear Jane); seeing in his mind a set of big brown eyes, pools of some potential that no-one else could see, not even her. (Come to me. Come to Sonny, he'll unnerstan.) See in them eyes the hauntedness of that borstal experience, when she shoulda been a girl, a teenage girl growing up normal. Which Sonny unnerstans, he really does, and Jane'd get to unnerstan too if she'll put her faith in a man his own potential. He'll know of her pain and confusion at having her teenagehood locked up in a penal institution when she was — (how old, Jane? Sixteen? Seventeen? Me, I was sixteen. You dig where I'm coming from? Sixteen, Jane, and they had me in there, a prison of grilles and tiered landings of cell rows and bellowing guards and going mad kid crims.) It ain't right, ain't natural, it's a fundamental violation of womanhood, specially young womanhood, to make her a prisoner. No madda what she's done. Not 'nless it's murder, and even then check it out, check it out, it might be her rotten old man she done in. (Oh Jane. I've suffered the same. I had my teenagehood taken from me too.) It just ain't right that a young woman (or a young man age sixteen) should be locked up, have a card stating her sentence in a metal frame on her cell door, saying who she is and what she's done. Oh Jane. Talk to me, hon. I'm listening.

And I'd have her on the bed here, naked but not dirty naked like I'm Jube ready to attack, to sexually spear her. Naked and snuggled up under these blankets and clean sheets. And giggling at the smallness of the bed forcing them so close together, Now don't you be touching me, Sonny Mahia. Hahaha. Making out she's coy, and not the (apparent) slut she's been her sexually active life. But Sonny with his touching hand on D for don't, let her tell her story first.

. . . of herself. Telling of herself. But only because a man kept urging her, gently he urged her. Tell to me, Jane. My hand's fixed on D, but oh, I can't help my fingers just barely touching the hair down there of you. It ain't moving, my hand ain't. So talk.

He'd move his hand away, from down there, as she did talk, because of what was coming from her. Moving up to under her breasts, resting flatly and neutrally there. Sonny? Sonny? Yeow? Ya promise not to tell? Ya promise you won't tell no-one I tell you my story? He was hearing it as clearly as if she was real, he surely was.

Oh Jane, I wouldn't tell no-one. Ya promise? I promise, Jane. Cross my heart — Don't cross your heart, that don't mean nothin. Just look at me — no, don't look at me, I'll get embarrassed — just tell me in my ear you promise not to tell. (I promise, darling.)

Sonny, I — Choking on it, her story only got to opening point. Jane? Jane, it's alright, Sonny's here. I won't be laughing or nothin. It don't madda — But it does! It does madda, Sonny. I know it does, I know it does, I never meant it like that — Reaching out his arms in the reality of room dreaming and hugging the object, the person in his mind. Tenderly. With love in his heart. And his hand on D. Oh Jane.

Turning the pages back on her past. Juss this lil girl I was Sonny . . . in the dark. The dark meant to her her sleeping place. Her comfort and resting and thinking place. Of, you know, Sonny, innocence? Oh I unnerstan, Jane. Ya do? Oh I do, honestly, Jane. Innocence, ya know? Innocence, like, exploring itself. Thinking about the world. The world the child lives in. You know? (I know, hon. I know.) My dreaming place too, Sonny. The dark, the dark I might have a bad dream in and so I call my daddy: Daddy? Daddy? You know, Sonny?

Daddy, Janey's scared, Daddy; she had a scary dream. Ya know, Sonny?

Called from the dark, meant to be her sanctuary that Daddy is allowed to come into but only to comfort Janey had the bad dream. Juss a lil girl, ya know, Sonny? (Oh!) Sonny stifling a real sob escaping from his unfettered imagination. Oh Jane.

The dark that Daddy was meant to come rub a girl her forehead, whisper to her everything's alright, it's alright, darling, Daddy's here, Daddy's here. The dark. Daddy. Daddy in the dark. Daddy? Daddy? I had a bad dream, Daddy.

144

Daddy in the dark groping — Uh! Ya know, Sonny? (Oh Jane.) Daddy in my dark room making it darker, ya know? Rubbing me — *uh*! Oh, it hurting so, Sonny, it hurting so much. My thing. But my heart more. So please, Sonny, don't you be touching me and probing me; not me the kid wanting to have the bad dream rubbed away, a daddy hand on forehead, on little kid cheeks all flushed with pain and confusion. Not there, Sonny, ya unnerstan? The dark, the dark my daddy came into — *he came to give comfort to himself.* You unnerstan, Son? So please please don't touch me there, not tonight, not when I've told you my story. Morning eh? I'll let you have it in the morning?

No! Not have. It. Not have it, Jane. I don't want *it*. You unnerstan? I want your story. Tha's all. Feeling sleep taking him even as he dialogued in his mind. Jane? Ya hear me, Jane? I got a story too. But you tell yours first. And Jane? I got something else. Right here in this room. It's, uh . . . well, it's hard to explain. You have to experience it. But it's so *unreal*, Jane. And I And I. Me and Jube, Jane. It was me and Jube one night, stealing. Ya know, Jane? Sure you know, hahaha, you're a Tavi girl, and I'm a Tavi boy. Was. Were. Both of us *were*, Jane. Not soon. Not even now. Not after you've seen these tapes, Jane. Jane, I stole em. I stole my own life back from out of nowhere. Ya know, Jane? Yes, you know, I can tell. Oh Jane, don't make me keep my hand on D for too much longer. I won't hurt ya, ya know I wouldn't. I do it gently. Gently, Jane. Come to me, come to me. Jane . . .

14

He went through the big wooden gate, with barbed wire on top running the length of ironclad walls, right round the perimeter that Jube could see; first checked out by a tv camera eye, closed-circuit job Jube figuring; his escort speaking into a mike that he'd brung someone to do business with the Prez; someone the other side unlatching something steel-sounding on the gate and the big door swinging open. Remarking to his escort that it was hardly different to the big ole gate to the slammer, hahaha. Though the escort didn't laugh. Nor did he when Jube commented that the compound they crossed to the main headquarters, which was really a house changed a bit to suit the purpose, that it was like a jail exercise yard. Escort only mumbled, yeah, if you're lookin for that sorta thing, and Jube thought the man's manner had suddenly changed from when they stepped onto his territory. Different from the easy manner of Jube meeting up with him in the bar they drank at, the escort's gang, of having a few beers with him, telling the man, Billy, the nature of his business and then they'd driven here in Jube's car. Didn't seem the same man.

But Jube was buoyed by the money he carried on him, as well amazed and delighted at how sustained was the feeling of having money, the air it put under his feet, the cockiness it gave to his walk, the feeling of invincibility it gave him, even here, right inside a gang headquarters. (So fucking what?)

Across the compound Jube noticing how well kept the lawn was, was going to make a joking remark on that but decided better not. Up some steps and across a short stretch of olden-day verandah, Billy led them inside.

Place was like the lawn, surprisingly neat and tidy. Spotless. The gang emblem in form of big red and black flag with a motorbike in profile outline, skull and crossbones with the skull wearing a

146

helmet centred the flag, and SKULL RIDERS arched over the whole emblazoned in black over red. The room could have been quite a good-sized hotel bar; there were speakers set up on the stage, and a stand, like at a church, from which Jube figured the president himself must make his speeches, or whatever it is presidents of gangs make when they're talking to their men.

Yeah, just like a church (where the tired prison priest steps up to deliver his tired sermon to a bunch of crims who aren't there to hear his waffling crap, they're there to get out of their cells, they're there to play swap and trade and buy and sell games, of tobacco and dope and chocs, that could just as well and better take place elsewhere in the prison, and with less risk, but that's boob for you, and boob-heads, they seize on anything elaborate to justify their stupid existences, it's drama they want more'n not getting caught at illicit and illegal goings-on) there might even be something sacred to the place that Jube wasn't yet aware of, so he'd better mind his p's and q's. Not that he was frightened or nothin. How could he be? These were his own kind, more or less. In a way. Sure, they were ganged up, with membership dependent on how ya fared at being a hard nut as well bold and criminally inclined, but that ain't no big deal to an old hand like Jube McCall, not as if he's come in from a monastry, hahaha. (If I wanted in with the Skulls, I could.)

Billy led them to a bar. How about this. Billy went around the serving side asked Jube what he wanted to drink. Oh, a beer'll do, Bill. What kinda beer ya got? But Billy's eyes narrowed defensively for some reason, only one kind isn't there? (Huh?) Uh . . . Jube didn't know how to answer that one, so he flicked his eye to the chiller where the labels all lined up DB, so he said, DB, bud. My beer too, hahaha.

A quart bottle plonked on the counter. That'll be four bucks, Jube. And Jube started grinning — till he saw Billy was serious, he had his hand out. You're not — Four bucks, man. House rules. No-one's exempt, not even the Prez. And Jube felt sure he saw a fervent light in Billy's eyes that wasn't there before. He paid, And have one for yaself a course. Thanks. Jube hoping Billy'd be impressed with the size of the wad he peeled a fifty off; disappointed that Billy wasn't.

He watched as Billy rung the till for eight bucks, took the change out from the drawer, came back handed it to Jube, counted aloud as he did, Forty, and two dollars, thank you. So formal. And not self-conscious about it. Discipline, it appeared, ruled in here. (Okay? HAHAHAHAHAHA!!) Jube inside at his quick-thinking humour, and he had stifle his giggle.

Only him and Billy and not much chat from Billy's end, so he must be just a junior around the place. Same reason he was the contact for the dope wholesale; the man was a soldier. But Jube didn't mind being in the conversational chair, not with the high he was on with having four grand in cash; and he talked about this and that, a bit of rugby league, big-hit tackles and spear tackles, hahaha, and stiff-arms and all-out brawls, hahaha, and then he was on about making contact with the Skulls, with Billy here, that he'd chosen them rather than one of the Maori gangs cos he wasn't dealing with no Maoris, no fu — When he saw Billy's face go cold. Staring at Jube. Hey? I say sumpin wrong? What'd I say?

Ya said a word't don't never gets said in here, man. And I mean, *never*. Those people, they're blacks. Or niggers. Or coons. And Jube nodded (I get the picture). Or black cunts, eh Billy? Hahaha. Yeh, you could say that. Or coon dogs, hehehehe, Jube catching on real fast. You got the story, Jube, Billy's face lightened up.

HAHAHAHAHA!! Oh I got the story alright, Billy. Jube leaned forward, Bill — all earnestness of facial expression — I *hate* the black cunts, I do. Pointing to a scar under his right eye, another one slicing his top lip in two, See these? Who do ya think did that to me? Was Ma — Was fucking coons, mate, that's fucking who. I hate em, mate. You know how the arseholes are: one minute they're almost normal, almost civilised, next they're nutting off at nothing. You're telling me, Jube. Yeh, you know don't ya? It's in their blood, Billy. They're bad. Bad. Got no principles. Hah, they couldn't even spell that word, though — hahahaha — nor can I, come to think of it. HAHAHAHAHAHA!! Jube glad that Billy joined him in laughter.

He swept an arm around him, take this place. Neat as a pin. Be too clean for them black animals. And they stink. You ever been close to one? (Oops. Careful, Jube, careful.) Smell em from ten feet away. In here they'd feel right out of place. Know why? Too clean for em. Jeezuz, I don't have to tell you, do I, Bill? You've been around. Jube eyeing knowingly the tats on Bill's rolled-up sleeve-exposed arms. He pointed at the tats, I know them tats, mate. I know where you're comin from. We both know what the cunts're like when they're inside ruling the joint when outside ya can't gettem to organise a decent shit. They're fist merchants, mate.

Oh? Bill looking askance. And what makes ya think we white guys ain't? Oh, not saying that, man. Not. Hell, wasn't that long ago I had a brawl with four ofem — and the minute Jube made the exaggeration he knew he'd made a mistake, that this guy wasn't buying it that he, tall and mean as he knew he looked, he would have to be one hell of scrapper to handle four, specially if the four were Maoris, and he felt his face redden but had to finish it even though it ended lamely — all on my jacksy, and they got stuck into me over a game of pool. As usual, eh Bill? Trying to rope Bill in, to sort of smother the lie, and inside cursing himself for not telling the truth that it was three on one, and he had held his own, very well in fact. (Why the fuck did I have to throw in one more?) So naturally I went down. But I gavem sumpin to think about. Pointing to his right eye scar again, as if that'd retrieve the lie, but Bill's cold eyes telling Jube no such thing. Anyrate, like I said, Bill, I hate the black bastards too. Black — Yeah, man, you said so.

Jube took the hint. Had to. Had to stay on his toes. Now that he was right inside gang headquarters, even if he was sorta like one ofem in that he was white and he didn't like Maoris neither, though he didn't have a thing about em that these guys must have, judging on Bill here. So he foot-shuffled about, stared at the gang flag, the floor, the ceiling, around him at the set-up of tables no different to an ordinary bar, the tables were probably stolen from a pub, one at a time over a period, because they were standard elbow-height pub tables with the hole in the centre for the ashtray and steel bits to put your feet on as you talked and smoked and leaned on your elbows and of course drank since that's one of the whole points of life, ain't it, to drink to get drunk, to smoke cigarettes, get stoned when you can, and oh, get a fuck when ya could. The whole point.

He took his sweet time with drinking the bottle, keeping just behind Billy, who wasn't doing much talking still; and when he did, it lacked sumpin, Jube wasn't quite sure, friendliness or sumpin. Then Bill bought Jube a bottle and they drank that one a bit faster, which loosened Bill, made him more the guy he seemed, and he didn't mind Jube asking about his life, what'd made him a Skull Rider; it was just two dudes chatting the time away at a bar that coulda been an ordinary pub bar on a quiet Monday arvo, nothin special.

Bill's story weren't no surprise, just a standard story same as everyone else's, you know, having a bad upbringing, hating his old man or his old man hating him, hardly any ofem hated their mums even when she was a bitch, it just never got said. The gang made him feel he belonged, that he was someone for the first time in his life. Everyone loved each other in the gang. No shit, we love each other closer'n brothers, Jube.

So they had another bottle on that one, and Jube got to tell his very similar story except it didn't end in him joining a gang, but he did know the legendary Ace, did Billy know him? sure Billy did, don't everyone? They laughed at their late friend in common and Jube was half drunk enough to tell Billy the poem he wrote and had put in the *Star* In Memorium column, his very own tribute to a good mate there in black and white for the whole of Auckland to read. Man, it kinda freaked me out, eh, knowing so many people would read it. But Ace, you know don't ya, Bill, he was worth it, weren't he, mate? Oh yeah, he was alright. No doubt about that. The first dudes started coming in, in twos and threes and fours, going up to the bar getting served by Billy and eyeing Jube over while they waited for their drink, though it was no big deal, not as if it was eyeballin or nothin, just kinda half-hostile curiosity, with no hellos or nothin; half ofem had shades so it was hard to tell if in fact it was half hostility, it might've been, it mightn't.

Jube chatting in between arrivals to Billy, and Billy chatting back quite another person. Glancing around him every little while, just to check out the human scenery, noticing how there wasn't one without a beard, it must be part of the uniform; how a lot of em had them cutaway-sleeve sweatshirts so the denim jacket over it, also without sleeves, looked more or less one piece, gave em a bulked-up look, so that the ones without real muscular or solid arms poking out from the prevailingly hairy shoulders looked like pinsticks, or with padded-up torso that hardly chilled a man with fear. (Fuckem.) Tats were the order of the day, which Jube had long ago in his life stopped noticing except for an indication maybe in familiar initials or names tattooed of a prison, a borstal lag with maybe dates, otherwise he never saw em, no reason to. Tats are tats.

So when's the Prez arrivin, mate, any idea? Soon. He'll be here soon. Think I should buy a round of drinks, Bill? Jube in a half whisper. Man, why'd you do that? They got bread. We ain't coon gangies here, we know how to look after our money affairs; you wait till you meet the Prez. You can buy me one you want, though. Sure, Billy. Whyn't ya move into sumpin witha bit more . . . Trailing off because Billy's look said that wasn't a good suggestion, dunno why, but it wasn't. So Jube changed to rum and Coke. Doubles.

He fingered the bulge of money notes in his jeans pocket frequently. Made him feel good. Like, real good. So was the rum starting to work, boy, was it working on a man's head today. Must be just topping up my alcohol-loaded system. (Hahaha.) Exchanging pleasantries with Billy the barman, nodding to the different gang dudes who arrived or came to the bar for refills — of beer, most ofem. Not one gave him a return greeting and a couple ofem gave him really heavy pegs. Though he weren't worried. Not really. Not with the dough in his kick and the double-charged rums working away. And he was here on invite, or he wouldn't be here now would he? (Hahahaha!) nearly laughing out loud at that. But checked himself.

He brought up the game of rugby league with Billy, did he follow the game? Nope. Sport sucks. (Oh.) Ya see some big hits in league, though. Still sucks. Too much training. Too much listenin to some prick telling ya run here run there; I'd givim run some coach starting shoutin in my fucking ear tellin me to run here run there. Only one guy I listen to and that's the Prez. And Jube could see the fanaticism in Billy's eyes. When Billy swept an arm out at his surrounding fellows, told Jube, Ask them, man, what they'd do for the Prez, his eyes wide, and quite mad, Jube got a touch nervous. Like someone'd turned on an alarm inside; this other voice, the one't exists in everyone and says things out of the blue might even be the true blue, saying the alarm shoulda gone off long ago. But Jube just one drink, it might even be several, too far gone to heed properly what his instinct was saying.

And when the Prez did arrive, big and bearded and impressive and self-assured that he was, he shook Jube's hand warmly when introduced by a deferential Billy, This here is Jube, Prez. He, uh, wants to buy some bulk dope. So Jube wasn't the slightest bit worried, not with the warmth in the Prez's smiling blue eyes. He looked a lot like Jube's late hero, Ace, the one he'd composed the ode to. Cept Ace was meaner-looking; not as big, specially not barrel-chested like this big dude, but Ace had something special about him.

The Prez asked Jube how long he'd been here in the place, he asked had Billy been looking after him like a good Skull Rider should, and Jube laughing said he couldn't've asked for better and smiled at Billy, who nodded gratitude back for Jube scoring him some points with his beloved Prez, and Jube asked the Prez what he was havin but Prez said no, on me, and bought Jube another double rum and Coke, which made, what, seven or eight he'd had, plus the beers, plus the beers he'd had at the pub where he got taken by Reuben to be introduced to this druggie contact cos they were a tight, organised group, hard to get close to, and they weren't free, open and reckless like the dumbo Maori gangs with their access to large quantities of dope, those black coots'd sell it to anyone, which is why they were always getting done cos some undercover'd busted em — again. Which reminded Jube: Course I coulda gone and done the biz with one of the black gangs . . .

Eyeing the Prez for a signal of approval that he was alright, show he was a black-hater like they were. But the Prez gave away nothing, just nodded. Then a sheila came in the front door. A real looker. Enough to give a horny dude like Jube a hard on the spot. Blonde, with tight black trousers that showed her great legs he could see the shape, slight protrusion of her fanny shaped there, her breasts didn't have no bra under that near-see-through white blouse; she had a smoke in her mouth which had her squinting one eye, which caught Jube in a withering glare of question so he looked away. And she, the looker, stepped up to the Prez and kissed his big bushy beard. He ruffled her hair, Hey, babe. Slid a big hand down her back and held her in a hug as he asked Jube, So how much ya lookin to buy, pal? I forgot your name. Jube. Jube, that's it. How much were you after then, Jube?

He took his time in answering straight away. Just let it drawl out, Oh, bout, what . . . Pulled out his wad, looked at it, up at Prez, then without fear or a sense of inferiority, Four thousand bucks worth? Had to fight to keep himself from breaking out grinning so proud, so *big* did he feel.

Or he did till the Prez merely shrugged, looked at his woman, tweeked her chin, rubbed his fuzzy face playfully on her face, she giggled, and Jube caught the Prez's big mit grabbing a handful of bum cheek. And he envied the guy sumpin terrible, wanted that babe for himself, to bury his nose in her cunt, shove that laughing gear down on his equipment (fucking choke the bitch ta death on it . . .) pretending he had his eyes on the floor but he was fixed on that V of twat outline. Okay, Prez breathed near in his ear. Four buys you a pound. Aw, come on. Four buys you a pound and two ounces.

I thought it bought a bit more'n that. Jube not worried, this was just negotiating, he knew the score.

One pound five ounces they settled on; so two ton an ounce with an extra ounce thrown in. They shook hands on the deal. Prez invited Jube to stay on for a few more drinks; anyway, someone had to go and get the dope. Only a dope'd keep it on the premises, the Prez joked, had Jube in stitches. The Prez ordered a round of drinks for the half-dozen or so who were at the bar servery; one was introduced as the sergeant-at-arms, and, man, did he look like one, the ugly prick, worse cos he wouldn't remove his shades even in here so Jube couldn't read the man's eyes. But what the hell, he was with the Prez himself so what was he worried about? Yet the voice kept whispering away inside him.

The Prez liked rugby league, used to play it, years ago when he was a bit younger, but sure, he loved the game and yeah he thought that fight between the Aussie and Kevin whatshisname, the coon cunt, was a real humdinger, though as a rule he hated blacks, hated em. So do I, Prez. So do fucking I. So Jube confined his league anecdotes to white players. The night came in.

At some stage the Prez gave whispered instructions to Billy, who then left; Jube assumed to get the dope. He offered to pay Prez the four g, but good ole Prez, he smiled, no, wait till we got sumpin t' give you in exchange. How's your drink?

Billy returned, came straight up to the Prez and said something in his ear. Prez didn't give nothin away in his face; he'd make a good poker player Jube assessed in his getting-drunk state. Prez heaved a big sigh. He looked for some time up at the ceiling then asked Jube The Tavi's your watering hole, right? Jube nodded, Sure is. Ya been there? Prez shook his head, Hardly, bud. Place's fulla blacks. Looked at Jube, them friendly blue eyes now lancing into a man's watering own. Jube gulped; wished he had a smoke going to hang onto, hide his nervousness. The eyes boring into him. Nowhere to look cept into them; he couldn't look away, not with every set of eyes on him; he knew why, too, this guy was the Prez. Why he was the one in charge of the show, of all this lot, there'd be plenty of nutcases amongst em, yet he was in charge. The president. Though for the life of him Jube couldn't figure out what he'd done or said to turn the situation like this. He just couldn't.

Prez jerked a thumb in Billy's direction — Billy was stood with folded arms adding his bit to the evils Jube was getting, and Jube hurt, hurt and hating Billy, even in the brief glance he caught Bill eyeing him like he was, he *hated* him — Billy here's juss been down to Tavistocks . . . he was telling Jube in a fairly ordinary-volumed voice, though not so the tone. And Jube was understanding what leadership is about. You know, to check you out, case you was an undercover, mean ta say — Man, do I *look* like one? Jube with outspread of hands and appealing face. The Prez shook his great head, shrugged huge shoulders, So what does one look like, man? Jube in an instant stabbing a finger at his tats right down his arm. Them, man. How many undies ya see with them. Angry. Hurt too. Then it struck him that if Billy had checked Jube out at the Tavi, then surely he woulda come back Jube's crim credentials all sweet as? A weight seemed to half lift off his mind, even though the Prez seemed to be building to sumpin that weren't necessarily gonna go Jube's way. (Hope. We all live in hope.)

Then the eyes, with bearded outburst encasing them, and reddened with booze or whatever, boring into Jube's eyes. But not sayin a thing. Not one word that'd explain why this shift and what'd Billy turned up with from the Tavi.

Uh, Prez . . . ? Like — like Billy here musta found out, you know, my form? Looking to Billy. Billy? What'd people tell ya, man? But Billy's hostile features tellin Jube right away what information he'd got weren't what Jube could possibly have expected. So alarm bells ringing in his head, his half-aching half-murderous heart. (Man, I could poke Billy's eyes out, I could.)

Then Prez bellowed out to his men, and his deep voice echoed and boomed in the hall-like room, cavernous of sudden perceptive change: He's white, right? A murmer of yeahs. He grapped an arm of Jube's rammed it ceilingward. For an absurd moment Jube thought it might be a welcoming ritual, that maybe they were so impressed with him this was the Skull Rider way of showing a man they liked his form, his style. Jube felt close to giggling. The grip on his arm tightened, and Jube could feel the man's strenght, hear him telling his men in that booming voice, He's white, He's white like us. The grip tightened painfully. Yet he's living with — now get this, guys — he's flatted up witha — witha — And Jube knew what was coming. He didn't understand it. Not in the context. It didn't seem fair. Or right. Not when he'd deliberately chosen this white gang for being just that. Because he thought they'd have the principles he perceived the Maori gangs as not having. He understood, though, leadership, what it was, what made it; it was a voice that summarised. The voice that put the direction in these ordinary guys' their hatreds their unsure classifications, this is what leadership is about: they sum up the followers, they — he, this leader, he sums up any given situation for these thickheads to understand. He says, this is a Thing, and we don't like Things, says I your leader. Then he orders the Thing to be attacked.

So Jube didn't hardly hear the Prez calling out his summarisation of Jube, Jube the Thing. Who is flatted up with a nigger.

Just as he didn't feel, not really, not as a painful beginning to a series of pains, inflicted pain. Just a thud. Boom. Sorta muffled. Like cannon fire in the distance. It mighta been thrown by the Prez, seein as how he was the most wild-eyed ofem in that split second of situational sum-up that man gets when he is under attack, or it coulda been Billy threw a king hit because of his own hurt at warming to this Thing, being fooled by It. Didn't madda who it was; only that Jube was still standing, and thinking, Don't they know Jube McCall can take a hit? All my life I been hit, and never have I gone down from the first blow, ask anyone. So Jube tottered. And punches flew at him from everywhere. And voices were yelling through clenched, enraged, fucked up teeth, *Geddim! Geddim! Kicktheniggerloversheadin!*

Then he fell from his six feet and three inches of gawky height. (I fall down . . . *And we all fall down!* hahahahaha!) A childhood nursery-rhyme line came to him, with it children's laughter, from out of the mind blue yonder; as did the adult voices chatter this mad cacophony that he wassa niggahlover come to him, and he wondered about that one: if he might not be in the wrong country? Maybe I been in America my whole rotten life and now known it till now? This ain't New Zealand. We don't have niggers. And anyrate, I'm one of the good guys?!

They didn't hurt. Not the punches. Not the boots. Not a one ofem. Just jolts, is all; jolts of electricity going off in a man's brain. Sparks, yeah. Lectric sparks of brain signal, thought event, word connection in the squiggle of brain mass with its highways and off-roads and backroads of tracks and unmapped ribbon routes of message conduit. Tha's all. Tha's all 't' happening to me: it's a brainstorm. It's an event happening from the outside to the inside; sumpin good'll come of it . . . sometime. Some day. (Oh . . .) *Ohh!* (. . . I'm sure it will. Sumpin good'll come of this —) *Ohhhhhhhhh.*

Boots stomping, heeling at his protective hands covering his face. (Sumpin good . . .) And: My, is that Sonny I can see? Hey? Sonny? Oi, Sonny, lookit what you don, man. You did this. You're why they're doing this to me. And me, all I was trying to do was help us. Me and you, Sonny. I was trying to double our bread. (Oh, but sumpin good always comes of even a beating — don't it?) Jube fixing on something in his mind. A thought. An idea. A notion — yeh — a notion, that everything gonna be alright, Jube boy. Everything.

Juss like Daddy tellin me. (Or did he?)

15 Sing to us, Boris. Sing to me and Jane, Sonny with the tape labelled in hand-written black ink on the box, 'Music from the Slavonic Liturgy'.

The snow fell. Frozen icicles suspended from the church eaves. Shingle roof was only just visible in edging of otherwise total snow cover, though the spire broke clear of it because of the angle. And snow whipped up in flurries from some deeply cold Russian wind, as worshippers hurried to the warmth of church inner sanctum, hidden behind thick fur hats and upturned collars and oversize coats, hurried to the window glow of candlelight in a semi-gloom of probable morning over there in that climatically terrible country. Sing to us, Boris, and choir.

Sonny having woken with a start to a just-before-midnight troubled dream where he was struggling to hold onto a kite for all he was worth, and Jube was on the other end trying to tear it away from him. Woke and immediately ached from the dream effect as well the voice of imaginary Jane in his mind as clear as if she was there, beside him. And wanting to hear, to see that music.

And, in time, to he sitting on the edge of his bed, the big man with the big voice and backing choir sang like at a dozen funerals of everyone Sonny ever knew, was close to, gone; transported by voice and voices alone to both that church in far-off Russia and to the gravesides, a dozen of them, and like in dream all at once, staring down into coffin-bottomed holes at life irretrievable, life forever gone (without having lived in the first place) so a man not sure what he was crying for: that or the thought of their twelve deaths, or for that snow-swirled cold village in remote Russia somewhere and nowhere; wanting a hand to hold, a woman's (my mummy's?).

So come to me, Jane, come to me. You're here and Sonny's here. Come, let us cry together for them lost two lives of ours, and for the dozen lives now being lamented by Boris there, and his choir of good true men and women. Amazing, eh Jane, how they can put so much meaning and musical order into so much apparent grief. But it's not grief you say, Jane? But I know that: it's glory to God, to the god they worship in secret Russia. Like we have our secrets, Jane, in this country.

But it ain't God so much, Jane, you unnerstan? It's the god in them, in his voice, Boris's, that he sings to first. Ya see? It's his voice, the creative outpour from himself, his own special inner workings that has him, you know, like singing praise to himself. To the fact of him having such a beautiful voice. And then, then, dear Jane, he next sings to us and for us; so he can represent of us and for us what we're feeling. Our own inner understandings, ya know? It's God but it ain't God. You unnerstan? Sure you do, Jane, you and me, we're peas from the same discarded, forgotten pod, aren't we?

Ya see, he and they, the choir, the collective of em are singing glory to being alive, as much they are to God if even to God. They call it God, sure they do. It's the excuse they use to strive and then reach those heights. Some ofem might be atheists, ya unnerstan, Jane. Like me and you, we're standing at these gravesides in our same sad minds and we're crying, right? But who're we crying for? Them one dozen lined up down there in each his and her separate hole? Or for us? For us do we cry? Oh, but now the women have changed it, ya see now, Jane? How things shift? How life itself has shifted on us? But we missed it before, didn't we? Didn't we? Oh but, Jane, not now, not now, it doesn't have to be like that anymore does it?

Burying himself in his hands. As the voice and voices throbbed on.

The times, Jane. The number of times I, Sonny, have sat here and soaked up what's going on on screen. Now you, you're sharing it with me, Jane. Even though you don't actually exist, yet you are real in my mind. I can hear you. You have a voice, it's a husky voice — from too much smoking, eh, hahaha — you have a face, your hands are soft, we're just a meeting away from loving each other. Looking at the screen again. Thinking of twelve funerals, of a dozen deaths of everyone a man (and a woman) ever loved, and twelve might be an exaggeration, a convict's cell-practised lie, though any number less didn't give the experience sufficient meaning, such was the huge grief Sonny felt inside.

Twelve good people, Jane. Taken by the same catastrophic event.

What would it be, an explosion? Yes, an explosion. Dead. So all of em dead. And yet, Jane . . . ? You know? And yet not dead, or how this tremendous mourn of song-voice rising up and above even death times twelve? It's the possibilities, is it not, Jane, of life ascending, rising above death? It ain't hope so much as it's triumph; triumph even in our darkest moments, lifting us above the grief even as we grieve. We know this now, Jane, don't we? It's the possibility of life triumphing over the goneness of life. And that's what this tape, these tapes, are: just one of life's possibilities put to me — no, us, Jane. Put to us — no. Stolen, Jane. Be honest. I'll be honest. It's life's possibilities found to me one night when I was out stealing.

The bells tolled then the screen went blank, but the bells tolled on in Sonny's (and Jane's) mind. Then outside a car arrival. Jube's familiar engine roar. Sonny keen-eared to what followed. For several minutes he listened, but no sound of doors slamming closed, and the engine was still rumbling. Sonny figuring Jube and someone or ones were talking. Having a joint. Picturing them, hearing the gaudy laughter in confines of car. Smelling the dope. Listening to the breaths, of intake, of held breath, of final exhalation. Imagining that, and adjusting himself for their soon entry, of having to laugh at their inane and mad comments and unfunny jokes and remarks. At having to be one of them when he wasn't, and had never been. Nor certainly, not now, could possibly hope to be. He was just Sonny. Sonny who was out one night stealing when — When the horn sounded.

And had urgency in it.

The two of them; suspended, two closed-up figures in a night frame. Of overhead streetlight. Stars arena-ed around. Bowled above. It's always the stars, even when the clouds're covering them: lights down on man his wretched condition. And too his moments of beauty.

An unevenly heighted picture of physical statures. And postures. The smaller frame supporting the taller, the head slumped taller. Hey, Jube . . . Hey, man, it's Sonny. Sonny, bud. It's Sonny. (It's alright, Sonny's here. Sonny's here, pal.)

A suspension of locked, entwined figures, shapes converged under lamplight. Just another night scene, man, 's happening all over. Here. There. The city. The country. The fucking world. Of creatures of the always night screwing up. Fucking up. Happens every time. (Everytime, Jube.) Man, it's alright, Jube. I'm here. Can ya walk? Wanna get on my back? I think I can make it. Hey, what's money, man? Don't be talking bout no money. We never had it to start with, did we? And we ain't got it now. Gotta get you inside, man. Who did this?

Juss another night. Another streetlight. Another pair done blown it again. Cos one man's blowing is his friend's blowing too. How it goes. Juss another night.

Of hurt sobbing and heaving breath in the lamplight dark. A possibility happened, Jube, tha's all, Sonny whispering and not meaning for Jube's ears. Though his voice rose as he continued — couldn't stop it seeing as it'd started — When sometimes the poss's're good, sometimes they're bad. Huh, Jube? So it wasn't our turn tonight, uh? So what? Come on, let's get ya inside, cleaned up. How it goes, eh Jube? Ya know? Holding Jube closer to him. How it works out sometimes, Jube. Ya win some, lose some, okay? Holding Jube tighter. And feeling love cos love was all he and Jube got right now. Seein as how the possibility had already been reached, and this was its bloodied outcome. Plus the money, Jube was mumbling out through teeth-broken mouth, was gone. Stolen. Robbed. I got mugged, Sonny, he was mumbling, by our own kind. And sounded so betrayed. So betrayed.

Getting Jube indoors, on the sitting-room floor, on his back, but he rolled over on his side because he'd started to gurgle with blood probably running down his throat. Is alright, bro, Sonny's here. The mess they'd made of the man. It was unfair. Criminal. Not right. And the fucking money's gone too, Sonny. I'm sorry, I'm s — Hey don't worry, man. Who's talkin money? I'm not. Get you cleaned up, man, we might have to take you to hospital. No, no hospital, no hos . . . The word fizzed out in a hiss of blood bubbling up out his mouth. But then he lifted himself to a sitting position. And he looked the more hideous. It was the fight left in him: it looked so pathetic at the same time it had this mad pride, this crazy will of effort and determination. Oh Sonnee! he groaned, No, he didn't groan, he cried it out, as he did again: OH SONNEE! Man, it's alright, Jube. I'm just getting a wet cloth. Oh, tha'ssa mean cut, Jube, you'll have to get it stitched. No, man, we're going back, the madman was protesting in his monumental courage.

Back? Man, you ain't going nowhere. And I ain't getting involved, you know I never liked drugs, and I always hated violence.

Look what it's done for you, Jube. Oh man, no, don't say you're going back. Please?

But Jube was shaking his barely recognisable head, the face part. No. No, Son. No, Jube. No! Ya hear me? Sonny getting angry, and maybe some of it was upset at what'd been done to his pal (the only pal I got). No Jane any longer in his mind, not at sight of this face-pulped hideosity. We ain't goin —

— To the house, Sonny.

The what? What house? Where they already done this to —

— The big house. Oh, don't be si — Man, you're hurt bad. You'll be better in a few d — well, a little while anyway. Sonny dabbing at the face with a wet cloth, but no matter where he wiped, blood kept springing forth from another source or the same place. (God, I hope it ain't his life leaking out of him.) The big house, Son. We're going back there. Member? Member what it did for us, Son?

And the penny dropped. The Harl — You mean — Man, Jube, you don't know what you're saying.

But the man hauled himself to his feet, staggered for a moment. Managed, somehow, to break out in a kind of macabre smile, as if despite it all he'd still triumphed. It didn't seem possible. Nor probable. Cept it was happening right in front of Sonny's eyes.

Back to where it all started, Sonny, the man was saying through his broken-tooth smile; these words, this seized hope in his world of bloodied abjectness croaked from his hugely swollen lips: Back, Sonny. We're going back. Soon's I've healed up a bit. Member, Sonny? How it was the same thing, near? And how it turned around?

But they'll have alarms now, man.

Back to that big house, eh Sonny, hahaha.

And why'd they have money sitting around now?

Then we'll see. We'll show em, Son. We'll fucking show em.

And one smiled with a mad triumph as if already he was on his way back. And the other fell eyes to the floor, and shook his head. Then lifted them. I'm getting you a doctor.

We're going back, Son, the voice harsh in its pained delivery. The smile bizzare for the hope Jube had vested in his promise. Let's get you into bed. Back, Sonny. Ya hear? Back to get ourselves on the high road again, uh? Sonny not answering. Uh Son? Maybe. Not time to be talking — It is!

Jube's swollen eyes the same slits of vision they'd been from the other beating. The total of it adding more to the macabre, to the fucking unholy mess they were in — again. (A-fuckin-gain.) Slits that the madness was able to glisten through. Or maybe it was just hope born of desperation, and of wanting to change things. To swing this life back on course that the original crime seemed to have promised, but it was now in ruins. Bloodied, face-pulped ruins.

Then Jube started coughing, and it sounded bad. Looked bad as blood came dribbling out his mouth. Like a statement. On both their behalfs.

16 Mrs Harland? (Mrs Harland? Mrs Harland? Mrs Harland?) A hundred times he'd practised that opening; in his mind, under his breath, self-consciously aloud in the couple of hundred kilometres of being driven in Jube's car from when Jube first got the idea. Mrs Harland? Mrs Harland? Sonny had the opening imprinted on his brain.

And now, it was about to become reality, as Sonny Mahia stood in a Wellington city telephone box listening to the dial tone going *brr-ip brr-ip — brr-ip brr-ip*. With sweat popped out all over his forehead, hand holding the receiver covered in the stuff. (Mrs Harland?) Mrs Harland? he'd practised to say, yet never had it occurred to him how she might respond back.

Brr-ip brr-ip — brr — click. The sweat flowed. He felt he knew her so well; from the countless watching of her and daughter in piano duet, first introducing herself then her self-assured daughter doing her introductory bit on that home-made video. Her voice, Mrs Harland's, slightly husky, and very posh. Now, it was echoing in his ear: Penny Harland speaking. And he, the caller, couldn't speak.

Heart hammering, brain spinning, and with Jube parked right outside watching everything, and a man couldn't get himself to speak.

He coughed — *arrgh* — to clear the restriction in his throat. He wanted to put the phone down: (I've done my job: she's home. That's what Jube wanted to know.) But there was more.

Um . . . is that Mrs Harland? Yes. *Arrgh*, again he had to fight the seeming swelling of throat. Yes? she asked again and in a voice sweetly innocent. Um . . . is Mr Harland there please? (Please *please* let him be home . . .)

No. Sonny could hear her as though from a vast distance. He's

163

at his office in town, do you have his number? No, I — What more to say? Just wanting to put the receiver down. Then he got the idea that he could lie to Jube, tell him Mr Harland was at home, that the office with his framed credentials — and punched out by Jube's mad fist shattering the glass enclosure — was indeed his workplace, so the whole plan was off since this wasn't going to be an armed robbery or nothing like that. But then again, what if Jube did the check for himself? What to say then?

Uh, no. No, I don't have that number. Stiffened when she asked, in a changed tone, May I ask who's calling? So Sonny put the receiver down. Slumped both hands against the wall. Watched drops of sweat drip from his face onto the phone. And his legs felt weak. And for some reason the voice of the bass singer came into his mind . . . as though some haunting, ill-omened musical passage trying to warn him. But then a car horn sounded, made Sonny startle; then anger. Out he went, wrenched open the passenger door, What's with the fuckin horn, buster? Glaring at Jube, who was staring calmly back, So how'd it go? He there? He's not, is he? Yes? No?

No, Sonny turned away, stared out at a row of warehouse buildings, the comings and goings of vehicles and people, mostly men in overalls. What, no he's not at home? No, he is. Come on, Sonny. No, he's not at home. And man, I don't think this such a good idea even though he ain't.

But Jube'd already started the engine, and a glance at him said he was raring to go. So did the speed at which they accelerated away from the kerb. But no smiles of the usual chicken counting before they'd hatched. Not even a hint. Just this picture of grim-something, Sonny couldn't even call it determination, it was more a kind of mad fixation. And so Sonny lit a cigarette and buried himself in the clouds of smoke. (I want to sink deep deep into the clouds. I want to be swallowed. My cowardice, my nothingness, my being thief, I want to lose it. Lose it. Just fuckin lose myself somewhere . . .) As an engine roared out front of him.

The night (last night) the Jube-driven night (and all the nights and anguished days of his fixed deciding) now come, of three weeks and a few days of physical healing and mental determining, the night the night was come. And now (now, Sonny) it was gone. They were transported, uplifted of home, of no prospects moving to the exaggerated hope of other town prospect. Face wounds mostly healed, cracked ribs near gone of their pain, infection staved off by the medicines prescribed by the doctor Sonny had summoned in; the nights, the days, the nights of nursing the man — you're the only friend I got, Son. (Yeah, man, sure. While you need me.) Sonny'd not been fooled — had to change his dressings, cook for him, even wipe his arse the first few days because of the rib injuries.

The nights and delirious days of physical pain — oh I hurt bad, Son — but the mental pain was even worse — we'll get em, Son. Every man jack ofem, we'll get em. Soon as we hit the front again, go back to our fancy house bank — HAHAHAHAHA!! — down there in the capital city, bro, we'll soon be doubling our money, Son. And then, bro. Then. The big house, Sonny, the big house'll save us again like it did the first time; member that, Son, hahaha. From a nightmare to a fucking dream, eh Son? That's how it was then, weren't it?

(How it was how it was, but what of the *is*? How do ya *make* of this fuckin life!) Sonny trembling close to bursting out yelling, or even screaming. As if he was going to crack. And as if he did not belong to the world. Not in any way unless it was negative. Laughing ironically inside to himself at himself. (I'm here on this Earth so people can throw stones at me, *hahahaha*. But whaddid I do? whaddid I do?) As Jube took a corner on a lean. And no chuckle came from him as it always did. (Mrs Harland? Mrs Harland, we're on our way. But not to hurt ya, lady. Not to do you no harm.) Turning to Jube, Man, no nasty business neither. And, getting no response, added, Ya hear me, man? In a voice that surprised himself for how commanding it sounded. I hear. Sonny waited for something to follow, and when it didn't: And? And don't gimme no fucking orders, man. Do *you* hear?

I hear alright. But I'm staying with what I said, man: no nast — Fuck up. Okay? No okay, I — Sonny, I'm warning you. No! Sonny turning fully in his seat so he was facing Jube. We didn't agree to nothing bad, man. *Look* at me, man!

Yeah, sure. And crash us while I'm at it? Juss so I can look at your ugly dial? Jube drawling. And who said anything about *nasti*ness? Not me. Well ya didn't not say nothing about it either. Didn't I? Jube gave him the sleep-eyed look. And drove.

(The nights, the days and nights of healing this guy. Him crying out in his pain, even in his sleep, he coulda been a baby. Oh Sonny, my ribs're on fucking fire. Oh Sonny, my heart feels torn apart with what them dudes did to me. Oh Sonny, oh Sonny don't leave me man.) Was this the same man? (Come sit on my bed, talk to me, friend. You're the only friend I got. Yeah, and you too for me, man. (And Jane. Jane of my sure mind that I'll meet her one day.) Dabbing at the sweat droplets constantly beading on his forehead, dabdab- dab. There ya go, man. Oh Sonny. What'd I do without you, man. But we'll be back on top, Son, just as soon's I'm better. The big house, bro, we're going back to the big house. You remember that, Son, with them angles of the dangles outside and in? Man, it was some weird pad, weren't it? But what a find, huh Sonny? Like, what a fucking find we found, hahaha. And it'll be the same, Son. I know you say it won't, that it'll be alarmed up, but it won't. It won't, not when we hit it it won't. Oh Sonny, we'll make it up, you'll see.)

Got the balies? Well, not nless someone's shifted em from down on the floor here at my feet, Sonny sarcasming as he reached down and took up the two woollen balaclavas every thief has lying around, two sets of gloves by them at the ready. The taking up of disguise jolting Sonny the more with this reality.

Driving alongside the sea for a bit, pretty flat; houses and apartment blocks other side. The fountain some ways out in sea surround in proud display of some straight's ingenuity and others' imagination. (Whilst we . . .) Jube slowing to make the turn up a hill, with houses stuck to it. Up a steep climb, a sharp hairpin, more of the climb, a church (hello, God), some shops, and a cigarette sign reminding Sonny to light up while he could since it'd be but a few minutes more if that. But not lighting as he customarily did for Jube, not this time, it didn't fit. Not an act of even mild friendship. Staring ahead as he waited for Jube to protest where was his smoke. But Jube said nothing, nor did he light up his own, they just sat beside him, between the pair, on the torn upholstery, a packet of Pall Mall filter and a Bic lighter a yellow one.

Sonny sucked in the smoke as deeply as he'd ever. Held it there for longer too. (Anyone'd think this was my last smoke.) As Jube slowed and Sonny's eyes went left, looking for the house, told Jube the number from the telephone book, it's thirty-five. Then there it was, just another letterbox with brass numbers on it: 35, and a dug- out of driveway deep into cliff face turned to a double carport, and Sonny heard Jube gasp as he went, oh well, swung hard left and parked beside a sleek car, a sports model with a soft top and red skin.

Jube switched off. They sat there for an eternity of only moments, waiting for something till it didn't happen, then they got out at the same time, paused, both, at their opened doors and looked at each other. One's eyes glistened with tear film, the other's were hard to read, empty and yet filled with something. Detached, that's how Jube's eyes looked. Detached and cold. Let's go, his mouth with its moustache removed from when the doctor said it had to go to lessen the chance of infection now a few days of stubble, light brown stubble. And the smell of the rum Jube'd been drinking on the way down of six and a bit hours of fast driving, with Sonny sipping tokenly so Jube wouldn't call him a piker, straight from the bottle, a forty-ounce one, and over half drunk, mostly by Jube, now fuming off him this mid-morning in autumn Wellington.

A last look at each other that just happened that way: of Sonny trying to read right into Jube and Jube in turn giving back, and mouthing the words, This is it, mate. And so for an instant his eyes looked warm and of a kind to those observing him. Out of the carport. Steps. Must be over a hundred of them. Concrete faced with grey stone almost black.

Stubbing his hardly smoked cigarette out on the ground, Sonny went after Jube. (Man oh man, but this don't feel right.)

Lawn bathed in a weak sunlight, chill air with light breeze in it. Trees studded everywhere off to their climbing left, a line of them along the boundary to the right. House visible only in part, owing to the angle as well obscuring of trees. Breaths the faintest of vapour cloud frequent in puffing expel. Smell of Jube's rummy breath like a continuous cloud Sonny had to step up into. Sonny getting the thought — absurd it was too — that his own breath was barely tainted by the same smell since he'd hardly touched the vile, straight-from-the-bottle stuff. Absurd because he got this image of himself kissing Mrs Harland. (Kissing? Me?) He wondered if he might be going (finally) mad.

Breath cloud and booze stench and labouring lungs rasping a three-part lifetime of smoking. Insects in the cool air. Sweat starting to feel like sloshing around in sticky liquid.

In constant tree shadow of boundary line, snatches of lawn in glittering dew jewel. Other parts dark patches of shadow and foliage overhang. So very private. Such a twinned intrusion, one of them thinking, though more as a feeling than in words since words had left him some little time back. Intrusion turning to violation when Jube began swearing, Fuck. Fuck. This is fucking hard work. Though he strode on, those long, grubby-jeaned legs stepping up, two at a time.

Flurry of bird disturbance from nearby tree. A pause in Sonny's stepping at eyecatching of birds on wing, an outburst of twitter from tree shape, soaring into safety of sky. Of blue sky gap between white and grey cloud islands. Background drone of city traffic a faint register. Not a neighbouring house to be seen, just trees. And well-tended lawn in between.

Sea slice. With tall building segment, or broken clear against a blue and white background of sky. Sky, and two thieves moving and panting in its lower reaches.

Nearing the top so Jube's head going from left to right. In animal mode, for danger signs. His breathing sounding like his original rib-broken pain. Couple more steps to go, house very visible from the angle, in cream and broken by timber brown and grey shingle roof in fan shape, a cleavage, an inventive imagination gone not quite wild since it all looked controlled. No, balanced. (Balanced.) Biggish tree on the left. Jube stepping off the pathway into tree shadow, and straight down on his knees with hands and heaving breath. And Sonny following suit.

Balies, Jube puffed, as he straightened and pulled his balaclava over his head and down around his neck. Sonny did same. On with gloves; Jube's black leather, Sonny's grey wool. Not planned, just what they'd found at home. Home now so far away, and yet as if they'd never left. (As if we're still there, but we're here too, we're in the everywheres of our thieving comings and goings, that's why this sense of being back at the flat: it's cos we bring ourselves with us. Our intentioned, but unchanged selves.) Breathing easier. Regained. Lessgo. Jube. Jube in command.

Up onto a paved area, a kind of big courtyard. The breathing much better but the sweat like he, and no doubt Jube too, was soaking in it. Clothing clinging to skin, salt taste in mouth, stinging eyes, and woollen-enclosed neck and throat throttling. Across the paved area, which they'd not noticed last visit, night that it was. Front door entrance, with its little overhang walkway of pitched roof with same grey shingle covering, on wooden poles that green plant curled from the ground to the underside of roof. Same as last time except the little light of doorbell didn't glow like an eye in the dark of last time here. Not in the broad daylight. And not when the door was wide open.

And music issued from the shadowed opening. Classical music.

Into Sonny's heart it floated, at first sweet and highly familiar, then it turned discordant as it somehow played against a clashing background of his own memoried recordings, stolen (stolen) from this very house. Like some messaging dreamscape message trying to tell him something, except he wasn't hearing, not with the clashing of sound between reality and memory; stolen memory. Jube? Man, I don't like this, his whispering seeming so stupid of this bright-enough mid-morning. But Jube was already moving.

Sonny still standing there; caught in this confusion of song-pouring memory, and sight too of that door, wide-open slab entrance it could be a cave opening; churn of pictures in his head, none of it marrying: snow coming down and a man's deep bass voice ringing out in his triumph of himself over God even as he seemingly sung to Him, but clashing with the stringed orchestral sounds issuing from the shadow cave-like opening that Jube was nearing, as though everything was slowed down even as things seemed opposite, inside his mind, a picture of piano being played, by her, her inside, unsuspecting, she was in the picture, as was her daughter, the one with the funny shortened nickname of Ants, she with the wiring all over her teeth how they do these rich kids, yet untouched of self-confidence for that.

Messaging. That he, this man caught confused here, and that man moving forward on his cautious creeping furtive toes, two dudes transported emselves a furious six hours' drive down the main state highway, two dudes come from a structureless social pit, from mess of meaning, ruin of lives, bereft of values, from a dark she could not possibly know. Let alone that it was upon her.

Sonny turned looked down the long steep of panting climb; it could have been some dark-tiled passage they'd ascended, into some kind of unknown and yet it was a known (if only I could tell myself what it is). Wondering if he should bound down the steps, get the hell out of here while he could. Back the other way at Jube, to see him stopped there and glaring at Sonny and mouthing obscenities at what the fuck did Sonny think he was fucking doing. While behind

Jube, coming out that door opening, stringed sounds so unrelated to him and Sonny. Sounds.

Head cocked just to one side, hands and half raised arms like a Mother Mary statue (from that school I used to walk past, and the everyday surprise of seeing Her there, enclosed in this little concrete surround, in blue-painted gown, woman, Woman in stone forever). Like that she looked. Except she had an apron, a tartan one, and her surround was the broad reverberating of strings, orchestrated strings.

And Jube moving swiftly across the brown-tiled kitchen floor. The woman still with eyes closed in her world of ordered sound, still with her arms bent at elbow in supplicated Virgin Mary posture. Then not a sound as Jube took her, with an arm around her throat and other hand clamping over her mouth. Turning her to Sonny, so he saw her eyes, how utterly surprised they were (lady, I'm sorry), the terror in them; Jube walking her back so he was against a timber-lined wall that had a painting part obscured by Jube's balaclavaed head. His mouth was moving but Sonny couldn't hear, not at first, till he realised Jube was wanting the music turned down. Or off. Sonny fixed on the woman, her changing of eye reaction: from utter surprise to terror then closing in a kind of despair, but opening again to a narrowing that looked like determination. All this in the space of a few seconds. A witness, Sonny was, to a process of social conditioning, he was certain.

He moved to the divide between kitchen and dining room, feeling so mixed up; as if in an instant he was thrust back to the worst of confounded childhood. Of not knowing anything. Of being this thing, caught between a nowhere and another nowhere. So he moved thinking only shit! (Shit, shit, *shit!*) Like a kid deeply upset without understanding at what.

Into the living room, going automatically to where they'd last time removed the stereo system. Replaced. Looked different. But a volume knob is a volume knob. Turned it down, not too much, figuring they might need some cover sound. Head spinning. Going back to the kitchen, eyes seeing nothing, not with clarity.

Lady lady, don't you be getting clever now and thinking you'll scream, ya hear? Jube talking in Mrs Harland's ear, his voice slightly muffled from the balaclava, and hissing through the gaps of

170

punched- and kicked-out teeth. Hand still across her mouth. His eyes roaming as he spoke as if indifferent. As if he wasn't doing what he was doing, and worse: as if he didn't give two damns.

Her eyes registered Sonny's arrival. He stopped a few feet from her. Could smell her. Familiar too. Of the perfume he took in of her bedroom last time. But not able to hold her eyes because he thought he saw pleading in them.

You the only one here? Jube asked her.

Her head moved she was.

Money, honey, hahaha, Jube even able to chuckle. We came for the money. Now, I'm gonna take my hand away and if you scream, then — he was shaking his head, he looked shocking with his head completely covered, as Sonny knew he too would look — then, lady, you are gonna get hurt. She shook her head. Her eyes said she knew better than that.

Jube's hand came cautiously away, hovered a little ways off, so Sonny had to move to his right to get her face. Of no lipstick, nor make-up, as fresh and natural as the vase of flowers on the bench behind her. Green eyes, confirming the photograph, the home-made video. Sonny feeling an aching for her, but of sympathy and guilt, not longing. Looking at her mouth as it opened, as though wanting not to upset Jube, so careful. I — I — I'm sorry, her mouth broke into an apologetic quick smile, and Sonny thinking please don't be sorry for my sake, since Jube was behind her, face too damned close to her ear for Sonny's liking. As if Jube was gonna do something typical of him, like feel her up. Sonny thinking he'd grab that glass vase and break it over Jube's head he got dirty about this. His eyes kept flicking from the contrast of faces, of the woman's clear skin and proud cheekbones, her beauty, and Jube's blue eyes with their scar-tissue marks and eyebrows both cut in two by scars, looking out from the slot in the bali. Reminding Sonny how he must look himself.

I'm sorry, I lost my voice. Pause. I hope you'll understand in the, uh, circ — Get on with it, lady. The money.

Well, it's like this — I said get on with it. I am trying. Then try harder. We don't want your life story. Eyes grinning across at Sonny.

Her breasts came up in a heave of sigh. (She must be sucking in courage, fortitude from herself.) Sonny unable to cancel out the picture he got in his mind of this woman naked; her breasts, not large not small, not perfect neither. Her. This person. (I've seen her naked?) But she was talking again, and the image went.

We were burgled. Sometime ago. Burgled? Jube came in all false mocking innocence, eyes smiling over at Sonny. Ya hear that, pal? she was burgled. Grinning behind the navy face covering. (That's funny?) Oh now that's a shame, lady, burgled. And what, you gonna say they cleaned you out you're now broke? Bankrupt? Eyes laughing away to Sonny again, and Sonny hoping his cold return'd tell Jube he wasn't funny.

Look, I — I'm trying to tell you there is no money in the house. Well there is, I have a couple of hundred in my purse. After the burglary we — You stopped leaving money around the joint, right, lady? Yes. Yes, she says. Ya hear her, man? Yes she says. So what we gonna do about this, lady? I — She stopped herself. Side to side head moving showing her frustration, not to mention the fear that'd be running through her.

Ya hear her, mate, she says — Man, I ain't deaf. So let's get the hell out. Out? Yeah, out. Out where? Come on, man, you know — No fucking way, bud. She's lying. You're lying, aren't ya? You just don't — I do not lie. She said it to Sonny since Jube was behind her, said it in a queenly manner, of pride and outrage that she should be so insulted. Man, she's not lying, I can tell, Sonny trying to end it. Ya hear my mate there, lady? He doesn't want to stay around. Again Sonny saw her breasts heave up; came out on the air she expelled. I should think that is wise. Stopped there. Oh? Jube wanting more. Oh? when she didn't offer more. Oh, yet again when still she remained silent. Hahaha, she's packing a sad now. Jube as if this wasn't really happening or it was but it wasn't real, wasn't for real. Just tv. A bit out of a movie. And this wasn't her house, it was all of theirs. And she wasn't afraid, she wasn't really being terrorised, it was just part of the act. How Sonny saw Jube's perception of this. Going back in his mind the past few weeks of Jube in his physical healing, hearing snatches of Jube in kind of confession, of personal aspect, of his childhood, how he could never figure if he loved his mother or hated her, but since he hated his father, hahaha, that'd do for both of the buggers, HAHAHA! That laugh of Jube's echoing in Sonny's mind. And the calm way he said, Well we'll all go take a look-see, shall we? telling Sonny he was right: that Jube was living this no different to a little fantasy, a dream sequence, an act straight from a tv screen.

Though it occurred to Sonny as he followed the two that his

own role had a distant dreamlike quality to it, and that he was half in this moving moment and half somewhere in his peculiar head. (I might even be crazy.)

The study. That's where Jube was leading them, or she was in front and Jube directed her from behind, That-away, lady, straight ahead, hahaha. Turning a look over his shoulder, eyes wrinkled in smug smile.

Passing into the fantastic scope of living area, but didn't look the same as last time. Not anywhere the same. Not with her in front, being pushed along by the denim-clad figure behind her. (In her own house.) Thisaway, Lady Muck. Still with that chuckle. And with an old familiar swagger straight from a prison exercise yard, straight from a study (comic) on crims, their mannerisms, how they each tell a different story and how every crim comes to the same body-language conclusion. (Of being this. Being that. But none of which they are. Can never be. Ya are what ya are . . .) Which was why, Sonny thinking, he was going along with this kind of kidnapping thing, hostage taking of a woman in her own home: (Cos ya are what ya are. No madda how hard ya try to be otherwise.) Resigned to it. This life. This way of living. Even as he followed the two he had this sense of deep resignation to life being just another dreadful situation, and what did it matter what the details were? Cells're the same, they're all the fuckin same, only have a different name of prison on the inmates' lips; only have a locational difference, like this is crime and only the play-out of it is different. As so will the sentence.

Piano. Wow. Really took Sonny when everything else was barely registering. Only Jube and the poor controlled woman in her own home. She who was in a man's mind sat at that instrument, with her daughter beside, talking, introducing themselves, then playing. And mirroring on its upraised lid not a bad day outside too.

Well here we are. Would ya mind pulling them curtains across, my good man? Jube breezy. Too breezy. Sonny stepping around both them, Oops, sorry, for brushing against the hip of Mrs Harland, and wincing with embarrassment at Jube laughing at that. Oh yeah, man: Oops, sorry. Oops, he's sorry, Lady Muck. His laugh cut short at her telling him, Do you mind not calling me that. This situation is awful enough without you adding insulting terms.

Ohh! HAHAHAHAHA! Did ya hear her, mate? Did you *hear* her? At the same time the room went into a gloom when Sonny

pulled the curtains across. Ooooo, it's gone very dark in here . . .
HAHAHAHAHAHA!! Jube's laughter seemed to echo in the small
confines. Sonny trying to find the switch for the desk lamp. Found
it. On. World a tiny and different place.

Let there be light, Jube in a flat voice, like the change of light
had got to him too, turned this moment into something else.
Cranked it up a bit, or down. And Mrs Harland's face a different
smooth-skinned hue: soft yellowish from flower bursts in the curtains, and bits of hair over her forehead doubled up by throwing
shadow. White blouse in the natural light more brushed with the
same yellow; so the breast outline and cleavage shadow more
marked. Sonny swallowing. And hearing Jube's breathing changed.
And since nothing was being spoken . . . Looking at Jube's eyes, now
harder to read; and his tall, denimed figure looking more ominous
when before he looked like what he was — a galoot. She kept
brushing at the strands of hair on her forehead, and they kept falling
back to where they were. Books and leather smell and woman scent
and booze stench and body sweat, and three's different breathing.

Hers a quickened intake and expel, from a face of self-control
that was more than admirable in the circumstances of Sonny's
observing. Jube's in contrast a kind of panting sniffing, through his
nose, maybe from the beating he took, maybe from all the beatings
he'd taken (maybe from the beating life in gen gave the man?): uh-
ihh-uh-ihh-uh-ihh. It might even be sexual, probably was. But the
man was no rapist. Close, but not the real thing.

Jube let out a long sigh and asked, So where's the key to the
drawers? I have no idea. But you're wasting your time if you think
my husband still keeps cash in there. Her tone showing sign of
frustration. I see, Jube rubbing his wool-garmented chin. So you
figured it was us last time? Yes. I did. Jube started pacing. Or so
Sonny believed. Till he brought to a halt before Sonny. Man, she's
got our number for the first hit. I know that, J — I know that, man.
Sonny feeling ridiculous having a team conference but a few feet
from the lady of the house. And she says there ain't no bread, just
the couple of hundred of her own. Man, I ain't *deaf*, Sonny's own
frustration mounting. Then Jube turned to the woman, What about
jewels? She shook her head. He let out another sigh, but this one
was different: it had anger in it. Jube stepped over to the desk,
turned and sat himself on it. So.

So, he said again. We got but a lousy two hundred. We know she ain't into jewellery cos she wasn't the last time we were here. So. His breathing quickened. So we have the wife of a rich lawyer — Excuse me, but he is not rich. No? No.

Jube's arms went out, Ya call this poor then? I didn't say that, I said he is not rich. No? He's not rich with a house like this? No, he is not rich. He's not rich with having six grand in his desk, another grand stuck under a fucking pillow, in *Ant's* room? Her face tightened at that reference. And her eyes went cold and unafraid. He's not rich having enough Persian rugs to fly to the fucking moon on? So how much does he make a week? I have no idea. Lady . . . how much does he make in a week? He doesn't get paid by the week. A month then? Nor by the month.

You trying to be clever? Playing the smart-arse? Huh? Huh? You think you gotta couple a druggie desperadoes on your hands, that what you're thinking? Huh? No. No, I am not thinking that. I'm only wishing this would end. That you'd accept we no longer have money in the house, and you anyway have stolen from us as it is.

Hahaha! What, you want us to feel sorry for you? No. No, I don't want you to feel sorry for us, just have some decency, some sense of wrong of what you are doing, and leave now before your actions get you deeper in trouble.

Deeper? How do ya mean, deeper?

Well I'm sure a court will take a very dim view of terrorising a woman in her own home. Terrorising? Who's terrorising? Have I terrorised you, Lady Muck? Well you've hardly — Oh you know what you're doing. But how much do you *want* from us for God's sake?

HAHAHAHAHA! That a loaded question? And Sonny just caught the undertone in Jube's tone. As if some little shift had taken place. No, it isn't a loaded question. Look, I can withdraw money on my bank card. I have a — now what's my credit limit? — two thousand. I have a credit limit of — So how much does your husband make in a week? A week? A week, lady. He's a solicitor, they don't get paid by the week, she in an almost haughty tone to Sonny's ears, as if it was something everyone knew. A month then? Oh, about — I don't know. You do know. Look, he's a partner in a firm. It varies from year to year. So how much did he make last year? I — she clamped shut. And for the first time Sonny thought she lost honesty. A glaze had come over her eyes.

How much?

But she shook her head. And her eyes were more on the floor.
None of your business, it came quietly from her. So she didn't see
Jube ease off the desk, step across to her. Only felt his gloved hand
jerk her head up by the chin. How-fucking-much? And still she
shook her head. You'd interpret it wrongly, she said. Would I? Yes.
How much? She shook her head. *HOW MUCH!*

Three hundred thousand.

Jube looked up at Sonny. And his eyes said what a million words
would not. And his words said, ever so quietly, I think we'll take a
look downstairs. Three hundred . . . three hundred she says. And
she shook her head in despair. I knew you'd read it wrongly. And
Sonny knowing a further shift had taken place. As well that old
feeling of no return, that here was the moment of no return. And
thinking he could walk out. Right now. Yet he couldn't. Wondering,
but why he couldn't. (Cos I'll be alone then. And so will she.) So he
followed. Them. Jube and her; being marched in her own house a
captive.

17 (I seen a movie like this) at Jube from the rear, holding the woman by the scruff of the neck at the end of her bed; hearing the words coming out through clenched teeth but that had gaps in them, of punched and kicked out space: *Ya like em, doncha!* Jerking her forward then back. *Doncha!* At the pictures he'd spread out over the bed. The ones from the brown envelope Sonny had found. Swapped (oh God forbid), exchanged for photographs of her, this woman, this very terrorised woman, in the nude. (But my intentions weren't filth. I didn't want it to demean you, lady . . .)

Come on. Which pose do ya like? Hmmm? Jube's voice calm, but only for the moment, then he jolted her head forward. (And me, standing here staring. Watching. The observer. This man's flatmate, I been his cellmate, of a thousand nights of his reckoning and my counting, and they're the same. They add up the same. His thousand and my thousand are the same. We're one. We've always been one. But he's swallowed me.) *Which fucking one!*

— *OOOHHHHHH! that one! Alright?* Her shrieking a terrible wail reaching into a man. Reaching in and tearing at his everywhere. That one? That your favourite? Hmm? No — *YES!! You just TOLD me!* Tell me again. His voice from quiet to that incredible intensity that wasn't so much shouting as it was a kind of controlled screaming. (Like it comes from his rotten, festering insides.)

Three hundred fucking grand a year huh? HUH, I SAID! Yes. Oh God, but what am I supposed to say?

(Me, I'm standing here watching this. I'm standing here watching this like the guy waiting for the bus that ain't coming. So I'm standing here waiting for something to come that ain't gonna come . . .) Everything churned up inside Sonny's mind. Words. The sight of Jube what he was doing to that woman. The picture of the woman herself. Here. In her own bedroom. With sexual pictures spread out before her forcibly held eyes as if some indictment, some court indictment of her and her husband's guilt. (I'm waiting for something that'll never happen. I know this now.)

So standing there. Almost detached. Except for his breathing, which was going rapidly in and out in and out. Except for his eyes, which had sting in them from tears wanting to break forth, except what was the point. And brain going over and over with words and wording and sight and sights and now snatches of music, the over and over and (sweet) over of music stolen from her over there, hardly visible, hidden by the broad of her captor's back. And the bedroom in the same peculiar light of curtains drawn and bedside lamp on and splashes of curtain and bedspread cover somehow leaping up and merging with the light. Film, that's what it was. Olden-day film with that grainy look to it. (Or was it a dream? A bad dream.) At Jube slowly forcing the woman's head right down so her face must be touching the photographed drawing of her nominating. That one? I said: That one?

Yeeess!! Oh G — But she didn't finish it as Jube snapped her head back up, and Sonny saw he held her by the hair. And Sonny in his state of still observing like it was truly and only film. That it wasn't real, it couldn't be real or why would he, someone like him with a nature, like he had, be watching?

He just stood there. Even as he sort of registered that his right arm was grabbing at his balaclava from behind, pulling it up and over. He just stood there. Even as he heard Jube order the woman to strip. He just stood there. Even when he kind of half registered that Jube was removing his head garment too. Even when he next half saw Jube fiddling away down at his jeans, at fly level. Sonny just stood there.

He stood there and watched the woman, heard the woman sobbing as she began removing her clothes. He just stood there. And he saw with some clarity the contrast of tartan apron as it dropped to the carpeted floor, criss-crossed reds and blues and greens against a light earthen brown. Sonny stood there.

He drew in breath when he saw the arms go up and Mrs Harland's head disappear for a seeming eternity of removing white blouse. And he held the same breath as she turned, on Jube's softly grunted instructions to do so, not letting go till he heard her ask, Should I take off my brassiere?

He expelled it till the breath was no more and the woman's breasts became exposed. Then he took gasping breath again. And just stood there.

Take a walk, bud, it came without so much as a glance over his jacket-stripped shoulder to Sonny. Repeated itself, Take a walk for a little bit, but he just stood there.

When the photograph reality became the flesh of no more garment cover and was briefly and forever exposed to a man, Sonny took quick takes of breath, and stirred. Stirred.

Of loin of loin of loin, but not so he couldn't come forward, then change his mind, but not at the first glance in ages of Jube telling him to go. Not that. He just turned the other way and walked. As woman (Woman) sounded in his ears of short cry, just an O! Like the woman that night in the park had formed the totality of her horror in just a single letter of cry.

O!

No more. Just O!

He heard, lastly, the instruction, said on a chuckle itself half choked with the main meaning of Jube McCall of the thousand-celled days and nights knowing yet never knowing. Get your leg up on that bed . . . As Sonny turned into the passage and the instruction got shut off by curve of wall, sweep of passageway. He walked. But not too far away.

Then he halted. And he just stood there.

Sometime of the silence broken occasionally by moans, and muffled man voice cursing and control screaming through the gaps of broken, busted-out teeth, Sonny cocked his head to a something in his mind. A something reasonably simple. Arrival. That's what it felt like.

Like the bus that wasn't coming, was coming. And everything gonna be alright. That's how it felt. And then it had voice, woman voice, but not of the weeping being muffled by the majestic curving sweep of her home construction. Jane. (It is you, Jane.)

Then the voice(s) grew stronger as the man approached, it could have been the coming of the bus that wasn't sposed to be coming. Even though the separated sound of woman in cry was about the most awful Sonny'd heard, even in dream, he walked an unchanging, relatively calm walk back.

He stood there. In the doorway to the event going on in the private domain of this kind of funny-lighted half-dark, he stood, he stood, he moved forward. He took up. Of object. Put aside object. Of him. His. Jube's. His proud-owned Croc Dundee. He did not but look at it for longer than the perfectly stealthed moment of its taking. Nor did thought any clearer than a picture, a simple picture of instruction, a simple image of deed done before it was done, come to a man of raised arm bent at the elbow plunging downwards.

(The place meant to be her dreaming place, huh Jane? Of your daddy called to your dark but come with the darkness of him, him ruined, him utterly soiled of heart, of love, so entered into your dark, Jane, so to enter you.)

How quiet, too, was the thing, this man, this creature, his exit. And how of worst indignity as he jolted, as though in premature climax at the poor woman beneath him, then he stiffened and a hand reached behind him and it burst through the dams of fingers crimson of himself, his ruptured self, as another rupture burst into his side so he was driven by the force off that beneath him, rolled, then curled, like a foetus, like a tiny child returned to itself, and flopped with a surprising quiet onto the floor, the dyed colour of light earth imitated, except it was sprayed in red. Just as his single cry of O! was an imitation.

And his penis swelling died rapidly in time to the breath hissing as though from the bodily ruptures, or perhaps they hissed too with the last of air escaping him.

And he didn't even look up, nor cry, Sonny, oh Sonny, but what have you done? Just stared unseeing eyes into the earth-like ground he was dying upon, took his unspoken brokenness of heart, his unspeakable misunderstandings turned sour then rotten then festering, he took his unloved, unloving definite daddy and not sure mummy into the last moment of him, and with no more than a single O! as last statement.

And the killer of him turned to her, to her huddled unto herself with drawn-up legs upon the bed of her own thousands of nights (and day surprise) lovings and makings, and could only say, Sorry, sorry, sorry. I'm so sorry, Mrs Harland. Before he turned and fast strode from the house, this house, of one night out stealing. (And I thought, I really believed, Jane, so much, so *much* was being made of me from the takings of this house — (Do you think she'll be alright, Jane, all alone in there with him, a corpse?)

Bounding down the steps, the dark-paved steps from heaven to, he knew, hell. Yet not hell. (Not hell, is it, Jane, if it ain't in your mind?)

Into the smudgy undercoat-grey-coated mean machine of the life he'd ended, Varoom Varoom, that's what he woulda said. Varoom, varoom, and HAHAHAHAHAHAHA!!

Hurtling along the road, machine like an immediately returned haunting of him who controlled it, this surging awful power of roaring (Jube-bellowing) engine afore him in ugly protruding snout with its head down and charging. Charging. And voiced: of her. And her. Them both. Sonny's Tavi-scrubber Jane of more than imagination. And her, Lady Muck Penny of the finest house a thief could imagine. And oh look, my hands're all covered in him, his leaked-out life. And soon Sonny was grinning. And it grew to something more. Something free. Of him — (of *him*!) — hahahaha! as the not-Jube-driven engine roared and tyres howled. And (oh?) was that sound of a siren in the distance?

HAHAHAHAHAHA!! Varoom! Varoom! Oh Jane. Oh Penny Mrs Harland. Oh, and Boris, and choir in cold world over there yet entered of this thief who was one night out stealing when. Oh the all of you, what becomes of us each? Varoom, varoom. (And I think that is a siren.) *Varoom!* Bedda get a hurry on, Sonny (my main lil man, hahaha.) So it must be something I done, Sonny in the rear-vision mirror. Nope. Can't see nothin. Then at the speedo — Hey! VAROOM! VAROOM! at the needle flickering over the Jube-magic ton. Then a shuddering starting. Maybe it's Jube already on the haunt? Hahaha, Sonny's chuckle a little weak. But pressing further down on the gas pedal.

Outside lane — *tooot-toot!* swing into the inside, come on, bud, I'm in a hurry. Charging down centre lane, vehicles either side, a gap to the right and one further up to the right. Which one? Right. So he gunned it, and the car surged toward the gap. (There, how ya like that, Jube?) Blue sky and cloud rolls and hill-line green and sea-blue white-topped, and the gap.

Needle climbing steadily to the right, mean machine poised to swing right. For the gap. Into the gap. World turning a shuddering blur, though the gap still stood as just this dark spot a man was intent on and aimed for — (I think.)

World turned again. To this moment of utter silence and a sense of being lifted. Raised up. Suspended somewhere. In a somewhere that seemed forever but then it wasn't. It was raining. And the rain tinkled. And it flashed before the eyes like snow falling. On screen. In far-off cold of some Russian winter of village trying to triumph over their mere mortality of being. Of being in a cold climate, and being ordinaries as ordinaries are the world over. Of trying to break free of their something hung over them, maybe it is everyone's Something. And succeeding, yes succeeding, if only owed mostly to the big man leading em, Boris. Boris Kristoff of the voice pretending to be singing to God, cept he wasn't, he was singing to the glory of his own God-given voice, to the notes he was able to reach, to the tone depths he was able to explore. The heart, the emotion, the mind even, he was able to strive for and reach.

Everything gonna be alright cos hell is only in ya mind. And this glass shattering all around of a man like snowflakes are snowflakes. Cos that's what this man's made of em.

And the ripping and churning tearing of metal and upholstery (with the holes picked in it by years of idle, unloved hands) that ain't what ya think it is, not if ya don't want it to be.

Nor the flesh being rolled up in its hurtlement nor the mind behind the eyes seeing the world in violent milli-moments of colour flash and movement sensation, as well body signals telling of ruptures to itself, nor did any of that be anything other than the meaning a man gave it.

And in the profound quiet of engine silenced and car body broken and silent wisps of smoke and heat offgivings, a man was not in his last moments of dying in incredible pain. Nor anguish. No. Jane. (Jane? Is that you?) Smiling up at her. Or what he perceived as her, and that was enough.

And when the all around became of yelling men and tear-eyed staring women, and shouted instructions and commands of lift and heave and just general effort of men helping man in his moment of mistake, of bad judgment, of bad luck, of bad (or good) birth, it didn't seem to the man to be that bad. If only, that is, he kept his mind's eye focused on the image of the woman who at last had grown clear features and wasn't bad, she wasn't too bad consider-ing . . . You know, that your daddy did what he did in your dark meant to be your resting your dreaming place, poor Jane.

But it doesn't madda, it don't madda, does it Jane? You're here. I'm here. So everything gonna be alright.

So when, eventually, he was taken from the wreckage (of Jube's car but not Sonny's life. No way. Not when them stolen experiences was making so much, so *much* of a man his inside) he took with him Jane. Tavi-scrubber Jane. And, too, women. Mum? Mummy? Oh Mamma, what'd I *do*? And thought he was putting his arms around the woman, his mother. But pulled away because she gave off the stench of her inadequacy. Oh Mum, poor Mum, what'd you do, what'd you do, what'd we both do? Please hold me, Jane. Hold me hold me hol' me ho'me ho'me, Sonny's coming home, I am come home . . .

Listen, Jane, and there was this woman but you would not believe, Jane, she had beauty, she had everything of this life. Oh, and Jube. You know Jube? We was out stealing one night, ya know? Hahaha, yeah, you know, you're a Tavi girl you ain't no Lady Muck of the fantastic house palace with all its conjoinings a perfection of constructional art and workmanship. So much to tell you, Jane, so much. She . . . she — I saw her naked before she was naked, ya know? Ya know, Jane? Oh but weren't that; I ain't no Jube McCall. They were just photographs, Jane.

And my mate — well he weren't really my mate, not when I think about it, and yet he was — he had a wrong head, his mind was fixed. You get preachers like that, Jane, you know about them, in prison, when we were in our separate borstals, Jane. Fixed. Who're fixed on something. Something single. So it becomes dangerous, and it can't see far. Not far at all. Well ya see, Jane, I coulda taken — just — what Jube was doing cos it's Jube, ya know? He was the beast I knew, so it wasn't no big surprise. Oh Jane, do we really wanna be talking about him? About this? Come to me, Jane. Kiss me here. An' don't worry, my hands're on D for don't till you're, uh, ready for me. Ya know.

But, Jane, she lost her child, that's what did it. It — she — died of something, her mother said, cept I forget what cos I got blown away. Cos I felt I kind of knew her, Ants her name was. You know, from that video tape I tole you about? She died, Jane. From when we were last there till we came back. So it shoulda been enough shouldn't it? We — he — shoulda walked then. But he didn't. And I nearly didn't.

When she asked for that one favour of mercy, I thought it wouldn't be enough, not on its own, not with a man like Jube McCall. I know him and I know his type. Over a thousand days and nights I've known him, and the type. And they're no different to the borstal preachers and the tired old prison ministers, Jane: they're fixed. Ya can't shift em. Even with proof, as ya know. Or even with something deserving of one act of mercy, ya can't shift em, Jane. So — *urrrrrghhhh* I'm sorry, Jane, something in my chest choking me. Like a weight, Jane. A fuckin great weight. You'd think I'd had my share, wouldn't ya? Hahaha, but who's complaining, Jane? I ain't.

He shoulda let her off. He shoulda let her . . .

. . .? Jane? That you? (It's a voice. I know that voice.) Mrs, is that you? It is? Oh, wow, this is unreal. Hey, I'm sor — Don't be. But I am, Mrs — Okay, okay, I'll rest. You're the boss, hahaha. Hey, are you for real? Yes? No?

(It's Penny. She says she's Penny, and How are you, Sonny? is what she said. Jane? You there too, Jane?) A great heaving up from ruptured insides. Of blood. Or just liquid. For what madda what madda? He (I) is juss Sonny Mahia. Ya know? Sonny of the thousand-celled and ten-thousand-imprisoned days and nights who was, one night, out stealing.

G'nite to you too, Penny. Say g'nite to her, Jane. Farewell to you too, Jube, while we're all at it. And is that snow falling? The sound of bells? Sing to me, Boris. Oh, and choir. Sing to Sonny. Sing for me, eh?